Nocturne

ALSO BY CHRISTINE JOHNSON

Claire de Lune

Nocturne

CHRISTINE JOHNSON

SIMON AND SCHUSTER

A **pulse** book

First published in Great Britain in 2011 by Simon & Schuster UK Ltd,
1st Floor, 222 Gray's Inn Road, London WC1X 8HB
A CBS COMPANY

Published in the USA in 2011 by Simon Pulse,
an imprint of Simon & Schuster Children's Division, New York.

A CIP catalogue record for this book is available from the British Library

ISBN 978-0-85707-184-2

10 9 8 7 6 5 4 3 2 1

Printed in the UK by CPI Cox & Wyman, Reading, Berkshire RG1 8EX

*This is for the woman I most admire,
most appreciate, and most adore.
This is for my mother.*

Nocturne

Chapter One

CLAIRE'S HUMAN FORM offered no protection from the chill in the moonlit clearing. She shivered as the early-October breeze licked at her arms and cheeks. Wrapping her arms around herself, she stared across the circle, wishing her mother would hurry up and start the ceremony.

A tangled pile of branches waited in the center of the pack. Marie kneeled down in front of it and leaned in, the mist of her breath kissing the outermost tips of the twigs.

Claire's mother closed her eyes, focusing. The graceful lines of her body tensed for an instant, and then it was over. The fire ignited with a roar, pulled into existence by the force of Marie's will.

The light and heat spread through the clearing, changing the texture of the air. The forest crackled with power—it was as though the fire had woven threads of lightning, tying the members of the pack together, linking them to something larger than themselves. As the flames grew, the feeling intensified, humming along Claire's skin, whispering to her about the things she could do.

Begging her to become a wolf.

The pack stood in a circle around the fire, all of them silent. Waiting. The flames leapt before them, the trees towered behind them, and the full moon shone down from above. Everything was ready for their transformation. Marie raised her arms, and with her voice full of the authority that came with being the pack's Alpha, she began to chant.

She called each of their names, and Claire shifted from foot to foot, aching for the warmth of her fur. As she edged closer to the fire, Claire noticed Judith staring at her. She quickly turned her attention back to her mother but kept Judith in her peripheral vision. From her spot next to Marie, Judith regarded Claire with narrowed, judging eyes.

Claire forced herself not to raise a what's-your-problem eyebrow and kept her attention trained on her mother. The chant was almost over, anyway. Anticipation tugged at Claire as Marie called her name. This was only her second full moon ceremony since she'd completed her transformation, but every second she spent in the woods—every time she looked at the moon hanging in the sky like an ever-changing jewel—she loved it more.

There were no secrets in the woods the way there were in her human life. There was just the pack. And the ceremonies.

And the hunt.

Marie lowered her arms.

"And now it is time. You may transform."

The words hung in the air, tantalizing as a ripe apple. Claire forgot about Judith. She forgot about everything but the unbelievable joy of slipping out of her human form and changing into her wolf self. Paws appeared where her hands and feet had been, and her skin gave way to thick gray fur. Claire's teeth grew sharp, and she felt the sudden, familiar heaviness of her tail.

The instant she changed, her senses sharpened. She could see the individual twigs high up in the trees. Could hear the rustling of something small—a mouse, maybe, or a chipmunk—in the undergrowth. And the smells . . . It was almost painful at first, how many things she could smell when she transformed. In her wolf form she could tell that there were four kinds of wood in the ceremonial fire tonight and she could smell the sweet, sighing scent of the autumn leaves dying on the trees above her.

And she could smell pain—the sharp, unbearable scent of pain. It startled Claire, and when she heard a worried whimper coming from Katherine, one of the other Beta wolves, she knew she wasn't the only one caught off guard by the odor. The scent was coming from Victoria, who sat on the forest floor, paws splayed awkwardly, panting hard. After Claire, she was the youngest wolf in the pack, but she was groaning like an old woman.

Sorry, she huffed, in the nonverbal language they shared in their true forms. *The more pregnant I get, the harder it is to change. I'll be okay in a second.*

She hadn't been pregnant that long, and Claire was horrified by how fast her belly had grown. Werewolf pregnancies didn't last as long as human ones, which made having a baby especially difficult, because it was so hard on the human part of the woman. Claire had seen it—the terrible way Victoria's skin had stretched, how the sudden change in her shape and weight had made her hips hurt so much that she could barely walk.

Beatrice, Victoria's mother, walked over and sat next to her, leaning against her flank like she was propping Victoria up.

Marie, can you hunt without us?

Victoria staggered to her feet, her belly swaying underneath her, dragging her spine into a bowl-shaped curve.

No, no, no! I'm okay. I can go. She licked at her muzzle anxiously.

You reek of pain. You will stay here. And your mother will stay with you. The four of us can complete the hunt on our own.

The weight of Marie's command made Victoria sink back down onto the ground. She looked relieved and disappointed in equal measures. Beatrice just looked relieved.

Marie turned to Judith, Katherine, and Claire. *Let's go.*

Without waiting for a response, Marie trotted off into the woods, her ears pricked forward and her nose high, searching for prey. The other three wolves followed. Claire kept to the back of the pack, since she was the newest wolf. She didn't mind—there was more to do at the back of the hunt than stuck in the middle, anyway. While Marie tracked in front, Claire kept her senses trained behind them, searching for an animal that might not have been able to find a good enough hiding place. Judith and Katherine loped along in between.

It was hard work, running along with the hunt. Marie set a punishing pace and expected the rest of them to keep up. Claire had taken to jogging in her human form, to make sure that she was in shape. She'd die of embarrassment if she was gasping for breath the way Katherine was. If Marie had taught her anything, it was that being a werewolf was a privilege, a life-and-death-risking double identity, and Claire had every intention of living up to that.

Behind her, there was a single, soft noise in the forest. The sound of a step.

A misstep, more like.

Claire whirled around, her head lowered and her shoulders hunched, sniffing the air frantically. The odor was not quite like deer—it smelled muskier. The animal part of her brain supplied the answer at once.

Moose.

Claire gave a soft yip. Her mother pulled up short and circled around, nearly colliding with Judith and Katherine, who scrambled to get out of the way.

Marie pressed close to Claire, her nose quivering.

Judith stared over Marie's shoulder at Claire, her lips drawn back ever so slightly, showing her sharp, pale teeth. It was a dominant move—almost an accusation. Everything in Judith's posture told Claire she should have stayed at the back of the line, kept her mouth shut, and let one of the senior wolves find the moose.

Before she could stop herself, Claire rolled her eyes. Judith took a warning step forward.

Marie's soft yip froze Claire and Judith in their tracks. Whether she hadn't noticed what was going on or she was just ignoring it, Claire couldn't tell. Either way, her mother's tail waved approvingly.

Excellent. Well-spotted, chérie.

The praise made Claire shiver. The anticipation of sacrificing a moose—even if it was a young one—zinged through her. The other two wolves shifted behind them, silent as the shadows themselves. Marie turned and acknowledged them with a look.

Claire, you circle around with Judith, and Katherine and I will cut off the path. The order was given noiselessly, all eye flicks and twists of her ears.

The wolves didn't waste any time. Judith and Claire ignored each other completely as they streaked through the trees toward the doomed animal.

In a matter of moments, the quiet of the forest was broken by the moose's panicked bellow. And then it was over. They dragged the heavy, lifeless moose back to the clearing, in preparation for the feast.

Later, when the moose had been disposed of and their whiskers were clean again, the wolves ringed the fire once more. Claire hated this part—squeezing back into her human skin after the freedom of being a wolf. It was like slipping into a scratchy set of bedsheets. She got used to it quickly enough, but she dreaded the initial, prickly discomfort.

And Claire still wasn't used to going through the full moon ceremony without Zahlia. Zahlia had been dead for two months, and though they were not allowed to speak of her— even to say her name—the ragged hole she had left in the pack sent a shudder through Claire every time she passed too close to the memory.

After all, Zahlia had been her friend. Before Claire had found out that Zahlia was murdering humans. Before her "friend" had set up Claire's mother for capture. Attacked Claire's boyfriend. Turned on Claire.

Before Claire completely disappeared into the black hole

of the Zahlia nightmare, Marie gave the signal and the wolves transformed. As much as she wanted to stay in her lupine form, her mother's command had to be obeyed. With a sigh, Claire slipped back into her human skin.

Victoria stood next to her, dressed, but with her distorted stomach uncovered. The hem of her shirt had twisted, and she struggled to yank it over her stretched belly. Embarrassed, Claire averted her eyes.

"Damn it!" The curse was quiet enough, but Claire could hear the tears in Victoria's voice.

"It's okay," Katherine soothed. "It'll be over soon enough. They say that the end is always the hardest part. Just think— probably only one more full moon to go, and then you'll be a mother. Oh, I'm so jealous. I always wanted a little baby to squeeze and hug."

Claire squirmed.

Marie cleared her throat, silencing them.

"As the Alpha of our pack, there are many decisions that fall to me, including when to hold the traditional celebration of our newly transformed wolves."

Claire forgot all about Victoria. She stared at her mother, her eyes wide with questions.

Marie looked over at her. "On the night of the new moon, two weeks from now, we will gather here especially for you. You will be expected to do a short demonstration of the basic skills—transforming, hunting . . ."

The tension drained out of Claire. She knew how to do those things. And she even had something extra: the ability to hear others talking even when they were miles away. Not all wolves had that sort of long-distance hearing. Sure, she had to focus pretty hard, but still, she could do it. It might even be sort of fun, to have the attention of the group like that. She started to nod at her mother, but Marie interrupted her.

"Of course, you will also be required to light the ceremonial fire."

Claire's head stopped moving mid-nod.

The ceremonial fire. Shit.

She couldn't do that.

She'd been trying for weeks, but in spite of all her efforts, the only way Claire could create a flame was if she had a match handy. Of course, she hadn't admitted that to her mother. She hadn't wanted to seem that inept. Not being able to light the fire was worse than embarrassing. She might as well be having trouble tying her shoelaces.

Without being able to light the fire, she wasn't a normal werewolf—she couldn't prove that she could connect herself to the foremothers and tap into their power.

Oh, crap.

Her mother smiled at her. "And to celebrate your success as a wolf, you will lead the hunt that night."

The idea lay in front of Claire, rich as chocolate cake. Just participating in the hunt was her favorite part of the gatherings. It was the only thing in either of her lives—human or wolf—that required her to use all her senses to their fullest. The wild intensity of the chase, the pride of completing the sacrifice to the Goddess, and the frenzied joy of the feast that followed were consuming. She couldn't imagine anything better than that.

Except actually getting to lead the hunt. She wouldn't let anything get in the way of that. Not even her mental block against lighting the stupid fire.

Marie interrupted her galloping thoughts. "You are ready for this, yes?"

"Um, sure." Claire swallowed hard. She couldn't bring herself to admit that she actually wasn't ready. "I mean, it'll be fun, right?" The last word came out as a squeak.

"It's not just fun," Judith snapped.

Claire took in her mother's lifted eyebrows, and concern crawled over her, spider legged and sharp fanged.

Marie gave Judith a grudging nod. "True." She turned to Claire. "It does confirm that you are a complete wolf. There's no need to worry about it, though." She laughed. "Incomplete wolves are practically a myth, even the consequences for being one are almost medieval. It will be a wonderful celebration. I've been looking forward to it since you first changed—I can't wait to see you lead the hunt."

The words buzzed around Claire's head, and she struggled to stay calm.

Marie dismissed the rest of the pack and put out the fire. As the embers turned to ashes, Claire took deep breaths, letting the achingly cold air dull her panic.

When the only light in the clearing was the glow of the moon overhead, Claire and her mother headed for home. The sound of their feet crunching quietly through the last of the fall leaves was the only noise—there was nothing else to distract Claire from the worried pounding of her heart.

After a few wordless minutes, Claire couldn't stand it anymore. "Why didn't you tell me before? About the new moon gathering?"

Marie reached up and fiddled with the silver chain around her neck. "Because I didn't decide until tonight that it was time. After Victoria has the baby, she'll be excused from her pack duties for a few months. I didn't want her to miss the ceremony, but it was clear when I saw her tonight that she will certainly be pregnant for a while longer."

Claire started to say something but snapped her teeth shut before the words could come. Talking would just get her into trouble. And it wouldn't make any difference anyway. She knew her mother. There would be no begging for an extension. No bending of the rules.

She had two weeks to learn how to light a ceremonial fire or she was going to utterly humiliate herself. In front of the whole pack.

Great.

* * *

When they finally arrived home, Claire made a beeline upstairs. She was still fired up from the hunt and on edge from the announcement about the new moon gathering. It was already after two—if she didn't find a way to unwind, she'd never get any sleep before school the next day.

She looked longingly at her running shoes. Going for a run, even in her human form, was the only thing that really calmed her down lately. But it was too late to go running. Anyone who saw her jogging at this hour was bound to think *something* suspicious was going on.

She kicked the shoes into her closet and grabbed her phone—there were two messages. The first was from Matthew, her boyfriend. He sounded exhausted. With only five days left until the state soccer finals on Saturday, the coach had them on a crazy practice schedule. Still, in spite of the fatigue in his voice, he told her that he hoped she'd had fun at the gathering and that he'd see her in the morning. And that he loved her.

The words sank into Claire like sunshine. Matthew always had that effect on her. No matter what, he made her feel like whatever was going on, she could handle it. It didn't hurt that he was the only human in Hanover Falls who knew about the werewolves. He was a secret-keeper for the pack, a *gardien*. He protected them, and they protected him. Being honest with him about who and what she was made it a lot easier for Claire to keep lying to everyone else.

Like her best friend, who had left the second message. Emily's words came out all in a rush. She demanded to know why Claire wasn't answering her phone at almost midnight, unless she was asleep, in which case Emily was very sorry for maybe waking her up, but she really, really needed the blue-black nail polish she'd left at Claire's the weekend before and could Claire bring it with her tomorrow, please?

Claire laughed, loving Emily's signature, caffeine-fueled intensity. She deleted the message and grabbed the little glass bottle off her dresser, stuffing it into her backpack. She looked longingly at her bed, but she was still too wired to sleep. Instead, she trudged into the bathroom and turned on the shower, hoping the hot water would help. With her mother's announcement tying knots of tension in her shoulders, though, there might not be enough hot water in the whole city to relax her.

School the next day was slow-motion torture. Her exhaustion from the gathering and the constant, nibbling worry about the upcoming new moon ceremony were a dizzying mix. Claire staggered through the halls toward her locker, having survived first-period history without falling asleep on her desk or chewing her nails down to the quick. Considering how she felt, that counted as a major success. She dropped her bag in front of her locker, sending a dust bunny flying.

"Oh, yay! Yayyayyayyay! You're here!" Emily bounced

across the floor with a huge smile on her face. Her hair still startled Claire. After Emily had gotten back from her forced exile at her aunt and uncle's farm last summer, she'd chopped off her hair. It was short and sort of spiky in an irregular way that looked good on her, but Claire couldn't quite get used to it. She kept expecting to see the long, smooth ponytail Emily had worn since the fourth grade.

Emily started talking well before she actually got to Claire, her questions flying out of her mouth like a flock of sparrows. "Did you get my message? Did you bring the nail polish? Are you okay? I waited for you before class, but you never showed and I got worried. . . ."

Claire blinked, trying to digest all the words. She ticked off the answers on her fingers. "Got the message, brought the polish, fine-but-tired. I was up late and I overslept." She grinned at Emily. "Okay?"

Emily held out her hand. "Polish first. It's an emergency."

Claire dug it out of her bag.

Emily took it and then pointed the bottle back at Claire. "So, if you were up late, why didn't you answer my call?"

"My phone died. I didn't realize it until I went to bed, and by then it was way, way too late to call." The lie was as easy as blinking. She didn't even feel guilty anymore. Not really. Not when she knew what the consequences would be if anyone found out her identity. The thought made Claire's stomach sway inside her.

"You look like you're going to faint or throw up or something." Emily leaned forward. Claire could smell the fake-sweet scent of strawberry Pop-Tarts on Emily's breath, and it reminded her that she'd skipped breakfast.

"Your pupils are all funny. Are you *sure* you're okay?"

Claire blinked. Swallowed. Shook her head, then nodded.

Oh great, Claire. Way to look totally together.

"I'm fine. Just tired, really. And hungry. So, what's with the manicure urgency?"

Distraction was always a good tactic. And with Emily, it usually worked.

"So, that's the other reason I was calling." Emily glanced around the hallway and dropped her voice. "That guy Ryan, in art class? The one who does all the charcoal work?"

Claire nodded again. It was hard to keep track of Emily's endless string of potentially datable guys, but she vaguely remembered something about a blond guy who'd been making Emily's toes curl in the art room.

"So, yesterday, he came over while I was painting, and he told me that I held the brush like it was an extension of my hand. And the way he said it . . ." She shivered happily. "Anyway, if he's looking at my hands that closely, then I should probably redo my raggedy polish, you know? Because—"

Emily cut off midsentence as a pair of arms wrapped around Claire's waist from behind. For a wafer-thin moment she tensed, but then the familiar hint-of-cinnamon smell that meant only one thing—Matthew—wafted over her. She melted back against his solid chest.

"Hey, babe."

"Hey, yourself," she said.

Emily was staring at her expectantly. It was obvious that she wanted to say something more about Art Guy but that she didn't really want Matthew around while she rehashed the goings-on in her romantic world.

Matthew bent down and tucked his chin over Claire's shoulder. "Can I talk to you for a minute?" There was a heavy, serious note in his voice that made Claire's skin prickle.

Emily's eyes widened.

"Hey, guys!"

From down the hall, Amy Harper's blond ringlets bounced as she waved frantically. She was loaded down with posters, and she had a roll of masking tape around her wrist. Even though she'd only been in town a couple of months, Amy had managed to get on practically every committee in the school. She had a dentist's-dream smile and boundless energy, and she was genuinely one of the nicest people you'd ever meet. She was also into pottery—seriously into it. Apparently, some gallery back in Pennsylvania sold her stuff.

She and Emily spent a lot of time together in the art room and had gotten close fast, which Claire had sort of appreciated, since it took some of the pressure off her. Amy was there for Emily when Claire couldn't be. Claire had to admit that it made her a little jealous—as much as she loved being a were-wolf, all the power and freedom and feeling of specialness that came with the transformation had come with a price. And having to share her best friend with the petite, perky-sweet Amy was part of it.

"What's up?" Emily called back.

"Can one of you guys please help me tape up these posters? I have a quiz in precalc, and I don't want to be late!" Amy shifted the stack of paper from one arm to the other, blowing an errant curl out of her eyes.

The "you guys" surprised Claire. Amy wasn't friends with Claire or Matthew, but then again, she was so nice, she probably automatically included everyone. Like a kindergarten teacher trying to make sure everyone got a turn.

"Sure thing. Be right there." Emily looked pointedly at Claire, let her eyes skitter over to Matthew, and then twitched her lips. Which was Emily-speak for *I'm going now, but you will* tell me what the hell he wants to talk to you about, and I don't mean next week.

"We'll finish catching up at lunch," Claire promised, distracted by the catalog of things that might make Matthew sound so serious. Emily zipped off down the hall, arms already outstretched to catch the sliding pile of posters.

Claire turned to Matthew, her heart doing a sort of hiccuping stutter-step as she looked up at him. Claire had spent her entire sophomore year nursing a huge crush on

Matthew—along with most of the girls in her class. Somehow, she'd been the one lucky enough to catch his attention. That he'd stayed with her after finding out she was a werewolf was nothing short of a miracle.

"You sound strange," she said. "What's up?"

Matthew nodded his head toward Emily and Amy. "It's about that, actually."

Claire looked at him expectantly. Her heart quivered against her ribs, nervous.

"The posters that Amy's taping up everywhere? They're for the Autumn Ball." He reached up and rubbed the back of his neck. "I—I really want to go. To take you. But I know that you're not exactly into dances, and I don't want to drag you if you'd be supermiserable."

Claire blinked, wondering briefly if she'd be less confused if she hadn't been so worried that he was going to tell her something terrible. "What makes you think I'm not into dances?" she finally asked.

Matthew cocked his head at her. "Well, I've never seen you at one before. Emily's usually taking over the dance floor, but I just thought . . ."

Heat rushed into Claire's cheeks. She cleared her throat, trying to get up the courage to admit the truth. Matthew was the one person she could always be honest with, so lying about something so small, so *human*—it seemed stupid. But that didn't make it any less embarrassing.

"I . . . um. Yeah. See, the thing is, no one's ever asked me before. And Emily always had a date, so I didn't want to tag along stag, and it was easier to just pretend that I didn't want to go in the first place."

There. She'd said it.

Matthew's mouth dropped open. If he laughed, she'd kill him.

"So, you're saying you'll go with me? You don't mind the dress and the corsage and the awkward photos and stuff?"

The girliest, most human part of Claire did a little dance of glee at the words "dress" and "corsage."

"Of course I'll go with you. I would love to!" She grinned, swatting his chest with her hand. "Geez, the way you looked before, it was like you were going to tell me that you were moving to Arkansas or something."

Matthew frowned. "Sorry. It's just—finals are on Saturday, and things have been—"

"Tense?" Claire interrupted. "Pressure filled? Insanely exhausting?"

"Yeah, those would work." He smiled the wide, genuine smile that made his eyes crinkle up the tiniest bit at the corners. "But after this weekend, it'll all be done, one way or another."

Down the hall, there was a series of high-pitched squeals as one of the show choirettes opened her locker and a flotilla of helium balloons drifted out. Claire wondered if she should stuff Matthew's locker before the state finals—usually it was something that guys did for girls and not the other way around, but she wanted to do *something*. Maybe she'd just make a sign to hold up at the game, the way the rest of the team's girlfriends did.

Claire stretched up and kissed him, just as the warning bell rang. "You're going to be fantastic. The match is going to be fantastic. And I'm going to be right there, screaming my head off. Now go, before you're late."

"Yeah, you're right. I hope you're right." He turned and hitched his bag up on his shoulder. "I love you."

"I love you, too." She threw herself into the scurrying mass of people who were scrambling for classrooms, and as she headed down the hall she caught sight of one of the leaf-framed posters. She was going to an actual dance. With an actual boyfriend.

Claire smiled to herself. Emily was going to die a thousand deaths of retail happiness when she heard.

Chapter Two

WHEN CLAIRE GOT to the cafeteria at lunch, Emily was already waiting for her, intently picking the raisins out of a bagel. As Claire slid into the chair across from her, Emily looked up, then grabbed an enormous, half-finished bottle of Diet Coke and took a swig.

"So? What was Matthew's deal? He looked like he was going to tell you that he ran over your dog."

"I don't have a dog," Claire muttered, distracted by Emily's busy fingers. "Why did you get a raisin bagel? You hate raisins."

"Yeah, well, the hot lunch was meatloaf, and the only other bagels were garlic." She wrinkled her nose.

"Oh, right. And you can't reek of garlic when you see . . ."

Crap. She couldn't remember Art Guy's name. Something short. Nick? Jack? Ian?

Claire's mouth opened and shut like a fish out of water. Emily raised a freshly polished fingernail and pointed it accusingly at Claire.

"You forgot his name, didn't you?"

Crap, crap, crap. There was no way out of this one. Claire squeezed her eyes shut.

"Sorry. Please don't kill me—I really was listening, but then Matthew sort of made me forget what you and I had been talking about."

Emily went back to her raisin excavation. "It's Ryan. And I'll forgive you this once, because I *know* you're going to help me analyze everything that happens in art class today." She dropped her mangled bagel and picked up her soda. "I really want him to ask me out. He's Arizona-in-the-summer hot, and besides, my lack of a boyfriend is making me depressed." She sighed. "So? What did your Prince Charming want to talk to you about?"

Claire bit her lip. "You're going to love it."

Emily put down the soda. "What?"

"I'm finally going to a dance! He asked me to go with him to the Autumn Ball. Like, officially. He thought I didn't like dances because he hadn't ever seen me at one before. That's what he was nervous about—can you believe it?"

Emily went very, very still.

"Oh my God," she whispered. "You're actually coming to a dance?" She let out a squeal and bounced up and down in her plastic chair, which shook on its scrawny metal legs. "You! At a dance! We are so going *shopping*. And I am totally going to get Ryan to ask me and then we. Can go. To a dance. Together! Finally."

Claire reached into her bag and yanked out a sandwich. "I know. I'm so excited. And I definitely need you to help me find a dress, just as soon as I can wrestle a credit card away from my mom."

Emily immediately began outlining a preshopping strategy and debating whether they should double or if it would be better for Claire to have a more "romantic" one-on-one before-dance dinner with Matthew.

Claire ate her sandwich, nodding along with Emily's increasingly complicated plans. She didn't care when they went shopping or whether they got a limo—things felt normal between her and Emily, and she just wanted to enjoy it. This was how she wanted the rest of the year to be, and she was going to work damn hard to make sure she didn't do anything to ruin it.

That night, Claire slipped off into the woods to work on starting a fire. She headed straight for her favorite practice spot, the little opening in the pine trees that was enough space to work in but so well hidden that she wasn't worried about being seen. She swept away the pine needles until she had a ring of bare earth large enough for a pile of branches. Starting small seemed like a good idea, so Claire gathered up an armful of twigs, making sure they were all dry enough to burn.

Just after her transformation was complete, Marie had explained to Claire how to light the fire, but since then she'd never bothered to ask if Claire had managed to succeed. In the clearing, Claire arranged the kindling exactly the way her mother had shown her. After everything was set up, Claire stood over the sad pile of sticks, clenched her fists, closed her eyes, and imagined a fire. She held on to the picture in her head, eyes still shut, and listened for the sound of crackling bark. Waited for the scent of wood smoke. For her shins to get warm.

Nothing happened.

She opened one eye and checked. Nope. No fire.

Okay, fine.

She shook out her hands and stretched her neck before trying again. She had to relax. Being so tense wasn't helping.

Hours passed in the cold, dark forest. Birds roosted in the trees above her, then woke and flew away again. Claire stood in the shelter of the familiar pine trees until her feet and back ached from being motionless for so long. She visualized fire until the image of leaping flames was burned into the backs of her eyelids, but as soon as she opened them, the uncharred pile of wood stared back at her mockingly. If it had a tongue, it would have stuck it out at her.

Claire flopped down onto the forest floor, her heart pounding from the frustration and the wasted effort.

In her pocket, her cell phone rang. The noise startled her. It sounded so alien in the quiet rustle of the night forest. She wasn't the only thing surprised by the sudden sound in the darkness. The tiny creatures in the woods around her fell silent as everything but Claire held its breath.

A breeze ruffled Claire's hair. With a sigh, she pulled her phone out of her pocket and saw that it was already after midnight.

And Matthew was calling.

"Hello?"

"Hey. How are—" He paused. "It sounds windy. Where are you?"

Claire stood up and brushed the bits of dirt and leaves off her shirt. With one swift kick, she sent the unburned twigs skittering across the clearing, so that they came to rest in a natural-looking scatter. Screw it. She'd come back the next night and try again.

"I'm heading home, actually." She turned and started to walk. "You're up late."

"Yeah. I couldn't sleep." His voice was ragged with worry. She could hear Saturday's game hanging over him.

Claire took a long breath. She knew that the state finals

were a big deal. A huge deal. Matthew had been recruited by some schools, even offered scholarship money, but he still hadn't heard from his top choice—UCLA. There would be a Bruins rep at the game. Watching him. Making little notes that could determine his entire future.

"Matthew, it's going to be fine. You're amazing—you've been amazing at every match this season, and there's no reason this game is going to be any different."

He sighed. "I hope you're right."

She laughed. "Of course I'm right. I'm always right. Don't you know that by now?"

"I know, I know. I wasn't calling to talk about it, anyway. So. Where're you headed home from?" He was trying to keep his voice light, but he wasn't completely successful.

Claire crouched low and slipped through the hole in the brick wall, stepping onto her lawn.

"The woods," she said, "but I just made it back to the house. Last night wasn't as fantastic as it could have been. I mean, the gathering was fine. But it turns out that the pack is having a special gathering for me. Like, where I'm supposed to demonstrate my—" She paused. "My skills." Her words were heavy with meaning.

"I don't see the problem. You're good at all of that, right?" He sounded distant, and she could hear him shifting around in an edgy sort of way.

Claire stared up at the dark windows of her house. "Except

26

lighting the fire. I can't do that part." Her voice came out in a whisper.

"I—oh. Well, I'm, uh, sure you'll work it out." His voice was as bright and fake as a cheerleader's smile.

Something tightened in Claire's chest.

But what if I can't? What if I screw up so amazingly that I can't ever lead the hunt?

Claire didn't say anything. She looked up at the moon. It was still nearly full, just the tiniest sliver missing from one side. She knew it would shrivel away to nothing all too fast, but she didn't want to add to Matthew's worry if she didn't have to. He was plenty anxious about his own stuff—after all, he was about to be judged too.

Claire shook herself. "Sure. Right. Anyway, I'm home, and I need to go to bed. And you do too."

"Yeah. At this rate, we're both going to be zombies tomorrow." He yawned. "I love you, you know that?" he asked, sounding like his old self again.

"I love you, too," she whispered.

The intensity of her worry rubbed against her, making her want to strip off her human skin and run until she was too tired to care about anything. But instead of transforming and sprinting through the woods until she had run herself out of her self-doubting, Claire flipped her phone shut and trudged into the house. Pretending she was just an ordinary human. Pretending everything was fine.

* * *

By Friday she was a wreck. Claire sat in the forest, surrounded by little unburned piles of kindling. Nothing would light. She wrapped her arms around her knees and stared at the stack of sticks in front of her, wondering what it would really be like to fail in front of the whole pack. If she couldn't figure out how to get *something* to catch fire, that's exactly what would happen.

She didn't want to ask her mom for help, mostly because she didn't want to admit just how much trouble she was having with something that was supposed to come naturally to werewolves. It would be almost as bad as admitting that she couldn't wag her own tail. Claire pressed her forehead into her knees, the denim blotting out the mocking, unlit wood in front of her.

Two more days. I'll just practice for two more days. Then, if I still haven't figured it out, I'll talk to her.

The idea that she might really be an incomplete wolf was so awful that she couldn't even think it any louder than a whisper. But there was a little voice at the back of her head that had started muttering ugly, doubt-filled things, and once it knew it had gotten her attention, there was no way to shut it up.

Part of her knew she should stay where she was and try again to make some sort of combustion happen. But Matthew's game was the next day. All the other soccer players' girlfriends would have flowers and cards and signs with their boyfriends' jersey numbers on them. Claire wasn't going to let

Matthew down by being the only one sitting there at the state finals with nothing. Even if it meant missing out on a little bit of practice. She still had more than a week until the gathering. That would be plenty of time to work things out—to keep herself from being humiliated, from having everyone think she wasn't as good as any of the other wolves.

At least, she hoped it would be plenty of time.

Saturday morning dawned, full of heavy gray clouds and the promise of colder weather. Claire was relieved. At least by nightfall Matthew's stress would be over. And the game would be a good chance for her to think about something else and blow off some steam. She was even looking forward to the traditional postgame celebration at the diner.

And then afterward, she promised herself, she'd head straight for the woods and practice.

She'd been up way too late trying to make a decent-looking sign, but she'd finally managed it. It was just Matthew's number inside a glittery heart, but it was big enough that he'd be able to see it from the field. After doing her best to drown her fatigue with coffee, Claire tugged on a pair of leggings and a T-shirt with a disintegrating collar. She had hours until the game, and the caffeine had made her way too jittery to sit around the house. The only thing she could think to do—at least, in the daylight—was go for a run.

She paused on the front porch, stretching out her left calf

and adjusting her earphones before taking off down the driveway. She loved the shock in her chest as the thud of her shoes against the pavement reverberated into her ribs and her lungs stretched, trying to keep up with her sudden effort.

Just when her muscles had really warmed and loosened and the running started to feel almost—but not quite—as good as when she was in her wolf form, Claire reached the edge of the forest. Seeing the shadows between the trees sent a flutter of anxiety through her, undoing most of her relaxation. She wanted to be there, in the woods, practicing. She turned her eyes back to the road in front of her, training her gaze on the cracked pavement. She needed to stay focused on Matthew right now. On her human life.

Besides, there wasn't anything she could do about her werewolf existence until it got dark.

With the road spooling out in front of her like a ribbon, Claire inhaled long and slow and matched her pace to the drum-beat rhythm of the song that poured through her earphones. She let the repetition calm her, numb her, until she wasn't worried about fire lighting or Matthew's scholarship chances. Until she was just running. Breath and motion and nothing else.

When she was sufficiently sweat-soaked and soothed, Claire jogged home and hurried to shower—she had time before the match started, but she wanted to be early enough to get a good seat.

After she was clean, she pulled on jeans and a long-sleeved T-shirt that was cute enough for Louie's. Then, for luck, she threw on one of Matthew's sweatshirts. She ran her thumb over the slightly frayed edge of the cuff, imagining all the other times he had worn it, all the times it had been his skin inside the soft fabric instead of hers. A happy little shiver ran down her spine. She grabbed her phone off her vanity, sending Matthew a quick "I love you and you're going to be fabulous" text before shoving it in her pocket.

In the kitchen her mother sat with her hands around a cup of coffee and stared out the window. There was an untouched sandwich in front of her. Claire took a deep breath, gripping the edge of Matthew's sweatshirt for support. She hadn't spoken to her mother much since the gathering, which wasn't such a big challenge. Marie worked crazy hours, meeting with clients, working her contacts, and playing with new equipment when she wasn't involved in an actual photography session.

Claire was mostly relieved that her mother hadn't seemed to notice how much time she was spending in the forest—that she wasn't questioning whether or not Claire was ready for the new moon gathering. Claire grimaced, wishing she wasn't going to be paraded around like a trick pony—or trick wolf. Whichever.

As if she could hear Claire's thoughts, Marie turned to Claire and took a sip of coffee.

"Good morning, *chérie*. Actually, afternoon almost, isn't it? Are you just waking up?"

"No. I went for a run. Did you need me to check in or something?" The last sentence came out with a fish-hook barb on the end of it, and Claire bit the inside of her lip, hoping it wasn't going to get her in trouble.

Just pretend everything's fine long enough to get through this afternoon. That's all I have to do. Then I'll spend every possible second getting a handle on the fire stuff.

Her mother raised an eyebrow, but she let the comment slide. "Matthew's game is today, yes? The important one?"

"Yep. I was wondering—um, is Lisbeth coming this afternoon? I sort of need a ride."

"Emily isn't going?"

"No. She has a family thing she couldn't get out of. Plus, she doesn't really love soccer, you know?"

In spite of the fact that Claire and Matthew had been dating seriously for months, Emily and Matthew still hadn't become friends. At first it had seemed like Emily didn't want to butt in. She'd made lots of innuendo-laced comments about a couple needing to "get to know each other" without interruptions. But lately Claire had been wondering if there was more going on. Interspersed with the eyebrow-waggling one-liners, Emily had been mentioning third wheels and unwanted spinsters.

"You look extremely thoughtful." It was a statement, but there was an obvious question underneath it. Marie was always worried about Emily—or, more specifically, Claire slipping and Emily figuring out the truth.

"I'm just not awake yet." Claire shrugged off her mother's curiosity. "So, can you drive me?"

Her mother shook her head. "I've got client calls starting in half an hour, and I'll be busy straight through dinner." She pursed her lips thoughtfully. "But they are sending a car for me for the dinner. . . ." She slid off her chair and padded over to the coat closet. When she came back, the shiny black oval key fob dangled from her hand.

Car keys.

The car keys.

Marie held them out. "Why don't you take my car? You have a license. There's no reason you can't drive yourself."

Do not squeal. Do not squeal. Do not squeal.

Claire cleared her throat as casually as she could. "Are you sure?"

Her mother stared at her pointedly. "I trust you with far more than a car on a daily basis. I know you will be careful."

Claire reached out and took the keys, reveling in the sharp weight of them against her palm. "Thanks," she said. "This is actually great—I'll be able to give Matthew a ride home after Louie's."

Marie smiled. "See? Better for everyone, then." She looked at the clock. "I'd better go prepare for my calls. Enjoy your afternoon."

"Sure thing." Claire grabbed her bag and headed for the garage before her mother could change her mind. She'd driven plenty of times—with Marie in the passenger seat. She'd even driven Matthew's car a couple of times at the very end of the summer, when he'd pulled a muscle in his calf.

But she'd never had a car all to herself before.

The Mercedes sat in the garage, all glossy black paint and sinfully soft leather. Claire hit the button that opened the garage door and slid behind the wheel.

This was going to be good.

Really good.

The match was intense. All the players knew what was on the line, and they were playing hard, not keeping anything in reserve. They weren't afraid to get injured—they were all hitting each other as hard as they could without getting thrown out of the game. By the midway point of the second half, Hanover Falls was up, one to nothing. That's when the right back came flying out of nowhere and slammed into Matthew as he dribbled the ball toward the goal. A two-footed hit in the box that meant a penalty. If it went in, it would come close to sealing the game.

Claire held her breath, curling her toes against the soles of her shoes. The adrenaline pulsing through her heightened her senses until she could hear Matthew's determined, nervous breath. The scent of tension—sharp, bitter—poured off the players on the field, strong enough to make her wrinkle her nose. Matthew took two steps back, squinting against the sun as he lined up for his penalty shot. There was a rip in the back of his jersey, remnants of the illegal hit he'd taken moments earlier.

Claire watched as intently as the rest of the fans. She'd never been really interested in a sport before she started dating Matthew, but the speed and athleticism of soccer appealed to her, and once she'd learned the rules, she cheered and hissed as loudly as any other fans, even when Matthew wasn't on the field.

Matthew shrugged one shoulder, and Claire gripped the cold metal of the bleacher as he ran at the ball. The solid *thunk* of his foot hitting the black-and-white sphere echoed across the field, and Claire—along with the rest of the crowd—jumped to her feet as the ball sailed past the goalie and swept into the back of the net. The free kick put Hanover Falls two goals ahead of Lawrence with twenty minutes left in the match. Claire sat perched on the edge of her seat, hoping they'd done enough to win. Willing it to be true. Her nose twitched and her confidence grew. There was no way Lawrence could make a comeback. Their players all reeked of exhaustion.

Claire watched impatiently as the time on the game clock ticked away. The sensation of a certain win swelled inside her, sending pinpricks of barely contained excitement into her hands and feet. When they entered the two minutes of injury time, she was on her feet, yelling with the rest of the crowd.

The referee's whistle sounded, signaling the end of the game.

Claire let out an enormous whoop and hugged the random girl sitting next to her, who hugged Claire back just as enthusiastically. She let go, turning to watch as Matthew celebrated with the rest of the team, slapping shoulders and getting cuffed on the back of the head.

He turned and caught sight of Claire. A grin spread across his face, and he jogged over to her. Claire climbed down the bleachers, stepping over people and purses, hoping no one noticed she was doing it a little more quickly, more easily, than a human would. Her feet hit the ground at the sidelines.

Heat spread through Claire's middle as Matthew came to a stop in front of her, smelling like clean sweat and grass and the sort of sweet-apple scent of happiness.

He scooped her up and swung her in a circle. "We did it! Can you believe it? We actually did it!" He set her down, leaned in, and planted a quick kiss on her lips.

His joy was so genuine and so all-encompassing that it wrapped around her, tight as his arms, filling her with a lemony-light giddiness. "Are you kidding?" She linked her hands at the small of his back. "Of course I can believe it. That free kick was absolutely amazing, Matthew."

"Thanks." He fidgeted with the hem of his jersey, looking uncharacteristically nervous. "I just hope it impressed the UCLA scout. I hope like hell he's writing the words "full ride" in there." Matthew's gaze flicked to the top of the bleachers, and Claire followed it. She spotted a man with an out-of-place tan and an unnecessarily heavy jacket scribbling away in a leather portfolio.

Matthew blew out a long breath, his normal expression—calm and confident—returning to his face. "Anyway, I guess I just have to wait and see. No use worrying about it right now."

Claire grabbed his hand and gave it a squeeze. "It'll be fine. It'll be more than fine."

"You ready to eat?" Matthew asked.

Claire nodded. She was always ready to eat. Ever since she'd become a full werewolf, her appetite had been insane. She was also starting to feel antsy about getting into the woods—as the sun slid to the west, she could feel the seconds ticking closer and closer to her practice time.

"Awesome. Let me just grab a quick shower, and I'll meet you outside the locker room, okay?"

Matthew. In the shower. Claire's insides quivered.

"Sounds perfect," she said.

She watched him walk away, his cleats throwing up little clumps of dirt as he went. In her back pocket, her phone started chirping. Claire pulled it out and glanced at the caller ID. It was Emily.

"Hello?" Claire answered.

"Claire! Hey! So, is it over? Did they win?"

"Yep, and mostly thanks to Matthew." Claire heard the pride in her voice.

"That's awesome. Tell him I said congrats." There was a

pause—it was tiny, but it caught Claire's attention. "So, I know you're doing the team celebration stuff tonight, but I wondered if you wanted to come over after? If the thing at Louie's doesn't go crazy late. You could spend the night, even."

Claire closed her eyes. She wanted to go to Emily's, but she really, really needed to get into the forest.

"I wish I could, but I think that the celebration at the diner is going to go pretty long. . . ." It was hard to outright reject Emily. She hated saying no to her best friend. She missed her. But she needed to figure out how to create fire, without having to ask her mother.

"No, it's okay. I knew it was a long shot." Emily's words were reassuring, but there was hurt in her voice, thin and bright and sharp as a needle. "Just call me tomorrow, okay? I want the dish. Something's bound to happen at Louie's. I just know it."

Claire's laugh had a note of regret in it. "You know I'll tell you, first thing."

"Okay, go do the whole jock's-girlfriend thing. I'll talk to you soon." Emily hung up.

Claire sighed and tapped her phone against her leg. At the top of the bleachers, the UCLA scout stood up and stuffed his portfolio into a battered leather briefcase. The stands were mostly empty—a couple of people from school were huddled around someone's cell phone, and a few parents were clearly waiting to drive their kids home. One of the adults glanced over at her, and the expression that flashed across his face made Claire jump. He looked . . . he was *looking* at her. Almost like he was checking her out.

His face was vaguely familiar. Sort of like one of the fullbacks'. Someone's dad, probably. Which was totally gross, but whatever. She was a werewolf. She could take him out without blinking if she needed to.

She returned his stare, her shoulders thrown back and her hands curled into fists at her side. It was a dominant posture. Fearless. Claire watched his piggy little eyes widen in surprise, and he dropped his gaze, studying his battered tennis shoes like the winning lottery numbers were written on the laces.

Satisfaction poured through her, hot and sweet. She couldn't fail at the ceremony. She couldn't stand to let anyone look at her the way that guy had—like she didn't count, like she could be used. She couldn't be some sort of incomplete wolf.

But before she could ensure that didn't happen, she had a date to go on and a best friend to worry about.

Chapter Three

LOUIE'S WAS BUZZING with people, and most of them had come over to say hi to Matthew at one point or another during dinner. Claire stole the last of Matthew's fries while Doug Kingman grilled him about the recruiter who'd been watching the match.

Doug shook his head. "Man, I'm just saying. If you get a full ride to UCLA, I will totally die of jealousy. I'd have the acceptance letter tattooed across my chest. Seriously. I'm already booking my plane ticket to visit you."

Matthew shrugged. "It's a long way from being a done deal. And it wouldn't be so bad to end up here at the university." He glanced over at Claire. "Closer to home is pretty good, you know."

Claire swallowed hard. She was only a junior. She and Matthew hadn't talked much about next year—what it would mean for them if he got into UCLA. If he left. Just thinking about it made her miss him, even though he was still within touching distance.

Doug slapped the table. "Well, you know you'd be a seriously big fish in a tiny-ass pond if you stayed. Everyone in this town practically worships your dad. Hell, maybe I should think about going into lycanthropy research."

Matthew smiled, but it was tight, fake. "Yeah. It's a really great career."

Claire stuffed a French fry in her mouth to keep herself from making a smart-ass comment. A suspicious smart-ass comment. She'd gotten a lot better at keeping her thoughts to herself over the last couple of months, but sometimes people were so ignorant that it made her want to scream. And anyone who thought that Dr. Engle was a good guy was definitely ignorant. The "cure" he'd developed for werewolves didn't really work. He'd only tested it on men, and since all werewolves were women, that meant he'd never actually tested it on a werewolf. The poor humans Dr. Engle experimented on were all in permanent comas. He'd used his clout in the scientific community to cover up his failures, to boot. How a man like that could have had a son like Matthew was beyond her.

Doug looked over at the door, where Kate-Marie Brown stood, tapping her foot impatiently.

"Whoops. The girlfriend awaits. If she's late for curfew, I'm pretty sure her dad will kill me. Which would make it really hard for me to take her to the Autumn Ball. Later, guys." He half-sprinted over to the door.

Claire's mouth dropped open. "Doug is dating Kate-Marie?" She stared at the two of them wrapped around each other in the entryway of Louie's. Kate-Marie was as close to royalty as the senior class got. She was pretty, she could sing, and she was the one who decided who was in and who was out. If you cared about your social standing at Hanover Falls High School, you cared what Kate-Marie thought.

Matthew glanced back over his shoulder. "Yep. It's only been a couple of weeks, though. He jumps every time she snaps her fingers."

"Yeah, well, she *is* kind of hypnotizing, in a bitchy sort of way."

Matthew snorted and grabbed the bill off the end of the table. "Come on. Let's get out of here."

Claire stood up and stretched, walking with Matthew toward the cash register. An itchy feeling crawled over her, her instincts telling her to be careful. She glanced around the diner, trying to find the source of the prickly sensation. Her gaze drifted to the far end of the counter, and she spotted the person who'd been watching them.

Amy was making her way toward Claire and Matthew, with a smile on her heart-shaped lips and a sparkle in her green eyes. Claire felt herself tense.

Though Claire was hardly some sort of gigantic oaf, Amy was about five inches shorter than she was, and wispy as a cloud. Claire instantly felt awkward. Clunky. She hadn't really felt that way since she'd completed her transformation, and it startled her.

"Hi, Matthew. Great game. That penalty you took totally clinched it!" Amy flashed him a blinding, orthodontist-white smile before turning her attention to Claire. "I didn't even see you until the end of the game, and you were way at the other end of the stands—I'm so bummed we didn't get to sit together! I was hoping we could hang out."

Hang out? A quiver passed through Claire. Why was Amy paying so much attention to her?

Claire gave her an apologetic shrug. "Maybe next time?"

If next time was in a million years and Claire wasn't a werewolf.

So, actually, maybe never, but there was no good reason to be bitchy. She gave herself a mental shake. Amy was Emily's friend. She was nice to people. She probably cried during ASPCA commercials.

"Definitely next time." Amy grinned, looking like she'd won the lottery. "You two off to the after party?"

"We haven't decided yet," Matthew said.

Claire slipped her hand into Matthew's and gave Amy her best, Marie-inspired fake smile. She braced herself. "Are—are you?"

Amy shook her head. "I'd love to, but I figure it's a team thing, and besides, I promised Emily I'd spend the night at her house."

Claire's smile crumpled. She knew that she had bailed on Emily a lot lately. It wasn't that she wanted Emily to spend Saturday night home by herself, but she couldn't help feeling a little bit replaced.

I'm the one who told Emily no. I can't be upset about this.

"I wish we could stay and chat, but I'm whipped." Matthew squeezed Claire's hand, interrupting her racing thoughts and bringing her back down to earth. "I think we're heading out."

"No problem. I'm leaving pretty soon myself. Talk to you guys on Monday!"

Matthew pulled Claire toward the parking lot, but she couldn't resist a quick glance over her shoulder. Sure enough, Amy was watching them go. Amy saw Claire looking at her and waved, and Claire waved back without thinking.

All at once, they were through the door, and the chilly air wrapped its fingers around them, pinching Claire's wrists and tugging at her ears. The parking lot was dark, and the two of them wound their way carefully through the cars.

"Are you sure you want to leave?" Claire asked. "I mean, we

have a good forty minutes before you have to be home."

Matthew grinned. "On a normal Saturday night, that might be true. Tonight I don't have a curfew."

"I . . . oh. Wow. That's, um, . . . ," Clare stammered. She'd counted on being able to work on her fire lighting. Really, really counted on it.

Disappointment crashed across Matthew's face. She made herself smile. She could give up one night of practicing. This was Matthew's shining moment—what sort of girlfriend would she be if she couldn't put him first for that?

"That's great," she said. "So, where to? The after party?"

Matthew made a noncommittal noise.

Claire hit a button on Marie's key chain, and the car's headlights flashed.

"Can I drive?" he asked.

"The Mercedes? Are you kidding? My mom will smell you on the steering wheel, and I will never, ever get ahold of these keys again."

She walked around to the driver's-side door. Matthew followed her, and she turned to face him.

"Very cute, but you're still not driving."

"I'm not trying to drive." Carefully, he edged her back until she was squeezed between him and the car. He wrapped his arms around her, cupping the back of her head with one hand to protect it from the metal.

He leaned in close and smiled at her. "We may have seen

everyone at Louie's, but I'm not quite finished celebrating," he whispered.

He kissed her, his full mouth warming hers before he caught her lower lip gently between his teeth. Claire's knees wobbled, and she heard herself make an incoherent noise.

"There is an after party, but I don't want to go." Matthew pulled her tighter against his chest. "I just want to be with you."

The tingle in her middle headed lower, and she sighed happily, forgetting about everything except him.

The next morning, Claire woke to the sound of pots and pans banging around in the kitchen.

What the hell? Is mom actually trying to cook something?

Claire stumbled out of bed and dragged herself downstairs to see what was going on. Lisbeth stood in the kitchen, dressed in lounge pants and an old T-shirt. She was halfway through cooking what looked like an omelet.

"Uh, morning," Claire croaked.

Lisbeth whipped around, her face a strange mix of happiness and irritation. "Oh, hi, Claire-bear."

Claire frowned at the nickname. It was cute when she was younger, but now it was just irritating. "Um, what are you doing here? It's Sunday," Claire pointed out, sliding onto one of the high stools around the island.

"I know. Your mother called me early this morning to see if

I could come stay for a day or two. Apparently, her dinner last night went so well that they all decided to fly to New York for some editorial meetings. They left late last night." She flipped the eggs in the pan with more force than was really necessary. "She didn't think it would be a good idea for you to be alone for too many days, even if she did leave you with the car keys." Sarcasm hardened Lisbeth's usually mellow voice. "I just don't get why she didn't call me before she went. What if something had happened to you last night?" She shook her head, clearly frustrated with Marie.

Claire shrugged. "Nothing did. It's fine, Lisbeth."

The truth was, if something had happened during the night, they had fire alarms and working telephones, and if someone had somehow gotten into the house, Claire was more than capable of defending herself. The real reason her mom wanted Lisbeth around was so that there would be someone to report back on what Claire did. For all her mom's proclamations about trusting Claire, she couldn't stand not being in control. Even if it meant using Lisbeth as a stand-in.

Claire rubbed her sleep-gritty eyes. It could be worse. She loved Lisbeth, and it would be nice to have some time together, just the two of them. Like old times. Besides, Lisbeth slept like the dead. Claire had snuck out plenty of times when Lisbeth lived at the house. She'd be able to get into the forest to practice without any trouble, and that's all that really counted. She glanced out the window and noticed for the first time that rain was splattering against the glass, filling the dip in the pool's off-season cover.

Crap. There was no way she could practice in the rain.

Crap. Crap. Crap.

She ran a hand across her forehead. Matthew's stress was over. His goal had won the game, and if UCLA had any sense, they'd be sending him a scholarship offer as fast as they could type it up. He had to be feeling fantastic this morning, facing a day with no pressure, no stress.

But Claire still couldn't light a fire, not the right way, and the new moon was barely more than a week away. The calendar weighed on her. The rain mocked her. And the worry about what it would mean if she failed burned through her veins, hot and achy and terrifying in its hugeness.

Lisbeth slid the enormous, fluffy omelet in front of Claire, interrupting her descent into a full-blown panic attack.

"I guess you probably want some of that vile coffee." She shuddered.

"Yeah, but I can make it."

"No." Lisbeth shooed her back into her seat. "Eat that before it gets cold. It won't kill me to make you one pot of coffee." She pulled the grounds out of the pantry. Claire took a tiny bite of her breakfast. It was delicious. Perfect.

But she'd completely lost her appetite.

She sighed and pushed away the plate.

* * *

Hour after hour, the rain poured down. By late morning the constant tapping of the drops had made her restless and edgy. She knew that Matthew had to be exhausted, and she didn't want to call him and wake him up. She settled for sending him a "call me when you're up" text.

She'd promised she'd give Emily any major gossip from Louie's, and the whole Kate-Marie Brown/Doug Kingman thing definitely counted. Claire picked up the phone and snuggled down into the couch, looking forward to a long session of rehashing the night before. The rain might be keeping her out of the forest, but it did have a bright side.

Emily answered immediately.

"Hey! You're alive! How was it?"

"Good—I mean, the match was fantastic, and then Louie's was fun. But I'm calling because I have serious news about Kate-Marie Brown for you."

"Oh, yesssss. Why don't you come over? We're having pancakes. Gossip is always better with maple syrup." Claire could practically hear Emily jumping up and down. And her mom's pancakes were legendary. Claire's appetite came roaring back. She had eaten those pancakes a hundred different times on a hundred different Sunday mornings, and the idea of something so familiar made her mouth water almost as much as the thought of the batter sizzling on the griddle.

"I'll be there as soon as I can get Lisbeth in the car."

Half an hour later, Claire waved good-bye to Lisbeth and

ran up the front path to Emily's door, grimacing as the rain pelted her face and snatched at the hems of her yoga pants. She pushed open the front door, and the warm, sweet smell of breakfast washed over her.

"Hello?" she called.

"Up here!" Emily's voice sailed down from her bedroom.

"Hi, Claire!" Mrs. Lucero shouted from the kitchen. "Pancakes are on the way. You want a cup of coffee?"

"No, thanks," Claire said over her shoulder, already halfway up the stairs.

At the door to Emily's room, she jerked to a halt. Emily sat on her bed, surrounded by Styrofoam leaves in varying sizes. She had a bottle of glue and a tiny brush in her hand. On the floor in front of the bed, Amy sat with a couple of huge bowls of glitter.

Something inside Claire broke—like a cracked fishbowl, shiny and dripping. Every time it seemed like *something* was finally going to be the way it always had been, it changed. Why hadn't Emily told her that Amy was here? The memory of Amy telling her the night before that she was spending the night at Emily's resurfaced. But it was nearly noon—why was Amy still here?

"Hi, Claire!" Amy looked up from dipping a gluey piece of leaf-shaped foam into one of the bowls. Her curls were piled on top of her head, caught there with a pair of chopsticks. A few errant flecks of glitter sparkled across her cheekbones, making her look sickeningly adorable.

"Uh, hi." Claire glanced down at her soggy running shoes. Imagined her sloppy ponytail.

Emily grinned at her, a smudge of white glue marking her cheek. "We're making fall look fancy." She pointed to an army of glittered Styrofoam leaves drying in ranks on top of the Arts and Leisure section of the Sunday paper. "Wanna help?"

Claire lowered herself to the floor. Emily's room felt strange—Claire was so used to it being just the two of them. Amy's presence shifted something in the air, knocking things off balance. "Um, sure."

"Oh, awesome!" Amy handed her a bowl of orange sparkles. "This is going to go *so* much faster with three people. Just scoop the glitter over them until they're totally covered." She looked down at her glue-and-glitter-smeared fingers and sighed. "We're going to be walking disco balls by the end of this."

"Can you believe Amy got roped into doing this?" Emily asked, handing Claire a glue-drenched acorn. "They're totally taking advantage of the fact that the word 'no' apparently doesn't exist in her native language—you know, Philadelphian." Emily shot Amy a meaningful look.

Amy laughed, an inside-joke sort of laugh that squirmed unpleasantly over Claire's skin. She and Emily were getting so close. Claire wanted that back. It would be too hard to keep her true identity a secret from Amy and Emily both, but watching the two of them start the sort of boundaryless friendship that she'd had with Emily, before all the secrets, before all the hiding . . . it made her chest ache so badly that her ribs were nearly cracking with it.

Claire dropped her Styrofoam into the bowl, turning her head as a puff of sparkles rose into the air and settled on her lap. "How many of these are you making, and why, exactly?"

"Five hundred," Amy announced. "They're decorations for the Autumn Ball. I know it's ages away, but I figured I needed to get a jump on it since I have so many to make. It's so nice of you guys to help!" She smiled at Claire. "You and Matthew are already going—now Emily and I just need to find dates and we'll be all set!"

The way she said it made it sound like they would all be going together. Claire looked up at Emily, trying to gauge her best friend's reaction. Emily was focused a little too intently on the half-coated leaf in front of her, and the tips of her ears were cotton-candy pink.

Slowly, Claire reached into the bowl and sent a drift of glitter cascading over the acorn while she chose her next words.

"Yeah. I'm excited about the dance." She tried to sound casual.

"You should totally join the dance committee," Amy said. "I mean, we need more people, and you're obviously good with glitter."

Emily laughed, and Claire did too, surprised at the wit peeking through Amy's perky veneer. An unexpected warmth flared in Claire, catching her off guard. For a moment she saw how it could have been—the three of them—if Claire hadn't had so much to hold back.

"I—that sounds fun, but I don't think that Kate-Marie Brown would approve of me having a hand in major school social events," Claire said.

Amy rolled her eyes. "Kate-Marie doesn't rule the world."

"She sure thinks she does," Emily groused, putting glue on another leaf. "God, Claire, remember when Yolanda wanted her to come to your birthday party last summer?" She looked over at Amy. "Kate-Marie blew her off just because she didn't want to deal with the pool thing."

Amy shuddered. "Well, that I can actually relate to. You really have a pool?"

Claire nodded, uncomfortable.

"Ugh. They terrify me. I can't swim at all. I'm a total solid-ground sort of girl. So, I guess Kate-Marie and I agree on one thing, at least."

"We'll try not to hold it against you," Emily joked.

From the kitchen came the sound of a griddle being thumped into the sink. "Girls?" Emily's mom called up the stairs. "The pancakes are ready! Come and eat them while they're still hot."

"Oh, yum!" Emily reached for a damp wad of paper towels and pulled off a handful, wiping her glue-coated fingers on them and handing the rest to Amy.

Amy wiped the glitter off the perfect ovals of her little fingernails.

"I'm starving," she announced. "And I totally want to hear about the after party and stuff last night. God, you must have been up all night—I can't believe you're not an exhausted mess today! What's your secret? Seriously. I have a billion quizzes next week. If you have a secret energy drink or something, I want in."

The questions sent an angry jolt through Claire. She worked *so hard* to keep her secrets hidden, and Amy, with all her cheerful and well-intentioned bonding crap, was on the verge of ruining everything. Claire had a sudden urge to snarl at Amy—to startle her into silent submission.

But this wasn't the woods, and Amy wasn't a wolf.

"Yeah." She cleared her throat. "I'm pretty much all about caffeine."

Claire's lupine side lunged inside her, pushing at the cover of her human skin. She was right at the edge of transforming, balanced on a thread-thin line between human and wolf. She stayed motionless as marble, tracking Amy's movements with her eyes, until she was a hundred percent sure she could control herself. Until she knew she could stay human.

With shaking hands she set the bowl of glitter on Emily's bed, her gaze sliding over the bedside lamp. The memory of the epic fight Emily and her mother had when Emily broke it last year swam into Claire's mind. How Emily had come storming over to Claire's house. How, later, they had tried to glue it back together, adding shells and buttons and bits of yarn to hide the places where the ceramic was missing. She could still hear the echo of the two of them laughing so hard over the deranged-looking results that even Emily's mom couldn't stay mad.

Last year. When Claire still thought she was human.

With her wolf self roiling and snapping underneath the tender barrier of her smooth, pink skin, last year seemed untouchably far away.

It tore at her to do it, but Claire knew she had to leave. The stress of being around Amy—with her intense scrutiny and the way she made Claire so achingly jealous of her relationship with Emily—it was too much. Claire could feel her control slipping. She couldn't afford that. The risk to Emily was far too great. After all, if she ever found out what Claire was ... It was against the laws of the pack to kill humans, except in cases of self-defense. Killing someone who knew a pack member's identity definitely counted as self-defense, since it was only by keeping themselves hidden that the werewolves stayed alive at all.

The thought of Emily—happy, bouncing, warm-skinned, very alive Emily—being hunted by the pack made Claire's insides tremble. She would do anything to keep that from happening. Including telling a skyscraper-high stack of lies.

Emily stood in the doorway, looking back at her with a confused expression on her face.

"You coming?" she asked. "You're about a zillion miles away."

She doesn't even know how true that is.

"C'mon." Emily jerked her head toward the kitchen. "It's *pancakes*."

Claire wanted those pancakes more than anything. Wanted a normal Sunday morning with Emily—just Emily— when she wasn't endangering her best friend's life. She stood up, wiping her hands on her pants. "I think I'm going to head out, actually. I'm not all that hungry. Lisbeth cooked this morning—you know how that goes."

Emily's mouth opened and then shut again. "But—but how will you get home?"

"I'll run. It's just a couple of miles." Claire shrugged. She tried to keep her face calm, but she was dying to leave before her mask slipped—before Emily guessed just how upset she really was.

"You'll *run*? God, Claire, you really have changed, haven't you?"

Hearing the question was like touching a live wire— painful and shocking and way too close to the truth.

"Hey, I'm still the same old Claire. I'm just in better shape." Claire fake-smiled, shifting from foot to foot, trying to get her wolf self to shut the hell up for a minute.

"Oh, sure. You had to go and get into something *athletic*." Something wistful drifted across Emily's expression as she fiddled with the door's hinge. "We didn't even talk about Kate-Marie, though."

"Yeah, I know." From the kitchen, the sound of Amy and Mrs. Lucero chatting pricked at Claire's ears. Made her feet itch to get moving. She edged toward the door. Emily noticed and stepped back to let her through. "Soon, okay?"

Emily caught up to Claire as she padded down the stairs. "We should go to The Cloister. We haven't been there since school started, even. The espresso machine is probably twitching from withdrawal."

The mention of the coffee shop on Fourth Street where Claire and Emily had been more regular than the regulars brought a smile to Claire's face. A sad, genuine smile full of years of history and meaningless secrets that she and Emily shared. All those things that had come before. She threw her arms around her oldest friend and squeezed hard enough to make Emily squeak.

"That's a perfect idea. Next weekend, okay? You and me and our old table by the window," Claire whispered.

"Emily? Claire?" Amy's voice called. "Are you guys eating or what? 'Cause I'm starving here."

Emily turned to answer her, and Claire slipped out the front door like a shadow and ran off down the street, relishing the stinging chill of the rain on her face. She willed herself not to turn around and check whether Emily was watching. Forced herself to move forward, step after step, until she was too far away to look back.

Chapter Four

TUESDAY MORNING, CLAIRE woke from an uneasy sleep and lay in her bed, trying to put her finger on what had woken her. Something was different.

Quieter.

It had stopped raining.

Claire's breath came rushing out in one long whoosh. Tonight, finally, she'd be able to practice. And with her mom extending her stay in New York, it would even be easy to sneak out to do it while Lisbeth slept.

The day dragged, but the afternoon finally faded into evening, and Claire sat in her room, half-doing her homework, rereading the same page in her history book three times without absorbing a word of it. She was itching to get into the forest.

Cracking her back, she stood up and headed to her closet. She had to move—going for a run was the only way she'd be able to stay sane until Lisbeth went to bed. Claire slipped on her shoes and bounced down the stairs.

Lisbeth was curled up on the couch with a cup of tea and a book.

"I'm going for a run," Claire announced. "I'll be back in a little while."

"Are you finished with your homework?" Lisbeth asked.

Claire shifted from foot to foot, aching to feel the rhythm of her feet against the asphalt—four feet against the forest floor would be better, but running in her human form was still better than nothing.

"Not exactly," she said, "but almost. I'll be back in plenty of time."

Lisbeth glanced out the window. "You'd better—it's dark out there. Wear something reflective, okay?"

"I'll put on my white jacket," Claire promised, backing out of the room.

She grabbed the jacket off the hook, and then she was outside, in the chilly, still-damp air. She took a deep breath and started to run.

Five miles out, she finally felt herself start to relax. Her thighs hurt from the pace she'd been keeping, but it was a good hurt. A distracting hurt. From the trees along the side of the road came the quiet sounds of things settling down for the night. It was better than listening to music.

The sound of a car's tires thrumming over the road came up behind her. Claire moved to the side to let the car pass, but instead it slowed, crawling past her and then coming to a halt. The darkness and solitude that had seemed so calming a minute before suddenly seemed precarious. Her senses flared as the wolf inside her swam to the surface, her instincts grabbing hold of her. Shaking her. Taking over.

Claire wasn't scared. Not exactly. She was mostly afraid of someone doing something to force her hand, putting her in a situation where she would have to defend herself. She widened her stance, ready to bolt into the woods.

Dr. Engle stuck his head out the window. "Claire? What are you doing out here by yourself?"

A rough-edged relief spread through her. Figuring that the danger she knew was better than the danger that she didn't— and also because it would look weird otherwise—she straightened up and walked a little shakily toward Matthew's dad.

"Just out for a run, Dr. Engle. Is that a new car? It looks really nice," she said. Her voice was a shade too bright. But she was already out of breath from jogging, which would probably be enough to hide her discomfort.

"A loaner," he said. "The brakes are out on the other one. Can I give you a ride home? This stretch of road is too deserted for a girl to be running alone on." As usual, his attempts to be concerned were too patronizing to ring true.

"Don't worry, there are plenty of bushes to hide in if the bad guys come driving up," she joked.

Dr. Engle leaned a fraction farther out the window, peering into the trees beyond Claire. "The woods aren't always safe, either. After last summer, you should know that."

The words froze Claire's blood, and she stood gaping at Dr. Engle. His lips thinned into a satisfied-looking line. She knew that he didn't intend the double meaning she heard in his words. He wouldn't be offering her a ride if he had any suspicions about her being a werewolf, but it still made her shudder.

"Thanks for the offer," she simpered, hoping a sticky-sweet act would get him off her back. "But I'm not that far from home." She'd been planning to run awhile longer, but she just wanted to get out from under Dr. Engle's probing gaze.

"Well, be careful," he admonished, pulling his head back into the car like a turtle retreating into its shell. "I suppose I'll see you at the house sometime," he called through the window. Slowly, it slid shut, and he drove away.

Claire could practically feel him watching her in the rearview mirror.

She turned and ran back toward her house with the ice from Dr. Engle's comments still chilling her veins.

There was no room for error with him around—he was too vigilant. Too committed.

And much, much too scary.

Claire sprinted up the drive with her sweat-dampened shirt slapping against her as she went. Lisbeth was going to freak out about how long she'd been gone, and Claire wanted to have time to shower and shake off her encounter with Dr. Engle before she headed back out into the woods to practice. The minute Lisbeth went to sleep, she promised herself, she'd be out the door.

She opened the back door and stepped inside, wavering the tiniest bit from the weird sort of vertigo that came with stopping after a long run. Lisbeth was waiting for her.

"Forget something?" she asked Claire in her best I'm-the-grownup-here voice.

Claire blinked, looking down at the white jacket she'd put on before she'd left.

"Like, your phone?" Lisbeth held it up and Claire reached for it, as if she could erase the mistake by getting the phone into her hand—as if her fingertips could apologize. She was supposed to take her phone with her when she went for a run.

"Um, sorry?" she offered.

Lisbeth shook her head. "I swear, keeping you safe is like trying to make the rain fall up." She held out the phone. "It's been ringing off the hook. Since I know you're not dead in a ditch somewhere, I'm going to bed."

"Okay." Claire took the phone and checked the screen. Five missed calls. "Good night."

"Come get me if you need anything." Lisbeth sighed, heading for the stairs.

Claire nodded, only half-listening. Her voice mail icon was flashing frantically. All the missed calls were from Emily. She dialed the number.

Emily answered on the first ring. "Finally! Where have you been?"

"Sorry," Claire apologized. "I went for a run and forgot my phone."

"Again? Seriously, Claire, the phone only works if the battery is charged and you have it with you."

The memory of Dr. Engle's pale eyes peering into the woods shivered over Claire's skin. "Trust me, I know. Is this a bad time? Is it too late?"

"Nah. I'm just trying to make a green glaze to put on this pot that Amy helped me throw yesterday."

Amy's passion for pottery was right up Emily's alley. Nothing artsy held any appeal for Claire, but right then she wished it did. Maybe she should take another crack at sculpture.

"So, what's up? Why all the calls?" She glanced out her bedroom window at the night-covered woods. Just a few minutes and she'd be out there.

Emily took a little, hitching sort of breath. "It's Ryan."

The guy from art class. At least this time Claire remembered. "What about him?"

"So, you know we've been flirting like crazy for days, and I really thought he was on the verge of asking me out. But after the last bell today, I saw him in the parking lot with Lindsay McCracken."

Emily was crying. Claire could hear it. She went into the bathroom and sat down on the edge of the counter, not wanting to lie on the bed in her sweaty clothes. "Okay," she said slowly. "Well, maybe he needed a homework assignment or something."

Emily choked out a little laugh. "Unless she wrote the vocab words on her tonsils, I don't think so. They were steaming up the car windows, and they weren't even in the car."

Claire made a face. "Ew. Ouch."

"Just wait," Emily sniffled. "It gets worse."

Claire looked at the clock. She was dying to get into the forest, but Emily's voice had that just-getting-warmed-up sound to it. Claire stared at the shower, wondering if she could put Emily on speaker while she cleaned herself up.

The choked sob that came from the other end of the phone answered her question. Emily needed her. And not on speakerphone.

"Worse how?" she asked.

"I ran into Yolanda—like, literally ran *into* her because I was watching the PDA horrorfest, and she said that Ryan asked Lindsay to the ball today." The last word was more of a wail.

Claire took a deep breath. "Oh. Wow. That sucks."

"I know! I mean, I really, really thought he was going to ask me out, but apparently he's just an outrageous flirt." Emily bawled.

"Well, then, aren't you better off with someone else?" Claire offered.

"Not necessarily. I mean, as a long-term boyfriend, obviously he's not a good choice. But I need *someone* to take me to the dance, and it would have been nice to have a couple of warm-up dates first. I could have dumped him afterward if he was still playing Prince Charming to half the school. Now what am I going to do?"

"You have time to find another guy to go with." Claire bit one of her cuticles, trying to think through some possible dates for Emily.

"Not really. People are mostly paired up. The posters Amy plastered all over school kicked everybody into date-finding high gear. I *so* don't want to go stag, Claire, not when this is the first-ever dance that you're actually going to. Stupid Ryan with his stupid flirting. Hang on." There was a muffled sound as Emily dropped the phone and blew her nose. "Sorry. Anyway, I'm going to end up being that lame-o dateless chick who's hovering by the DJ during all the slow dances. I just freaking know it."

A mix of sympathy and frustration rolled through Claire, sweet-sour as a lemon drop. She wondered if this was how Emily felt all those times she'd gone to a dance while Claire stayed home.

They spent awhile batting around possible date ideas, none of which went very far.

"Hey! What about one of Matthew's friends? The whole soccer team can't possibly have dates. I could ask him—see if he could put out some feelers."

"Okay, first of all, don't say 'put out some feelers,' because it sounds squicky. Secondly, I do *not* want to be that über-desperate loser friend who needs a mercy date. I have *some* dignity left, you know."

Claire squeezed her eyes shut. "I didn't mean it that way. Really. I was just thinking it might be an easy solution is all."

Emily's exhale hissed and rattled in Claire's ear. "I know. I didn't mean to be so edgy. I'm just not used to being in this situation. I swear to you, this is the last time I *ever* put all my eggs into one potential-date basket."

They talked awhile longer, until finally, Emily quit crying and started to pull herself together.

"Okay," she said. "Maybe you're right. Maybe it's not the end of the world."

"Not even close," Claire assured her. "We'll fix it, I promise. Tomorrow is another day and all that, right?"

"Right," Emily said. "Actually, shit. Today is another day.

Oh my God, it's already after midnight. I'm sorry—I didn't mean to keep you up so late."

"It's okay, I didn't have anything else to do," Claire lied. "But you'd better go to bed or you'll be all puffy in the morning."

"You're right. You, too. I mean, not the puffy bit, but the rest of it."

They hung up, and Claire stared through the open bathroom door at the clock on her nightstand.

Damn.

She hopped off the counter. She'd shower later. If she hurried, really hurried, she'd still have a little time to practice.

Claire knelt on the damp ground, focusing on the tiny pile of sticks that lay in front of her. She'd searched the thickest parts of the forest to find branches that weren't completely sodden. She'd made a little circle out of stones and everything. There were dead leaves underneath, for tinder. But the sticks were in exactly the same state they had been an hour ago.

Not burning.

Frustrated, she tossed her head, attempting to get her bangs out of her eyes. She was going to have to get home, and soon.

Claire stared at the little pyre she'd made. One of the leaves fluttered in the breeze, and a shower of leftover raindrops pattered down onto her.

Why couldn't she *do* this?

She could hear her mother's voice in the back of her head

admonishing her to move inside the wood and leaves with her mind. To bring in a hot little spark, the same way she could hold a feeling of heat in her wolf form when it was cold. Claire groaned in frustration. She'd tried imagining a spark. She'd tried picturing big flames and little flames and freaking house fires' worth of flames. Nothing ever happened. No matter how hard she tried to visualize the branches getting hot enough to light, they never so much as twitched.

She wanted to just reach in there and start rubbing two of the sticks together until they caught. At least she'd be able to say she started a fire without a match. That would almost count, right? Of course, she didn't really know how to start a fire that way, either. She was pretty sure it was something about friction, about the way the edges of the wood rubbed up against each other until they made so much heat, a little spark just sort of appeared between them.

Just then, a sensation she couldn't quite place slipped through her muted human senses, bringing her sharply to attention. It was like she was standing on a boat that had suddenly listed just a bit—a shifting.

Something had changed.

A tendril of smoke drifted up from her pile of kindling, and Claire froze, watching it. The misty gray curl rose into the air like a hot breath, then broke apart and disappeared. Nothing caught fire, but there had been smoke. And that meant *something* had happened. A wild little giggle rose in her throat, and she had an insane urge to dance around the clearing.

Because even though something had been holding her back from starting the fires, the smoke scribbled across the sky told her that she might not be an incomplete wolf.

She wished she knew exactly what she'd done differently, so that she could push it further, into actual flames.

She straightened up and cracked her back. The moon had moved farther than she'd expected across the sky. It was so late that it was practically early. She'd come back and try again, but right then, she had to get home.

Claire crept up the stairs toward her bedroom. She could hear Lisbeth snoring—all she had to do was slip into her room and pretend that she'd been there all along. She tiptoed over the creaky board in the eighth step and steadied herself against the wall with her fingertips.

She took a deep breath and nearly choked. She reeked of smoke—the smell of success. Her throat was raw with it, and her eyes stung every time she blinked. Miles away, deep in the forest, the stack of dead twigs lay, rigid, like victims of some bizarre crime.

Suddenly, Claire heard the nearly inaudible swish of a door opening, its bottom edge brushing over the thick carpet. She froze. Over the last few months, she had gotten too used to being the hunter. She had forgotten the immobilizing terror of being the prey.

"Claire?" Her mother's voice whispered from down the hall. Claire could barely hear her over Lisbeth's snoring. "Come in here. Now."

What the hell was her mother doing here? She wasn't due home from New York until tomorrow. The tone in Marie's voice was unmistakably punishing.

Damn, am I actually going to be in trouble for this?

She blew out the breath she'd been holding, crept past Lisbeth's door, and headed for her mother's room.

Marie sat on the edge of her bed, looking displeased. Her slender arms crossed over her chest. Even though it was the middle of the night, she looked impeccable, her crow-black hair wound into its usual sleek bun, her clothes smooth, and her makeup unsmudged.

"You're home," Claire said. As soon as the words left her mouth, she wanted to kick herself. It just made her sound guilty.

"As are you. Do you have any idea what time it is?" Her mother's foot jiggled impatiently.

"Um, sort of late?" Claire answered.

"It is *very* late." Her mother's voice was clipped.

Claire hung her head, trying to look as submissive as possible. "I was out practicing. It's been raining since you left, and I had to wait until Lisbeth went to bed—"

Her mother's eyes narrowed. "Practicing what?"

Claire bit her lip. She didn't want to lie to her mother, but she really didn't want to admit that she hadn't quite managed to light the fire.

Even if it is only a matter of time. The next time I get to try, it'll be right there.

"All the stuff for the ceremony. I just want everything to go okay at the new moon."

Her mother's posture relaxed a fraction. "I suppose I can understand that. And I appreciate your commitment to your role. But I still don't like you being in the forest alone so late without anyone knowing where you are. Werewolves are not invincible. You know that as well as anyone."

Her mother's reference to last summer hit home. It all came rushing back—the horrible, panicked anxiety Claire had felt when her mother had been captured—the suddenness of the memory half-drowning her.

"I know we're not invincible. Matthew knew I was going to be in the forest tonight. And I had no idea you were coming home from New York, or I would have told you where I was going too." Her voice had started to rise, and she caught herself—the last thing she needed was to wake Lisbeth.

Marie's expression softened. "Well, it's good to know that you took some precautions. I—I suppose I might have over-reacted a bit. I was not expecting to find your room empty, and I—" She hesitated, spots of color appearing high up on her cheekbones. "I suppose I'm not used to worrying about you this way."

Claire scrubbed her sleeve across her tired eyes. It was as close to an apology as she was likely to get. "Okay. Well, I'm glad you're home. I'm going to take a shower."

"Yes. Of course. Good night, then."

Alone in her room, Claire tossed her forest-dirty clothes into the hamper. She was exhausted, which meant that tomorrow was going to suck, but it didn't matter. She wouldn't embarrass herself at the new moon gathering next week, and right then, that was more important than being tired during chem.

Way, way more important.

The slam of locker doors and the jostle of a thousand students trying to get to class echoed around Claire. She closed her eyes and rested her forehead against the metal shelf at the top of her own locker, breathing in the musty smell of textbooks and ancient gym socks. Her head throbbed, and she promised herself that no matter what, tonight she'd go to bed early. She was used to getting by on much less sleep than a normal human needed, but she'd had too many late, frustrating nights in the forest.

"You okay?" The warm, low voice spread through her, speeding up her heartbeat and easing the pounding behind her eyes. She peeked over at Matthew, who was leaning against the locker next to hers. His backpack was slung over one shoulder, and his hair was still wet. He looked amazing. As usual. Claire smiled, tilting her face up for a quick good-morning kiss.

"I'm fine," she said, "but I'm kind of tired."

Matthew's forehead wrinkled the tiniest bit. "Okay. Why?"

"So, I was, um . . . practicing?" Claire gave the word some weight, letting it hang there, so that Matthew would know what she meant.

"Yeah?" He leaned in close, his eyes looking worried as he scanned the faces of the people walking past them.

She glanced around, wondering what was making him act so weird. It wasn't like anyone could guess what they were talking about. She wouldn't take a risk like that. She couldn't. "I got it to smoke," she said. "On my own and everything." The words were sweet as frosting in her mouth.

"Wow. See? Everything works out."

"Well, I mean, it's not quite—"

The edgy look disappeared from his face, and Matthew turned his full attention to her, interrupting her midthought. "So, please, please tell me that means you'll be free on Friday night?" His eyes glittered.

Claire hesitated. She hated to turn him down when he was looking at her that way. By Friday she should have had plenty of time to do the fire thing again. To make sure that it would work at the gathering.

"I guess so. Why?" Claire grabbed her history book and shoved it into her bag.

"Yolanda's parents are out of town, and she's having a party." He hitched his bag higher up on his shoulder.

Claire bit the inside of her cheek. If Yolanda Adams was having a party, it would be a madhouse. A huge, pulse-pounding, wall-shaking, keg-in-the-kitchen event. Yolanda never met anyone she didn't like, and everyone loved Yolanda. Especially when she was throwing one of her famous "my parents are on another weekend trip" parties.

"Do we have to go? I just—there's a lot on my mind." The words slipped out before Claire could stop them. It wasn't that she didn't have time to go to Yollie's, but with the gathering so close it just felt so trivial, so . . . human. She couldn't really afford that much distraction when she needed to stay focused on the fire lighting that was looming ahead of her. "Maybe we could hang out a little bit, just the two of us? Then I'd still have time to do that, uh, thing I've been working on."

Claire slammed her locker door and looked up at Matthew, waiting for him to say something.

"You could still do . . . whatever, after the party," he said. "And I maybe sort of already promised Yollie we'd be there?" An apology lurked in his eyes, like a fish caught in a net.

"So, I guess we're going to Yolanda's?" she asked.

Matthew reached up and slid a hand through her hair. "C'mon. It'll be fun." He gave her the sort of smoldering look that made her forget her own phone number. "And I promise to completely distract you from everything else. But right now, we're going to be late for class."

With her knees still less than solid, they turned and

headed down the hall—Claire's history class was only two doors down from where Matthew had economics.

"So, what time? On Friday, I mean?" she asked.

"Eight-ish? Any later and there won't be any street parking left."

Claire sighed. Everyone really was going to be there.

"We'll have some time soon, just the two of us," Matthew said, stopping in front of his classroom door. "I swear. Triple swear. Take-me-out-in-a-field-and—"

Claire rolled her eyes and smiled at him. "You don't have to take it quite that far. What about Saturday night? My mom has a work thing. You could come over, and we could watch a movie or something."

"Deal." Matthew smiled back and disappeared into econ.

Watching him walk away made Claire's mouth water. She was already looking forward to Saturday.

Claire flopped down at her usual lunch table and waited for Emily. She yanked a soda and a sandwich out of the front pocket of her backpack and opened them, scanning the cafeteria. Matthew was in physics—he had the late lunch. But at least that gave her some time alone with Emily. It was sort of weird, how much less time they'd been spending together since school started. As long as they'd known each other, Emily had been the busy one. The one who constantly had a (constantly changing) boyfriend. The one who was always involved with some project in the art room or tied up with after-school activities. Claire wasn't used to being the one who had to schedule in her best friend.

She craned her neck, checking the soda machines. Emily usually fed her Diet Coke habit before showing up at the lunch table, but she wasn't anywhere to be seen. Claire pulled off the bean sprouts that Lisbeth had tried to hide underneath the cheese, and watched the lunchtime buzz while she waited.

Emily came racing in, winding her way through the tables. She came within millimeters of clipping one of the basketball players with her overloaded messenger bag, which she promptly tossed onto the floor next to Claire.

"Sorry I'm late!" She was breathless and panting, eyeing the line in front of the soda machines. "English was horrible, and then I was talking to Amy about the disaster in the parking lot yesterday. We were making plans for this weekend, and I just totally lost track of the time. Oh my God, I've got to go get a Diet Coke, or I will never, evereverever survive Spanish this afternoon. Be right back!" Emily plunged her hand into her bag, pulled a handful of change out of the front pocket, and sprinted toward the soda machines, cutting in front of some poor freshman who was studying the drinks indecisively.

Amy. So that's who had stalled Emily. Claire was a little surprised to hear that Emily had rehashed the Ryan incident with Amy. She thought the two of them had already sorted it out.

Emily hustled back to the table clutching two Diet Cokes and slid into a chair across from Claire. "Okay. Sorry. God, what a week! I so cannot wait to go to Yolanda's on Friday. And no matter what, I *will* find a date for the dance there, so help me God. Even if I have to go with a monosyllabic football player or something. You and Matthew are coming, right?" She opened the first can of soda and drank about half of it in a single swallow.

"You're—you're going to Yolanda's?" Claire blinked in confusion. She hadn't known that. Yolanda's parties weren't usually Emily's thing.

"Yeah, I know. They're usually a little bit too jock-beer-fest for me, but Amy really wants to go, and so I thought, what the hell, you know? I need a date, and it's the perfect hunting ground. Plus, I know Matthew's usually more into that stuff, so I figured maybe I could actually spend a Friday night with you for once."

"That sounds great." Claire's sandwich suddenly tasted better. She didn't even mind the stray sprouts. Having Emily at the party would make her feel a lot better about abandoning her practice plans.

"Awesome!" Emily took another swig of her drink. "So, are we still on for coffee Saturday afternoon?" Her eyes were jumping around in a way that made Claire instantly suspicious.

"Yeah, we're still on. Why?" She kept her voice light.

Emily spun the soda can around in her hands. "So, um, the thing is, Amy heard us making plans last weekend, and I sort of ended up inviting her along. Is that okay? She's never been to The Cloister. Can you believe it? And since she heard us talking about it, she's dying to see what it's all about, so . . ."

"No, that's fine. Whatever you want. I'm sure she'll . . . She'll . . . I mean, I can't wait to hear what she thinks of Yolanda's famous parties." Claire bit her tongue to keep herself from saying anything else. She shifted in her seat, trying to shake off the irritation that spread through her like a thorn-covered vine, pricking her ribs as it grew. She knew Amy was Queen of the Nice Girls, but suddenly it seemed like she'd pushed herself into every corner of Claire's life. She couldn't exactly get mad at Emily for changing their plans, though, especially when it sounded like Amy was doing everything in her power to get Emily to bring her along. Claire had been unexpectedly changing plans on Emily for months.

"Thanks." Emily looked relieved. "I really think it'll be fun." The first bell rang, and she shotgunned the rest of her soda. "Caffeine for lunch. Yummmmm."

Claire laughed.

"Okay, I'm off to the torture that is Spanish class. I'll text you later, and we'll figure out what we're wearing to Yolanda's."

Claire faked a smile. She couldn't care less what she wore to the party. It would be clothes, not fur, and that was all that mattered.

"That sounds great." She stood up and grabbed her bag. "Talk to you later."

Emily waved over her shoulder and swept out of the cafeteria, which had turned into a mass exodus.

Claire turned and headed for class. A few more days. One

lousy party. Then she could get through the new moon gathering and back to normal life.

At least, as normal as a werewolf's life ever got.

That night, Claire was planning to slip off into the woods, but her mother eyed her running clothes with suspicion.

"Are you going for a run or into the forest?" she asked.

Claire hesitated.

"You are ready for the gathering, yes?" she asked.

"Yeah," Claire said, with more confidence than she felt. "I mean, I'm sure it's going to go fine."

She didn't want to see the disappointed look that she knew would appear on her mother's face if she admitted she was having trouble.

"All right. Well, enjoy your exercise."

"Thanks," Claire mumbled, slipping out the door.

She ran the long way into the woods, jogging a couple of miles down the road to a quiet spot where the trees strayed close to the pavement. It was a perfect cover—she'd be able to tell her mother, truthfully, that she'd been for a run, but she could still go make sure that she was ready for the new moon ceremony.

She hurried to the main clearing, the one where they met for the gatherings. It was closer than her practice spot. She stepped into the open space beneath the trees, which was darker than usual since it was lit only by a thin arc of the crescent moon.

Only, she wasn't alone.

Chapter Five

"OH! I'M SORRY." Claire froze at the edge of the clearing.

Victoria was sitting on a log, her arms wrapped around her enormous belly. She looked up at Claire. "Don't be sorry. I heard you coming, and you're allowed to be here as much as I am." Her voice was flat, lifeless, and Claire began to worry. Victoria had always been so nice—timid, maybe, a little nervous, but nice.

"Are you okay?" Claire asked.

Victoria shrugged. "I guess. Mostly. I can't sleep anymore—that's why I walked over here. My hips hurt, and I get heartburn and—" She stopped suddenly, looking up at Claire with a miserable smile on her face. "Sorry. There's no way you want to hear about all this pregnancy stuff."

"No, it's fine," Claire protested as sincerely as she could. She *didn't* really want to hear about it, but she didn't want to make Victoria feel any worse than she obviously already did.

"Nah," Victoria said. "It's boring. But it's completely taken over my life, and I can't think about anything else." She sighed. "I feel like I'm barely part of the pack anymore—I can't do half the things I'm supposed to."

"But you're *pregnant*," Claire protested.

"Exactly!" Victoria huffed. "That's all I am anymore. 'The pregnant one.' I miss being just *me*. I miss participating." She shook her head. "My mom's so nervous, and now *your* mom's nervous. It's like it's a requirement for being the Alpha—that suddenly you have to be paranoid about everything. It feels so awful to watch everyone else run off to hunt while I'm left behind. You must've felt the same way last summer. I can't stand seeing the rest of the pack doing all the things I would be doing if I weren't stuck behind this belly."

Victoria had never been this honest with Claire. Claire lowered herself onto the hard ground and stared over at Victoria. It made her miss Zahlia, being with Victoria, just the two of them. Not the crazy, death-hungry wolf that Zahlia had turned out to be, but the friend that she'd seemed like in the beginning. Claire missed having a wolf friend. Someone she could talk to—really talk to—who knew what it felt like to be in wolf skin. To change back and forth. To feel the pull of the moon.

"I'm sorry," Victoria said. "I shouldn't be dumping all of this on you...."

"It's okay," Claire said. "I understand. I—" She hesitated. If she was honest with Victoria, Victoria might run straight to Marie, making Claire look like even more of an idiot.

But maybe she wouldn't do that. The possibility of being Victoria's friend glittered in front of her, close enough to touch. Dazzled by the idea, Claire reached out.

"I've been having some trouble, too. I know how it feels to watch the other wolves doing something you know you should be able to do." Her voice was barely more than a whisper. "I haven't lit the ceremonial fire. I tried for weeks and weeks, and I finally made some twigs smoke the other night . . . but that's the only time."

Victoria's mouth fell open. "But everyone can do that."

Claire felt her face crumple like a used tissue.

Victoria caught herself. "Sorry. I—does your mom know?"

Claire stared up at the sky, her eyes going everywhere except to Victoria's shocked, sympathetic gaze. "I didn't want her to be disappointed. And I've been sort of embarrassed about it. I mean, Judith already looks at me like I'm some pigtailed kid who's tagging along for the ride. I didn't exactly want to reinforce that idea, you know?"

Victoria made a scoffing noise. "Judith just has a hard

shell. She's been through some difficult things. Last summer didn't exactly make it any better."

"Well, anyway, I don't mind if you know, but you won't say anything, will you?"

Victoria shook her head. "I know what it feels like to be the Alpha's daughter. Everyone expects you to be perfect, and there's always the threat of someone running to your mother." She smiled. "I'll make you a deal. I won't tell your mom about your trouble with the fire if you won't treat me like some sort of delicate flower just 'cause I'm pregnant."

"Deal," Claire said.

"You know, if you want, I could help you with the lighting—give you some tips," Victoria offered. She looked excited for the first time in ages.

"Sure," Claire said, though her palms were damp with self-consciousness.

"Awesome. Let's find some kindling."

They made a small pile of twigs, and Claire crouched in front of it while Victoria sat back down on the log. Claire focused on the wood in front of her, trying to block out the humming of her nerves and the itchy feeling of Victoria's watching eyes. She tried to remember the sensation of the branches rubbing against one another—the heat that came with it.

But nothing happened.

Victoria waited. Claire felt a fresh bead of sweat form on her brow.

"Maybe"—Victoria paused—"try in your wolf form. It's easier, I think. You don't have to fight through that human layer."

Claire hadn't thought of that. Since she'd have to do it in her human form at the ceremony, that's how she'd been practicing. But Victoria's idea seemed worth a shot, since all the things that she did in her wolf skin had come easily, as though she'd always known how to do them.

She transformed quickly, feeling a little awkward about being unable to communicate with Victoria, who sat patiently in her human form while Claire bent her snout to the twigs. They were more real to her in her wolf form—more complex. Like their matter wasn't as set as it seemed when she was a human.

She reached out with her thoughts, pushing the sticks to light, to burn.

The clearing stayed every bit as dark as it had been. There was no fire.

"I feel you working at it, but something's just *off*," Victoria said. "You have to push them to transform, but the fire's already in there. The way your wolf self's always inside you, even when no one else can see it. Like this." She narrowed her eyes, and the pile in front of her burst into flame so quickly that it was more like an explosion than an ignition.

Claire made a low noise in her throat to show that she understood. It was the closest she could come to talking.

"Transform back," Victoria suggested, "and try again." She stacked up a new pile of small branches while the other fire crackled and died, already using up its meager fuel.

Claire pulled on her smooth-skinned form, slipping quickly into her clothes. "At least that felt different," she said. "It's like I can see what I need to do but I can't quite reach it."

Victoria pursed her lips, thinking. "Maybe I can try with you." She lowered herself to her knees across from Claire. "Okay, just do what I do, step by step." She stared into the tiny pile of tinder. "Look right into the middle. I think it's easier if you keep your eyes open. Focus on putting a layer of fire over the top of it the same way you put a layer of fur over your skin."

For several long moments, the twigs lay cold and dark in front of Claire. Panic rose inside her, ugly and prickly. But then she felt something tug at her, like the wind tugging at the leaves.

And a spark caught.

The sudden light broke her concentration. The crackling of the twigs spread like a whisper through the clearing.

Claire rocked back on her heels, shaken and uncertain. Her eyes met Victoria's across the flames.

"Did I do that, or did you?" she asked.

Victoria's surprised expression mirrored hers. "I really don't know. That was weird. I mean, it was like it sucked the fire out of me or something."

Something inside Claire twisted. "So, that's not how it's supposed to feel?"

Victoria pushed her hair back off her face. "It's not how it feels when I do it, but maybe that means it was you? Or . . . maybe it was because we were both trying?" She stretched. "Ugh. I'm getting knotted up from sitting too long."

Claire's eyes went straight to Victoria's enormous belly, and she suddenly felt ridiculously selfish.

"You've stayed out way too long, and it's all my fault. I'm sorry. You should get home."

Victoria frowned. "I don't want to leave you when it seems like you're so close to being able to do it." She rubbed her hips like she was testing them.

"No, it's fine. I think I get it. Really. Besides, I need to head back before my mom gets suspicious," Claire said, standing up and brushing off her pants.

Victoria waddled over and gave her an awkward, sideways hug. "This was really nice," she said. "Having someone else who knows what it's like to be the Alpha's daughter—it makes me feel a lot better about things."

"Me too," Claire said, returning the hug. "Be care—"

Victoria gave her a sharp look.

"I mean, have fun getting home," Claire finished.

Victoria laughed. "You too."

Claire turned and jogged back through the woods, heading for home and praying that her mother would believe she had just been for a really, really long run.

* * *

Friday night, Claire sat in her room, staring at herself in the mirror and trying to decide if big silver hoops were too fancy for the party. As she got dressed for Yolanda's, she grew more and more excited. She was ready for the new moon gathering, and without that stress, she was dying to see Matthew and Emily.

There was a knock at the bedroom door and Lisbeth poked her head into the room and glanced around.

"Your mother's not in here, is she?"

Claire shook her head. "I have no idea where Mom is."

"Huh. She was looking for you—I figured I'd find you together. Anyway, I'm leaving for the weekend. Mark actually cooked eggplant curry from scratch, and I sort of have to be there to eat with him." She sighed.

"You don't sound all that excited about the eggplant curry." Claire wrinkled her nose.

"'Vegetable' is not a bad word, Claire. Mark just likes to spend a *lot* of time together. I'm not used to it, I guess. I miss hanging out with you." Lisbeth looked at her, the rejected clothes splayed on the carpet, the tube of opened-but-unapplied lip gloss in Claire's hand. "But it doesn't exactly look as though you're going to be sitting home pining for me."

Claire rolled her eyes, ignoring the nostalgia that was inching its way over her. "Just because I'm not 'pining' for you doesn't mean that I forget you exist the second you walk out the door or anything."

"Especially not when I leave you with these as a reminder." Lisbeth opened the door a little wider and revealed a plate full of chocolate heaven. "Triple fudge nut brownies. Can I come in?"

Claire nodded and sat up. She really wanted to finish her makeup in peace, but Lisbeth's brownies were impossible to turn down. Besides, she needed to get ready to go, and Lisbeth was likely to leave her alone a lot sooner if she said yes.

"Is anything special happening at the party tonight?" Lisbeth slid the brownies onto Claire's vanity and pulled one off the stack.

"Just too many people gossiping too much with too many camera phones involved. You know, the usual," Claire said, picking up a brownie and taking a bite of the dense, still-warm chocolate.

"Well," Lisbeth said around the food in her mouth, "if there's ever anything going on—or going to go on—or that you're . . . thinking about, you can come talk to me if you want to. I promise not to freak out."

Claire choked on her brownie. She didn't know whether Lisbeth was talking about drinking or sex or what, but she didn't want to find out.

"Well, I'd better go. Apparently, Dr. Engle's taking some new fancy researcher on a tour of the woods tonight, so I've gotta drive home the long way to get around the news vans."

The words closed around Claire like a cage. Penning her in. Trapping her.

The burned-out fires she'd left in the woods blared in her mind like a warning siren.

Lisbeth gave Claire a quick hug. "Mark's probably already wondering where I am. I'll see you on Monday, okay?"

Claire's phone chirped at her, and she picked it up. There was a text message from Emily.

Claire waved, focused on Emily's text, while Lisbeth closed the door. The message started off with OH MY GOD!!!!!!!

Emily liked to text in all caps. She said it gave her messages more excitement.

Claire glanced at the clock. It was a little after seven thirty, which meant the party had probably just started picking up.

This should be good.

She opened the message. It said, simply, THE STREET IS ALREADY FULL! WHEN ARE YOU GETTING HERE???

"Is everything okay?" Her mother appeared in the doorway.

"Just Emily. About the party." Caught off guard, Claire put the phone down.

"Ah. You look ... stressed. Is everything all right?"

Claire hesitated. The two choices hovered in front of her, waiting. She could either tell her mother and deal with the fallout of Marie knowing how much trouble she was having with the fire lighting, or she could sneak off into the woods alone and hope that she didn't get caught by some eager reporter or research-happy lycanthropist.

*If researchers are in the woods, I'll hear them coming . . .
I should be able to outrun them.*

"Um, yeah. It's fine. Just—Emily's wondering when I'm getting there is all."

Marie nodded, spinning her tea mug thoughtfully in her hands. "Well, I have some work to do. Enjoy your party." She ghosted away from the door, and Claire let out a long, thin breath.

She wasn't at all sure she'd made the right choice.

On the bed behind her, Claire's phone beeped.

Oh, crap. What am I going to tell Emily?

Claire snatched her phone off the bed, ignoring the texts, and dialed Matthew.

"Hey, babe. I was just leaving to come get you. What's up?" He sounded so upbeat and relaxed that it just highlighted how tense Claire was.

"Something came up. I don't have time to explain, but I have to go into the woods for a little while."

He cut in. "So, you're bailing on the party?"

Claire blew out a long breath. "No, but I'm going to be pretty late to Yolanda's. Can you tell everyone that—I dunno—that my mom dragged me to dinner and it ran late or something?"

"Sure," Matthew said, and she wondered if she was imagining the edge of irritation she heard in his voice. "I can do that. What about Emily?"

"I'll text her," Claire said, "which I need to go do right this second, 'cause if I'm not downstairs in exactly two minutes, I'm going to be cutting this way too close. Thanks for covering for me. You're the absolute best." It sounded like groveling, but she meant every word.

They hung up, and Claire sent Emily a text saying that she was stuck with her mom but she'd get to the party as soon as she could. She added some smiley faces and exclamation points, hoping that it would keep her desperation from showing, and sent it. She was already halfway down the stairs by the time she got the phone back into her pocket.

After a brief glance toward the basement, Claire slipped out of the house.

In the woods, Claire stayed in her human form. It was earlier than she usually went into the forest, and the noises of the daytime animals settling down to sleep made her edgy. She was used to more quiet.

With her ears straining for any sign of reporters, Claire maneuvered her way into the clearing. When she stepped out of the pine trees, the sight of the tiny, blackened pyres made her throat tighten. They looked so ceremonial, the way they were so perfectly centered in the ring of trees. It was horrifyingly obvious that they weren't leftover campfires or lightning-struck patches, and Claire had no doubt that they would have been suspicious of the fires if Dr. Engle and his entourage had stumbled across them.

As quickly as she could, Claire scattered the burned sticks, tossing them into the underbrush. When the charred remains had been dealt with, she got down on her hands and knees and swept her fingers through the pine needles, mixing the ashes into them until it looked as natural as any other tiny clearing in the woods. The whole time she worked, she listened to the sounds of the forest, becoming more comfortable as the familiar night sounds took over. She knew the creak of a branch settling beneath the weight of an owl and could recognize in an instant the *patter-swish* of a raccoon moving through the bushes.

She sat back on her heels and looked over the clearing one more time. Maybe she should transform, just to see if she'd missed anything. She'd be able to smell any big patches of ash she might have left. Without hesitating, Claire struggled out of her clothes, cursing the hook-and-eye closure of her shirt for slowing her down. She practically ripped the tiny pieces of metal apart, yanked the top over her head, and transformed before the fabric hit the ground.

She stretched out her hearing over the miles of forest, just as a precaution. Since in her true form she had the ability to hear over insanely long distances, she might as well use it. She scanned the forest. Without a specific person to focus on, it was harder to hear than usual. Her senses spun like an old-fashioned radio dial searching for a signal. And then, somewhere off to the southwest, she heard it.

A nasal female voice.

"We're already in the trees—I am *not* hiking through there in the dark just so that you can get a more 'authentic' shot, Jim."

Shit. The reporters.

Claire gave a hurried sniff in the direction of the clearing. She could smell one imperfect bit at the far edge, and she hesitated.

It wasn't worth getting caught over.

Claire grabbed her clothes with her mouth and ran through the woods, praying that Dr. Engle and his entourage weren't coming the other way through the forest. She tried to listen—to see if she could hear the scientists—but she couldn't focus enough to hear and run at the same time. It was almost worse than running from something—at least then she'd know for sure where the threat was and which way meant escape. All she could do was run like hell and hope that she made it out.

When the trees thinned enough that she could see a deserted stretch of road, Claire practically whimpered with relief. Only the fear that someone would hear her kept the noise from rattling in her throat. Quickly, she transformed, tugging on her clothes. Claire pulled her cell phone out of her pocket. It was damp from where she'd held it between her teeth—she'd been more afraid of losing it than drooling on it.

It was eight thirty. The party would be in full swing, but she was pretty sure she was only about half a mile from Yolanda's. It was going to be a long walk, though, since she was wearing heeled boots and didn't have a jacket. Still, the party was the best alibi she could have, for Marie and the lycanthropists both. She toyed with the idea of calling Matthew to come get her, but that would be even harder to explain to everyone, and she'd already asked an awful lot of him for one night, anyway.

She smoothed her shirt over her jeans, wrapped her arms around herself, and started to walk. The rhythmic ringing of her boot heels against the pavement sounded too loud against the obsidian silence of the night, and Claire shuddered, chilled by more than just the wind.

Chapter Six

FIFTEEN MINUTES LATER, Claire stood at the end of Yolanda's driveway. The front door to the house had been left ajar, and a strip of yellow, music-filled light sliced across the lawn like a beacon. Claire edged her way into the party, overwhelmed by the rush of heat and the crush of bodies. The rooms on either side of her were dark. And loud. And crowded. Down the hall was the kitchen, where she glimpsed a dented silver keg sitting in an enormous tub of ice.

She headed in that direction, scanning the faces for Matthew or Emily, nodding to people she recognized and trying not to wrinkle her nose at the smell of beer and desperation and excited sweat that filled the house. Yolanda came out of the den, where the flickering blue glow of a gaming system flashed across the faces inside. She spotted Claire and threw her arms around her neck.

"You're here! Oh, I'm so glad. Matthew said you had to do something with your mom. Oh my God, you're freezing! Did you walk here, or what?" Her eyes were sparkling, and her teeth were bright against the smooth, dark skin of her face. This was Yolanda in her element, throwing the best party of the year, flitting from person to person like a butterfly in a roomful of flowers.

Claire untangled herself from Yolanda's hug. "It's just really hot in here, I think. Sorry I couldn't get here sooner. Hey, have you seen Matthew or Emily?"

Yolanda pursed her lips, thinking. "They were in the living room a while ago. You might check there."

"Thanks." Claire wound her way back to the living room, where the pulse of a bass beat shook the pictures on the walls. In the corner next to the stereo, a couple of people with flashlights were joking around, sweeping the beams of light over the group in the middle of the room. One of the glowing strands darted across Matthew's smiling face. Claire took one step forward before realizing that he was dancing with Amy and Emily, the three of them goofing around on the dance floor like they were the oldest friends in the world. None of them were looking over their shoulders. Not looking for her, not worrying about anything.

A ripping sensation tore through Claire's chest as she watched the three of them. She should have been the one out there with Emily and Matthew. But it wouldn't be the same. Things wouldn't be that easy if she were with them. Amy could be Emily's friend without hiding anything—without worrying what would happen to Emily. And Matthew didn't have to keep any of Amy's secrets.

Claire took a step back and collided with someone.

"Claire! Hey, you made it!" Doug Kingman slapped her shoulder. "Matthew's in here somewhere. Have you found him yet?"

"He's, uh . . . dancing." Claire nodded in the direction of the dance floor. Maybe if she acted like it was no big deal, it wouldn't be.

Doug shook his head. "That boy *seriously* can't dance. You need to get over there and save him from himself."

Before Claire could protest, Doug grabbed her elbow and dragged her into the throng of people.

Matthew spotted them coming, and his face lit up. He hurried over to Claire, picking her up and spinning her around.

"Hey, babe. I'm glad you finally made it." His smile was genuine, and so was the kiss he pressed against her mouth.

Amy appeared next to them, smiling, her hair a tumble of sexy-messy curls.

"Hey, Claire. I'm so happy you're here! You missed all the drama—there was an *incident*, and Matthew and Emily had to rescue me."

"Robert Gorman found his way into the party. He roped Amy into dancing," Matthew explained. "I don't think she really knew what she was getting into."

"Oh. Ew." Claire tried to look sympathetic. "Well, I'm glad Matthew saved you, then."

"Hey! What about me? I was a knight in shining armor too. Or, a princess in shining armor. Whatever. You know what I mean." Emily swayed a little bit at Claire's side. She was drunker than Claire had thought.

Amy rolled her eyes conspiratorially at Claire and shook her head in Emily's direction. She leaned closer to Claire.

"Matthew said you were going to be late because something came up with your mom. That's such a bummer. What happened? Is everything okay?" She was trying so hard to be nice. But keeping Emily safe was hard enough—Claire couldn't imagine spinning enough lies to hide her secrets from another friend.

"Oh. Yeah. Fine. Just, you know, one of those stupid parent things." Claire waved a hand, as though she were only being vague because the details were so boring. She hoped that Amy would take the hint and drop it. She so didn't want to spend the rest of the night ducking Amy's questions about what Claire liked to do in her spare time and avoiding the I'll-share-if-you'll-share sort of confessions that she knew would follow. In another reality she'd probably really like Amy, but her world just wasn't big enough for that.

The curiosity in Amy's eyes gave way to hurt, and Claire grew tense, her toes curling against the soles of her shoes. Amy looked over at Emily and said in a half-joking way, "So, she's *your* best friend—is she always this wildly communicative?"

Claire felt a little muscle in her jaw jump as she clamped her teeth together. "It was no big deal, that's all."

Emily looked at Claire and bit her lip. Claire could see it in Emily's eyes—the memory of last year, of all the other years, when Claire would have complained to her in excruciating detail if a Marie-related incident had made her hours late for a party.

Damn. Damn, damn, damn! Claire struggled for a way to rescue the situation—to make Emily forget that she'd even been late. Amy cleared her throat and linked her arm through Emily's.

"Being saved from a potential stalker makes me super-thirsty. Come get something to drink with me?"

Emily squinted down at her cup. "Yep. I like that idea."

Claire sighed. At least Emily getting drunk was probably a pretty good way to make her forget about Claire's weird late arrival.

Well, "good" isn't quite the right word for it. "Effective," maybe. God, I sound just like my freaking mom. Fantastic.

Amy and Emily wove their way toward the kitchen, and Matthew caught Claire's hand and dragged her back into the crowd of dancers. She wove her fingers through his, trying to shake off the awkward, bad-friend moment.

"C'mon. Let's dance." He pulled her tight against him, his

clean, cinnamon-laced smell making her sigh happily.

It only lasted a few seconds.

Someone near the front window yelled, "Cops!"

"Shit. Let's go." Matthew grabbed her hand and pulled her toward the hall.

Claire's heart skipped a beat. Adrenaline flooded her veins, making her want to change. The light in the hallway hit them as she struggled to remain in her human form. Getting arrested would be bad, but transforming would be deadly. She bit down hard on the inside of her cheek, forcing herself to stay smooth skinned.

Around them, the party was half chaotic escape attempts and half drunk-and-ignorant partying. Since Claire and Matthew were sober, it was pretty easy to wind their way through the mess.

"Where are we going?" Claire asked as they broke into a jog.

"Garage." Matthew's face was grim as he pushed open a door and the cold, dank smell of cinder blocks and motor oil washed over them. "I figured this might happen, so I parked two blocks over," he said, his voice echoing a little bit. "We can cut through the backyard if we hurry. The cops never come in right away, 'cause then they have too many people to deal with. They give the people who are mostly sober a minute to make a run for it, and then they just haul in the really drunk ones." He sounded like he'd done this before.

Claire hoped he was right. And she hoped Emily and Amy were getting the hell out of the house too. Once she and

Matthew were outside, her senses took over. She heard the whine of the sirens, saw every welcoming hiding place. Faintly, she heard the crunch of hard-soled shoes on the gravel walk at the front of the house.

"They're almost to the front door," she whispered, her pulse thudding in her ears.

"Then we'd better get a move on."

They darted across the lawn in the shadow of an evergreen bush and jumped over the picket fence into a neighbor's yard. Claire turned toward Yolanda's and saw people streaming out the back doors like rabbits scattering, hopping in crazy patterns, hiding in stupid places. She wanted to wait for Emily, to make sure she was okay, but getting caught would mean too much for Matthew. His scholarship hadn't come through yet, and Claire wasn't going to be the one responsible for ruining his chances at UCLA.

Her senses sharpened, begging her to run. Her fingernails itched to become claws, and the dull edges of her human teeth ached to turn sharp and pointed. Struggling against the pull of transforming, Claire forced herself to look away. She grabbed Matthew's hand, and the two of them dashed around the neighbor's house, across a street, and through another set of yards. In the last one a golden retriever came around the corner, and Matthew jumped a mile. The dog's ears went back, though, when it caught Claire's scent, and with a quiet whine it slinked back around the corner with its tail dragging on the ground.

Submissive, her mind said first.

And then, *prey*.

The thought went through Claire like an electric charge. A painful shudder rolled over her. She could feel her fur, painful under the confines of her skin. Pushing its way out.

"Oh, shit," she whispered, frantically scanning the yard.

"What?" Matthew hissed.

"I—I—" The words caught in her throat. "Don't look at me! I'm going to change. Just—just leave me alone." She had to find a place to hide, but she didn't want him dragged in by the cops in the process.

"What, *now*?" A horrified look crossed his face.

She didn't answer him. She couldn't. Claire bolted behind a little barn-shaped storage shed at the far corner of the yard. She wasn't even close to being hidden, but it was the best she could do.

She tossed off her clothes, pressing herself close to the rough wood, willing herself to stay human. The fur crept out along her hands as they cramped themselves into paws. Her nails lengthened into claws.

And that's when she heard the footsteps.

"Claire?" Emily's voice rang out across the yard.

Oh, no. Oh please, no.

"She's—she's not here, Emily."

Claire could hear Matthew step toward Emily, heading her off.

"Is she hiding back there? Are you guys hiding back there?" Emily's words were half-slurred. Claire could tell from the direction of Emily's voice that she was looking at the shed, where Claire stood, caught between her two forms, struggling to get back into her human limbs.

If Emily saw her, there would be no way around the consequences. The pack would kill her best friend, and it would be all Claire's fault. Because she lost control.

That is not going to happen. I am not going to let that happen. She glanced over her shoulder, wondering if she could jump the chain-link fence without anyone seeing her.

"No. Claire took off ahead of me. I'm—I'm meeting her, uh, somewhere."

God, he's a terrible liar. Claire licked at her whiskers. She'd never heard him trying to cover for her before, but Emily was bound to see through this. Even if she was drunk.

"Emily?" Amy's voice came from somewhere far off and to the right. "This way! Come on, run!"

"Oh! Sorry, Matthew. Gotta go. Um, good luck." The thud of Emily's footfalls receded into the distance. Claire lay panting behind the shed, the fading rush of adrenaline sending shivers through her limbs. She took a long, whistling breath in through her nose—gaining just enough control over herself to change back into her human form. She did it quickly, yanking on her clothes just as Matthew's head appeared around the corner.

"Damn, that was close." His eyes were wide, and there was a tremor in his voice.

"I know. She almost—" Claire's voice broke, and she sagged against the splintery wood. "You should have left. I told you to leave!"

Matthew's jaw tightened. "She would have seen me anyway. I didn't know what else to do—what else to say." His voice shook. "But she didn't see. You're . . . you again, and she's off hiding in the bushes with Amy."

Claire just shook her head. Emily had been feet—*feet*—away from finding out exactly what Claire was. And Claire would never be able to live with herself if the pack came after Emily because of something Claire did—because she was so stressed that she hadn't been able to stop herself from transforming.

It was never going to happen again. She would do whatever it took to make sure that Emily stayed safe, even if it meant keeping Emily at arm's length. Just the thought of it made Claire lonely, but it was better than the alternative.

Matthew interrupted her wandering thoughts. "I know it's been a rough few minutes, but we are sort of running from the cops here, remember?"

"Right. Sorry." She could see his car from here. It was parked just on the other side of the bland, two-story house in front of them. They crossed the yard, the crunch of fallen leaves loud under their feet. Matthew hit the button to unlock his car, and they both slid inside.

It was over. They'd made it. Matthew drove them out of the neighborhood, taking a convoluted way around Yolanda's block to avoid the cops.

Shaking from the adrenaline, Claire leaned against the window. A stray wolf hair shimmered on the leg of her jeans, and Claire plucked it off, opening the window just a crack and dropping it into the cold October air. Getting rid of the evidence.

Matthew drove her home. The tension in the car was so thick that Claire could barely breathe. When she got home, Claire hurried upstairs before her mother could see her. She didn't want to explain why she was flushed, and if her mother knew—smelled—that something Claire had done posed a danger to the pack, there would be hell to pay. That was the only time Claire's human side really mattered to Marie—when it endangered the precious, protected bubble of her wolf life. And Claire was never going to let that happen.

There would be no more close calls. Ever. Even if it meant becoming a hermit.

Upstairs, Claire got ready for bed and sent Emily a text, asking her to call or text or something to let Claire know that she was okay. A text seemed safe enough. Normal. Human.

She flipped her phone shut and slipped into bed, where she dreamt restlessly of jealous dogs and ringlet-crowned intruders. And running.

Lots and lots of running.

Chapter Seven

THE NEXT MORNING, Claire had a text from Emily. It was time-stamped at nearly two thirty in the morning, and from the number of bizarre typos, it looked as though Emily had still been pretty wasted when she sent it. But at least she'd made it home, and she promised to tell Claire the whole "ftory" when they had coffee.

She went downstairs and flipped on the TV. The local news was on, doing some story about adopting shelter puppies. The next segment started with a shot of a nervous-looking reporter standing in the forest. Claire tensed, her fingers curling around the remote control.

"We're here live in the woods on the west side of the city, where visiting lycanthropist Dr. Masaharu Otsuke took a tour early this morning. Dr. Otsuke's visit represents a major coup for the university's research department, whose international funding has dropped sharply in the wake of this summer's failed attempt to cure a local werewolf. Dr. Otsuke will spend the next few days assisting the Federal Human Protection Agency's investigation into the werewolf's death, which occurred while it was under the care of local lycanthropist Dr. Charles Engle."

Claire leaned against the back of the couch, her teeth clenched.

They cut to footage of the night woods. The glare of the television lights bounced off the tree trunks, making the forest look stark and menacing.

The reporter droned on. "In addition to touring the forest, Dr. Otsuke will be the guest of honor at a dinner hosted by the Rotary club, and a special fun run is scheduled—"

Claire clicked off the TV, a pleased relief spreading through her. There was no mention of anything having been found in the woods. No evidence. Nothing weird. Her secret was safe.

At least, for the moment.

That afternoon, Claire's mom actually let her take the car—again—so that she could meet Emily and Amy at the coffee shop on Fourth Street. She didn't have a ton of time before she had to get ready for her date with Matthew, though, since Emily had texted her and pushed back the time. Twice. Apparently, having a hangover the size of Montana made it pretty hard to get out of the house.

When Claire walked into The Cloister, Emily was already sitting at their usual table in the front window, nursing an enormous latte. There was a long, thin scratch across her right cheek. Her eyes were puffy, and she had the pale, sallow look of someone who's had a rough night. Besides which, Claire could smell her hangover. The poisoned, cheap-beer scent seeped out of Emily's skin.

"Hey." Claire shrugged out of her jacket and dropped it onto the chair across from Emily. "How're you?"

Emily winced. "Not so loud, okay?"

Claire bit back a smile. She hadn't exactly been yelling.

"Let me go get my coffee, and I'll be right back."

Emily nodded, reaching for the cup in front of her.

Claire got her own drink and settled herself at the little table. "I'm so sorry we got separated in all the craziness. What happened to you and Amy?"

Emily snorted. "It's a little tough to remember all of it. I ran and found Matthew, but he was waiting on you, I think. Anyway, Amy was more sober than I was, and she managed to hide us and a couple of other people behind a hot tub in Yolanda's neighbor's yard. The cops walked right by us. We got really, really lucky, 'cause according to what everyone was posting and stuff this morning, they snagged a *ton* of people. What about you and Matthew? You guys found each other and everything?"

Claire could still feel the rough wood of the shed against the palms of her hands. She could still taste the terror that had flowed through her when she transformed. It had been so close. Emily had been so close. The coffee swirled unpleasantly in her stomach, and she resolved yet again to keep Emily out of harm's way.

Claire worked to keep her face casual. "We were both sober—we got separated for a minute, but we found each other. He'd parked a couple of streets away." She shrugged. "We drove home. No big deal."

Emily grunted. "Lucky. Why wasn't he drinking, anyway? I thought the soccer season was over."

"It is, but he's still waiting to hear from UCLA about scholarships. If he gets caught drinking—if he gets in trouble—it could ruin his chances. He's worked so hard that he's not going to screw it up now, you know?"

Behind Emily, the door swung open and Amy walked in. She looked like she was in better shape than Emily was, though her hair was slightly less perfect than usual and there were delicate lavender-colored circles under her eyes.

"Hi, guys." She stared around the coffee shop, taking in the worn and pitted church pews in front of the pastry case, the collection of fancy crosses that lined the walls. Her eyes widened when she spotted the handwritten menu of drinks with names like Liturgical Latte and Antichrist Americano.

"This is wild." She took a deep breath. "Ooooh, and the coffee smells fantastic." Amy wandered over to the counter and returned with a steaming mug that held something frothy and vanilla scented. "Wow. This place is really great. I can't believe I haven't been here before!" She slid into the open seat between Claire and Emily.

"It's good coffee, and they don't care how long you stay," Claire said. "We've been hanging out here since freshman year."

"Really?" Amy looked confused. "I'm surprised I haven't heard Emily mention it more, then."

Claire flinched. "Well, we haven't had as much time to hang out here lately, I guess."

"We hung out here a lot pre-Matthew, is what she means."

Amy shot Emily a meaningful look that made Claire instantly uncomfortable. It was the sort of look that said she and Emily had talked about Claire's lack of Emily-time before. "Yeah, boyfriends can be a huge time suck. Plus, if there's anything, you know, *complicated* going on, then it's doubly distracting." Amy looked like she'd just pinched Claire and was waiting to see if it had hurt.

Claire rubbed her arm distractedly. *Anything complicated going on?* What was that supposed to mean? Was Amy trying to convince Emily that there was more behind Claire's disap-

pearing act than just Matthew? If she was at all suspicious . . .
Oh, hell.

Claire cleared her throat. "So, um, other than the cops barging in and hiding behind hot tubs, what did you think of Yolanda's famous party?"

Amy lit up. "Oh my God, it was so fantastic! The music was awesome. And Matthew is so nice, Claire—you're so lucky."

"Uh, thanks."

A teasing smile spread across Amy's face as she stared over at Emily. "Ooooh, and guess what? Emily has a date for the Autumn Ball!"

Claire stared over at her best friend. "What? You do? Why didn't you tell me?"

Emily groaned and slouched lower over her cup. "Because it's Randy Steigerson."

Claire felt her mouth fall open. "Ran—wait. Seriously? You're going to the Autumn Ball with Randy Steigerson?" Randy was the editor of the yearbook. He was tall and sort of gangly. And he had a weird habit of leaning too close to whoever he was talking to.

"He was trapped behind the hot tub with us. Like, for hours. And he gave me his jacket when it got cold. . . . I don't know. I'd had an awful lot of beer before we got stuck back there." Emily put her head down on the table. "It's weeks away. Maybe I can get out of it."

"You look sort of green," Amy said.

"The Randy Steigerson reminder sent me over the edge. This coffee's not working. I need greasy food. Like, now."

"Why don't we go to Louie's?" Amy suggested.

"Perfect." Emily picked her head up and looked at Claire. "You in?"

Claire glanced at her cell phone. Matthew was going to be at her house in an hour and a half, and she still had to shower and change before he got there. She wasn't really finished talking to Emily, but maybe she could use her plans to convince Amy that the only complication in her life was a boyfriend obsession.

"Um"—she hesitated—"it's just . . . it's gotten sort of late, and Matthew and I have plans. . . ."

"Can you call him?" Amy asked. "We haven't even told you what happened with Kate-Marie yet!"

Claire bit her lip. "I know, but we already had to reschedule once because of Yolanda's party. . . ." She did her best to look torn yet love struck. "Why don't you two go ahead?"

Emily scowled into her coffee. "Fine. I'm going to the bathroom. I'll be right back, and then we'll go."

Claire watched her best friend walk away, each step driving the sadness and shame deeper into her heart. Each thud of her pulse made it worse. How could it have come to this? She wanted her best friend back—wanted to sit in the familiar coffee shop and have the sort of long, tangent-filled, soul-baring conversations they'd always had.

Amy glanced over at Claire. Curiousity and disappointment glimmered in her green eyes.

"It's too bad you can't come with us." Her voice was soft, gentle, but Claire could smell her suspicion.

Crap.

"Yeah. Sorry. Maybe I can make it next time," Claire said.

Amy took a long sip of her sweet-smelling drink. "I hope so," she said, turning to face Claire. "I think Emily's awesome. But it's weird, because even though you're her best friend, I know pretty much nothing about you. We should hang out more." Her earnest look startled Claire. There was nothing hidden in Amy's expression—no double-speaking smile, no Morse-code glance.

A year ago, Claire might have given someone the same look. But not anymore. Now she was always triple-checking her expression and weighing everything she said, making sure that a secret didn't slip out between her teeth while she wasn't paying attention.

Before Claire could recover enough to say anything, Emily came out of the bathroom.

"Okay, kids. I need fries. Now."

Claire scooped up her car keys and looked at Emily. Seeing her best friend standing there obviously trying not to look dejected, her defenses weakened. "Call me tomorrow? Maybe we can go shopping or something next week." Claire's voice sounded small. Emily looked over at her, surprised.

"Sure," she said. "Of course."

"Good." The miserable knot in Claire's middle loosened. Maybe it would be okay if they could hang out, just the two of them, away from the stress of Amy and all her suspicions and curiosity and general interfering.

A mischievous smile spread across Amy's face. "Yeah," she chimed in, wrapping her arm around Emily. "You have to find a dress suitable for Randy Steigerson."

Emily groaned and buried her sea-green-tinted face in her hands as Amy dragged her out of The Cloister, shooting Claire a scrutinizing sort of glance as they went.

Claire sagged as the door swung shut behind them. Amy was right about one thing: Claire's life was definitely complicated.

After a quick shower followed by a long session of try-things-on-and-pile-the-rejects-on-the-floor, Claire was mostly ready for Matthew. The doorbell rang before she could decide if her ballet flats were too dressy for a movie night.

Whatever. Bare feet are sexy, right?

She looked down at her unpainted toenails. Nail polish looked ridiculous on wolf claws, and after one transformation ending in pink-tipped paws, Claire had abandoned pedicures. Better to have plain human feet and look not-insane in her wolf form.

Claire hurried down the stairs and flung open the front door.

"Hey." Matthew grinned at her.

"Hey, back," she said. "Come on in."

Since Lisbeth had left hours ago and Marie was off on a shoot, they had the house to themselves.

Up in Claire's bedroom, Matthew flopped down on the bed, rolling onto his back and tucking his hands behind his head.

"So, did Emily make it home okay from Yolanda's last night?"

Claire sat next to him, leaning back against the headboard. "Yeah. Drunk, but okay. Sorry again that I was late to the party. It turns out that your dad took some Japanese researcher into the woods," she said simply. "I—" She hesitated, embarrassed. "I accidentally left some stuff around that I shouldn't have. I had to go fix it, and it's a good thing I did, because some reporters came and everything."

Matthew's mouth fell open. "I'm so sorry! I knew he'd gotten a last-minute meeting with that other researcher, but I had no idea they were going into the woods, I swear. I would have told you—"

Claire held up a hand. "I know. It's not your fault, Matthew."

"What sort of stuff did you have to clean up?"

"Burned things." The memory of the other night sent a tingle through Claire's middle. "From when I was working on how to light the fire the werewolf way."

His eyes darted around the room. "The Matchless Wonder, huh?"

It sounded like he was joking, but he was uncomfortable. She could smell it—an edgy, hungry sort of smell. Like he thought she was bragging. Or like she'd told him something she should have kept secret.

But he's a gardien, she reminded herself. *He's allowed to know this stuff.*

"Anyway"—she cleared her throat—"I'd accidentally left the burned-out piles in the woods. I didn't want my mom to find out and be pissed, and I didn't want your dad . . . Well, at least it's fixed now." She fiddled with a loose thread on the edge of one of her pillows. "Maybe when I get it—like, really get it—I can show you."

"Are you supposed to do that?" Doubt swam through his voice.

Claire froze. Her insides had gone all shivery, and not in a good way.

"I mean, you are a secret-keeper," she stammered. "The whole point is that I don't have to hide stuff from you, right? But I guess . . . it is just supposed to be for ceremonies and stuff. Maybe . . . Maybe at a gathering sometime?" Claire said.

"Yeah, sure." Matthew reached out and tucked a strand of Claire's hair behind her ear, a concerned expression on his face.

Claire swallowed hard. He'd seen her in her wolf form before. He'd watched her transform, even. But it had been a long time since he'd witnessed any of that, and all of a sudden, he didn't seem anxious to repeat the experience.

She looked up at Matthew, forcing herself to smile. "Let's just drop it, okay?"

"Sure," he said. "Come on." He stood up and held out a hand to her. "I'm starving. Let's go downstairs and find something to eat."

She reached out and took his hand. The two of them headed for the kitchen, but the feeling of Matthew's warm fingers wrapped around her own wasn't sending the usual rush of sparkling-hot blood through her veins. The longer the little knot of tension held on, the more freaked out she got. She'd never felt this way around Matthew. Ever. If anything, she'd always been *too* relaxed around him—too connected. She didn't understand what was happening. It was like everything had shifted just enough to make it hard to keep her balance. She didn't like this new, slant-floored world, but she wasn't sure how to straighten things out.

Matthew headed straight for the fridge, pulling out a pan of lasagna that Lisbeth had made the night before.

"God, I love your house. There's always something amazing to eat."

Claire hopped up onto the counter and perched there. "I think Lisbeth just feels guilty that there's not as much for her to do around here anymore, so she cooks."

"Well, I still love it." Matthew hummed to himself as he slid the pan onto the counter. He moved in front of Claire. "You're blocking the plates."

"Oh. Yeah."

She hadn't exactly meant to sit in front of that cabinet, but the teasing intensity of the look Matthew gave her made her glad that she had. The tangle inside her melted under his gaze. Gently, he nudged Claire's knees apart and stepped closer, wrapping one arm around her hips and pulling her against him. His lips grazed her neck, tracing a path from just underneath her jaw to the top of her collarbone. She wrapped her arms around him as his mouth met hers with the sort of burning kiss that sent electric tingles through her every time.

"What about the lasagna?" she managed to whisper.

"Screw the lasagna." She wrapped her legs around him, and he lifted her off the counter. "Couch." He kissed her. "Now."

She laughed as he carried her to the den and dumped her unceremoniously on the deep, fluffy couch. She stretched out on the welcoming cushions, and Matthew lay down next to her, picking up exactly where he'd left off in the kitchen.

Sometime later, Claire heard the faraway crunch of tires against gravel. She pulled away from Matthew, tugging down her shirt and sending up a tiny prayer of thanks that her mother had never paved the driveway. Matthew sat up blinking at her as she smoothed her hair.

"What's wrong?" he asked. "Did I do something?"

Claire reached behind herself and flipped on the side-table lamp. "My mom's home," she said, turning on the TV and searching for something she and Matthew could believably have been watching.

Matthew cocked his head, listening hard. "Are you sure?"

Claire raised an eyebrow at him. "Your hair is sticking up."

As soon as the words were out of her mouth, the unmistakable sound of the garage door opening rumbled through the house.

Matthew swiped at his hair. "I may never get used to your supersonic hearing." He grabbed a throw pillow that had fallen onto the floor and shoved it behind his back. "Right. So. What are we watching?"

There was a clank and a thud in the kitchen.

"Hello?" Claire's mom sounded tired. And vaguely grumpy.

"In here," Claire called back.

Marie poked her head around the corner. Her face was paler than usual, the contours of her cheekbones painfully sharp underneath her skin. She smiled when she saw Matthew, though Claire noticed her nostrils flaring ever so slightly. Claire willed herself not to blush. Other people only had to worry about not looking guilty when they got caught making out. Claire had to worry about smelling guilty, too.

"How was the shoot?" Claire asked. Talking about photography was the only sure way to distract her mother.

"Miserable." Marie pursed her lips. "They could hardly afford me, so the rest of their budget was nonexistent. The space was terrible, and the lighting was worse." She closed her eyes briefly.

"You okay?" Claire asked, concerned.

"Just tired and hungry. I noticed there's some lasagna on the counter. Have you eaten?"

"Um, not yet," Matthew admitted, a pink flush creeping into his cheeks.

"Well"—Marie cleared her throat—"why don't you join me, then?"

Claire opened her mouth to say no, but Matthew, who was clearly experiencing some sort of embarrassment-induced insanity, leapt in first.

"Sure," he said. "I'm starved."

"Wonderful." Marie smiled. "I'll get the plates."

The three of them sat in front of identical dishes of scalding-hot lasagna, the noodles hard at the edges from being microwaved too long. With the tines of her fork, Claire toyed with the fossilized cheese at the edge of the plate. No wonder her mother never cooked—she couldn't even heat things up without ruining them. Lisbeth's job was safe forever.

Marie eyed Matthew in a way that made Claire's stomach flutter to the ground. There was a thoughtful crease between her mother's eyebrows that Claire didn't like at all.

"You know, Matthew, it has been some time since you've been to a gathering. Perhaps we should make arrangements for you to attend the special ceremony we have planned for Claire."

A needle of panic pierced Claire, making her bolt upright in her seat. Matthew was already being weird about the pack stuff, and now her mother—her *Alpha*—was inviting Matthew to the new moon gathering? To watch her demonstrate her abilities?

"Oh, I wouldn't want to—I mean, I'd probably just be in the way." Matthew was gripping his fork so tightly that his knuckles had turned white.

Claire froze. There was no way she could complete the test if he was there freaking out while he watched her transform. Not to mention the hunt.

Oh, holy crap. I cannot let him see that. It will totally push him over the edge.

Marie spoke carefully, her voice carrying a note of command. "You won't be in the way. Quite the opposite—you're important to the pack, and I'm looking forward to seeing you there."

The words sent a shudder through Claire.

Matthew glanced over at her. "You okay?"

She forced herself to smile. "Yeah. Sure. Just not that hungry after all."

"How can you not be hungry for this—" Matthew's focus

drifted over her head, and his face paled. "Oh my God, is it really eleven o'clock?" He picked up his half-empty plate and carried it over to the sink.

"I've got to get home or I'll be in serious trouble." He turned to Marie. "Thanks for dinner and all."

Marie waved her hand dismissively. "It was Lisbeth's doing. I'm glad you were here, though. It's good we had a chance to talk."

Matthew turned to Claire. "Walk me out?"

"Sure."

She slid off her seat, carefully avoiding her mother's too-curious gaze, and followed Matthew to the front door. He grabbed his coat from the little chair where he'd tossed it and shrugged it on. When she wrapped her arms around him, she breathed in a whiff of his warm skin mixed with clean wool and the faintest hint of woodsmoke—an autumn version of the Matthew scent she knew and loved. He didn't lean into her embrace, though. Claire noticed it and stepped back.

Matthew edged toward the door. "I'll call you, okay?"

"Absolutely." With a last, lightning-quick kiss, he headed for the driveway. The icy air that swirled in behind Matthew chilled Claire, but the sudden distance that had appeared between them froze her to the bone.

She had to find a way to rescind her mother's invitation. And she had exactly forty-eight hours to do it.

Chapter Eight

"WELL, *CHÉRIE*, YOU'RE the one who talked with him about the new moon gathering." Marie stacked the rest of the dishes in the sink. "And he is a *gardien*. It makes sense for a secret-keeper to stay reasonably well-connected to the pack. Strong bonds make for strong loyalties, after all."

Claire crossed her arms in front of her.

"Yeah, but he and I were just *talking* about it. Inviting him to the gathering to see me change and stuff without even checking with me is not okay!" Though, to be honest, she was starting to think that she'd made a massive mistake when she told him about the gathering in the first place.

"I don't want him there while the pack is watching me—just me—like that."

It wasn't exactly true. But she wasn't going to throw Matthew under the bus by telling her mother that *he* didn't seem to want to be there.

Her mother turned to her. "He is part of the pack, Claire. Being a *gardien*, a secret-keeper, ties him to us. It is not wrong for him to be there."

Claire scrubbed at her eyes, frustrated. "I know that! I mean . . . it's just sort of complicated."

Marie stepped closer to her, cupping the back of Claire's neck in her hand.

"It will always be complicated, *chérie*. That is the nature of being what we are."

Claire narrowed her eyes and ducked out from underneath her mother's hand. Marie might be right, but Claire wasn't going to admit it. She stalked over to the stairs, looking back at her mother.

"He's not coming. I won't do it. I'll stand there and not do a single thing if he's at that gathering."

Her mother's nose twitched—an unhappy warning about Claire's commanding tone. She stared hard at Claire, the dominance of her position as Claire's Alpha and mother obvious in her eyes.

"You will absolutely perform as you are ordered. If you choose to disobey me, there will be extremely serious consequences. Matthew will attend, and you will find some manner in which to cope with your feelings." Marie's language got really stilted, which meant she was about three words away from slipping into French. She was seriously angry. She turned away from Claire, dismissing her.

Claire drew in a deep breath, stomped up to her room, and threw herself onto her bed. She stared up at the ceiling. The unfairness of her situation swirled around her like a fog, clouding her thoughts.

I could lie. Tell Matthew that he wasn't allowed to come after all and tell the pack that he got sick or something.

Claire wasn't above lying. She wasn't even uncomfortable with it anymore—not after months of living a life that was half-true at best. But she knew that if her mother ever found out, there would be hell to pay, in a very literal sense. And of course, she'd never lied to Matthew. Not about anything that counted, at least, and deep down she knew she couldn't start now.

She rolled onto her stomach and pulled the pillows over her head. All she wanted was to keep Matthew home, where he belonged, far away from the dead-eyed gaze of the new moon.

Monday morning, Claire stood at her locker, shoving the binders and books she needed into her bag.

A pair of familiar-smelling hands—freesia lotion and watercolor residue—snaked over Claire's shoulders and covered her eyes.

"Guess who."

"Hi, Emily." Claire spun around to face her. Emily's mouth was smiling, but there was something stiff and unhappy in her eyes.

"Wow. You sound cranky," Emily said. "And you never called me yesterday. What's the story with that, huh?"

Claire took a deep breath. True, she hadn't called Emily. But she'd been so worried about Matthew and the gathering, and then she'd gotten distracted with her homework—besides, she was the one who'd asked Emily to call *her*.

"Sorry," she said. "I was studying for my chem test."

Emily made a face. "Ew. Why? It's not until tomorrow. I thought maybe we could study together tonight."

With the gathering scheduled for late that night, there was no way Claire could make plans with Emily. Claire's mouth went dry as she searched for an excuse. "Um, I can't tonight. I have . . . Mom has a work thing, and I have to go help her with it."

It was such a thin lie that it was practically see-through.

A disbelieving crinkle appeared between Emily's eyebrows, and the little jingle that Claire's nerves had been playing all morning turned into a full-blown orchestral score. Today was not a day she could afford to screw up, and she was already making a mess of it. Lying practically counted as a werewolf ability.

She was failing before the gathering had even started.

"You've been helping your mom an awful lot lately. Marie's never exactly been a TV-perfect sort of mother—why so much togetherness all of a sudden?" Emily asked.

Claire shrugged. "I think she wants me to follow in her footsteps or something. But you know I can't take pictures for crap. Can I come over on Wednesday?" she asked, changing the subject.

The crinkle disappeared, and Emily's eyes lit up. It made Claire feel so much better, seeing Emily so happy.

"Absolutely! Anything special you had in mind?"

"Yep." Claire nodded. "It's only a few weeks until the Autumn Ball. Since I've never been to a dance, I need to start thinking about a dress, and you know I'm no good at making these sort of decisions without you. I want to make a game plan before I start the misery of trying things on."

Emily let out a little squeak. "Yay! Of course!" She was practically bouncing. "You know, it's almost worth going with Randy—at least you and I will finally be at a dance together!"

The warning bell rang.

"I've got to get to history," Claire said. "See you at lunch?"

"Absolutely!" Emily turned and disappeared into the hurrying crowd.

Claire watched her go, dying for it to be Wednesday. For the gathering to be over and to be able to just do nothing with Emily.

As the day wore on, Claire got twitchier. Edgier. She

tried to focus on the shopping websites Emily talked about at lunch, but she couldn't concentrate. She needed to think through everything she had to do one more time. How to light the fires. Transforming. Leading the hunt.

Werewolf 101.

At least she had the long-distance hearing. Not all wolves could do that, and it would probably impress Judith and Katherine. At least, a little bit.

She hoped.

Between classes, she looked for Matthew in the halls. She finally saw him ducking into government, just before the bell rang. He flashed her a smile like sunlight, but she barely had time to return it before she dashed to Spanish. Disappointment rumbled through her. It was the last chance she'd have to see him before the gathering. She wished they'd been able to talk—it would have been nice to hear him say he was excited or proud or *something*.

After her last class, Claire made it back to her locker and spun the lock, more than ready to escape school. Lisbeth was supposed to pick her up, and Claire wasn't even dreading the New Agey music that Lisbeth played in the car. She just wanted out of the hallway chaos.

But she hesitated before she pulled open the locker door. For years she'd watched other girls open their lockers and find flowers or balloons or tight-folded notes inside wishing them luck on something or another. Kate-Marie's locker looked like a gift shop half the time. It was the sort of thing that Claire had always been jealous of—that kind of obvious attention. And it was exactly the type of thing she thought Matthew might do, especially since they hadn't had a chance to talk.

A hopping little anticipation started in Claire's middle, and slowly she pulled open the locker door.

And saw nothing. Just books, and a stray sweater shoved onto the shelf. No half-wilted carnation, no card. Not even a "good luck" scrawled on a piece of notebook paper. Claire sagged under the surprising weight of her disappointment. She grabbed her books, slammed the door shut, and practically ran for the parking lot.

"You okay?" Lisbeth frowned as Claire threw herself into the car and swung the door closed with more force than was necessary.

"Yeah. Fine." Claire slouched down in the seat and closed her eyes. "I'm just ready for it to be Tuesday."

Lisbeth put the car in gear and headed for the exit. "I can still tell that something's bugging you. You can talk to me about it, you know. I don't bite."

That was probably true. If Claire actually told Lisbeth about all the things that were bothering her, Lisbeth would be too busy running shrieking in the other direction to bite anyone.

"I'm stressed about my chem test tomorrow." It wasn't a lie, and it would probably get Lisbeth off her back.

"Oh. Well, at least you have a whole night ahead of you to study, right?" Lisbeth's voice was so perky-bright that it made Claire want to scream. Instead, she nodded.

Once they were home, Claire escaped to her room while Lisbeth tackled a mountain of laundry. Claire tried everything she could think of to calm herself down—listening to music, watching bad TV, reading her English assignment. Nothing worked. The minutes ticked by at an annoyingly steady pace. She resorted to pacing the room.

She was on the verge of going to ask Lisbeth to teach her some sort of magical yogic breathing, figuring she could blame it on pre-chem-test stress, when her mom appeared in the doorway.

"You look tense."

"Hi to you, too," Claire snapped. Of course she was tense.

"You have no reason to be worried." Her mother's voice was softer than a whisper—a vibration on the air. "You know how to do everything—more than everything, with your extra hearing abilities."

Claire tried not to dwell on the fact that that wasn't entirely true. She'd come really, really close to starting the fire, but that was far from a guarantee that she'd be successful enough to lead the hunt that night. Especially with her boyfriend staring at her while she tried.

"But everyone will be there. Watching." She eyed her mother resentfully. "Matthew, too."

"You are my daughter." Her mother's voice was no louder than before, but it had a razor edge that cut Claire to the quick. "You are stronger than your nerves, and I expect you to be flawless tonight. Because I know you can be."

"Uh, thanks."

Her mother shot her a pointed look. "I will meet you downstairs at eleven thirty. That way, we will have plenty of time before the others arrive. I suggest you try to get some rest."

Marie turned and disappeared down the hall.

Claire walked over to the door, closed it, and resumed her pacing.

By the time eleven thirty rolled around, Claire had practically worn a bald patch in her carpet. With her nerves chattering, she threw on some old sweats and skittered down the stairs to meet her mom. Lisbeth had left hours before, after giving Claire a hug and a pep talk on the benefits of knowing how to balance a chemical equation. Claire and her mom had the house to themselves, but Claire still found herself moving quietly. She'd done so much sneaking in and out of the house over the summer that it had become a habit.

Her mother was waiting in the kitchen, dressed in high-tech light-but-warm running gear.

"Ready to go?" her mother asked.

Claire hesitated. What she really wanted was to have a few minutes alone in the woods before she had to face the judging eyes of the pack. She looked at her mother and shook her head.

"You go. I'll be right behind you."

Marie gave her an appraising look, but there was no disappointment or suspicion in it. In fact, she looked almost understanding.

"Fine. Don't be long, though, *chérie*. This is not a night to be late."

"I won't be." Claire crossed her arms, wrapping her hands tight around her ribs. She watched her mother slip out the back door and glide across the dark lawn, a shadow among shadows, all but invisible.

After giving her mother a few minutes' head start, Claire stepped out into the frosty night air. It was mid-October—soon they'd be starting the steep slide into the long, frigid winter. Overhead, the stars spit and sputtered in between a few wispy clouds, and there was a hole in the sky where the new moon hung, black and cold.

Claire stepped away from the house and faced the almost-leafless arms of the woods. Her heart crashed against her ribs. This was it. Her night to prove herself as a wolf. She squared her shoulders and hurried across the grass toward the waiting trees.

Once she stepped through the ragged opening in the brick wall that ringed their property, once she smelled the dying-leaf scent of the forest, everything changed. The swirling chaos of nerves she'd been dealing with all day became a focused determination. This was where she belonged.

She took a deep breath and ran off through the trees, following the path around the underbrush, over the fallen pines. In the distance she could just see the clearing. Without the fire, it would be invisible to a human eye, but Claire could see the starlight that penetrated the now sparsely leafed canopy.

As she stepped into the clearing, Claire's attention went straight to the flat, empty circle in the middle. The place where the fire would be. There was a small pile of branches stacked haphazardly off to one side.

"I started collecting the wood for you," her mother said, emerging from the trees on the far side with her arms full of kindling. She passed the awkward bundle to Claire.

"You might as well begin building it. The others will be here soon."

"Yeah. Okay." Claire arranged the branches the way she'd seen her mother do it before, creating a perfect little pyramid of wood. Behind her, there was a *crunch-swish* of footsteps against the forest floor.

Beatrice stepped out of the woods, her white hair gleaming. She turned toward Claire's mother, baring the side of her neck.

"Marie, I greet you."

"As I greet you, Beatrice." Her mother nodded solemnly.

Beatrice turned to Claire, her face cracking into a wrinkled web as she smiled.

"Claire! I greet you," she said, reaching out a gnarled hand to help Claire to her feet. "I greet you, Beatrice." Claire got to her feet. "Where's Victoria?"

"Here I am." Victoria bumbled out of the woods, her belly even larger than it had been the last time Claire saw her. "Marie, I greet you," she huffed.

"And I greet you, Victoria." Marie bit back a smile.

Claire greeted her, trying not to stare at her swollen middle.

Victoria hugged her. "Do not ask me about the baby," she whispered into Claire's ear.

"I wasn't going to. I'm too nervous," Claire whispered back.

"Good. But don't be. Now let me sit down." Victoria lowered herself awkwardly onto the ground.

Beatrice dragged Claire over to one side of the clearing while Marie and Victoria talked about the baby.

"I want to give you something," she said quietly, reaching into her pocket. She pulled out a square of cloth, unfolding it carefully. In the middle was a necklace. A perfect black circle of onyx with a tiny diamond set in its center hung from a delicate silver chain.

Claire's mouth dropped open. It was gorgeous.

"My mother gave it to me at my new moon gathering. To remind me that my power was there even when I couldn't see it." Beatrice pointed a twisted finger at the sky. "Just like the moon. That's why we do the gathering during the new moon, you know."

"I—I didn't know," Claire stammered. She felt her cheeks flushing with heat despite the kiss of the cold air. "I can't take that, Beatrice—I mean, it's beautiful. And it's so nice of you, but it's too much. And shouldn't Victoria—"

"Nonsense." Beatrice pressed the necklace into Claire's hand. "I gave Victoria a gift for her new moon gathering, but now I'm giving this to you. I'd love to see you wear it. And when you succeed tonight, it'll make me feel like I had a little part in it."

Claire closed her fingers around the pendant and threw her arms around Beatrice. "Thank you. I love it."

"Good." Beatrice squeezed her tight.

"Claire?" Her mother called. "The others are here."

Claire reached up and fastened the delicate chain around her neck before she turned to greet Judith and Katherine. Judith was eyeing her as though she were a piece of fruit that wasn't quite ripe, but Katherine was smiling at her in an encouraging way. Like she was a puppy at a dog show. Claire swallowed hard and made herself greet them confidently. Still, the reminder that not everyone believed in her the way Beatrice did sent a shiver of doubt through her, like a crack in a pane of glass.

Before she was forced to start making small talk, Claire heard something crashing through the underbrush. The flicker of a flashlight beam splintered the darkness of the woods, and the breeze brought Matthew's scent into the clearing. The other wolves stiffened, and Claire felt herself tense along with them. She'd never understood their hesitation before—had never gotten why a *gardien* would cause that sort of reaction.

But she could see it on their faces. It didn't matter that he'd been invited. It didn't matter that he knew their secret, that he kept it willingly.

He was human. And anything human in the woods was dangerous to them.

Matthew finally broke through the edge of the trees, his eyes going straight to Marie. "I'm not late, am I?" he asked. Worry shimmered across his face.

Marie stepped forward, wrapping an arm around him and pulling him into the middle of the clearing.

"Not at all. We were just getting ready to begin."

Marie steered him over to the edge of the circle and sat him next to Victoria and Beatrice. Judith and Katherine arranged themselves across from the trio, putting as much space between Matthew and themselves as they could. Claire ended up between Matthew and Judith. Her mother stood across from her, staring over the pile of wood. Matthew shrank into himself, barely even glancing at the other wolves. It was so obvious that he didn't want to be there. There might as well have been a neon sign buzzing over his head saying DESPERATE TO LEAVE.

Claire bit down on the inside of her cheek and forced herself not to stare at him.

Marie raised her arms over her head, and the group fell silent. She lowered her arms and stood in the darkness. With her shoulders square and her chin high, she began to speak.

"Welcome, all of you. Tonight we gather to witness the abilities of our newly transformed wolf. We will support her, but we will not assist her." She looked deeply, unflinchingly into Claire's eyes—a show of her status. Claire tore her gaze away, focusing instead on the waiting pyre.

She took a step back and motioned Claire closer to the pile of branches. "The first step in our ceremonies is the lighting of the fire. It connects us—spiritually and viscerally—to our ancestresses, and through them to the Goddess herself. The fire that comes from us, through our will, shows all who watch that we are part of the unbroken chain of werewolves that travels back to a time before memory. Their power gives us power—and the fire is the symbol of that strength."

Even in the darkness, Marie's eyes were luminous as she turned to Claire—like the spark of fire inside her shone so brightly that it was visible.

"Claire, you may begin."

Claire opened her mouth to say thanks, but the words caught in her throat.

She knelt, the ground cold and unforgiving beneath her knees. The stack of firewood was much larger than anything she'd lit before. It loomed in front of her, as if the ghosts of a thousand werewolves were staring down at her from the top.

Maybe I should have practiced on bigger branches.

Trying to stay calm, Claire picked two small twigs near the bottom of the pile, whose tips just touched. She took a deep breath, which was a huge mistake.

The smells in the clearing intensified in a blink-short moment. Support and excitement and doubt and nerves swirled together, choking Claire.

She could smell Matthew sitting across the clearing. His own scent, the maleness of it, strange in the protected clearing. It tugged at her attention, making it hard to concentrate.

"Claire?" Her mother prompted.

"Sorry." Claire turned her attention back to the twigs, focusing hard on the point where they came together. Seeing the molecules getting hot. She tried to give herself over and feel the same pulling sensation she'd had the night she practiced with Victoria.

Nothing happened.

She closed her eyes, trying to block out everything except the twigs. Matthew shifted, and the sound of his jeans scraping against the ground, the catch in his breath, drowned out Claire's own thoughts. She turned away from him and tried again.

She shook her head, her heart pounding harder with each second that passed.

She tried again, willing the flames to come. Behind her, she heard Judith clear her throat impatiently.

After several painful minutes, Claire looked up at her mother's shocked face.

"Can I transform? I think . . . maybe I can do it in my wolf form."

Marie shook her head slowly. Her eyes were wide. Horrified. "You must be able to do it in your human form. That is how the ceremonies begin. You—you cannot do this?" she whispered.

Claire slumped miserably in front of the branches.

"I've made smoke," she said. "I'm just . . . I'm nervous. Sorry."

"You'll get it," Katherine said in a too-chipper voice.

Marie shot her a silencing look. "All wolves can do this. All wolves have to be able to do this." Her voice was filled with an embarrassed rage that made Claire want to sink into the ground.

"Marie," Victoria said carefully, "she's trying. None of us are perfect, at the beginning."

Having someone speak up for her made Claire feel a tiny bit better.

But not much. Her cheeks still burned with shame.

"This is not about perfection." Marie was practically shaking. "This about doing the basic things we can all do. Victoria, I want you to take Matthew home, now." She turned to Matthew. "I am sorry. As you can see, we have some unexpected pack business to attend to. Victoria will make sure you get home safely."

Victoria made a disappointed noise. "If there is pack business, I want to be part of it."

"Matthew needs an escort, and I have selected you." Marie's voice was crackling with barely contained emotion. "I am your Alpha, and I am telling you to take him."

Victoria struggled to her feet, anger glowing in her cheeks. "Come on, Matthew. We've got to go."

Matthew stood up, looking like he wanted to say something but also like he wanted to bolt out of the clearing. He shot Claire an apologetic glance that made Claire's insides shrivel into dust. She had never been so embarrassed in her whole life.

"I'll see you," he said awkwardly, turning to follow Victoria.

"This way," Victoria said, steering him into the woods.

Claire and the rest of the pack watched them go. She was never going to get over this. She'd humiliated herself in front of Matthew and the pack. Leading the hunt was a lost dream.

When their footsteps faded, Marie turned to Claire. "Why did you not tell me you were struggling?"

"But I thought I could do it! I made the smoke before, and maybe sort of lit it another time. I just . . . It was hard to focus," Claire protested.

Marie looked over at Beatrice. Claire's mother had a look of uncertainty on her face, a hesitation that Claire wasn't used to seeing there.

"Is there any way around this?" she asked. "The consequences are so serious . . ." Marie's voice faltered.

Beatrice frowned, the wrinkles in her forehead deepening. "She must be able to do it." She looked sympathetically at Claire.

"I know." Marie closed her eyes, thinking, and then turned back to Claire. "The best I can do without violating out laws is to give you a bit more time. The naming of Victoria's baby will take place the night after she is born. Smoke is not good enough—nor, unfortunately, is your word. You will have until then to master this skill and perform it without error, or I will be unable to keep you from suffering the repercussions."

Claire's mouth went dry. "What happens if I can't do it? If I fail?" The words came out in a croak.

"You are not to fail." Marie pressed her lips together. They were white as snow.

"But what happens if I do?" Claire dug her fingernails into the dirt, steadying herself.

"Then you would be considered an incomplete wolf, unable to do the things that are part of a werewolf's nature. And we would have to"—Marie looked as though she were gagging on the words—"mark you as one."

The panic that swept through Claire was so cold that it numbed her and burned her at the same time.

"Mark me how?" Claire's voice was barely louder than a breath.

Judith leaned forward, her eyes bone hard and blood dark. "The top of your left ear. We cut it off. That way, any pack—

any wolf—who sees you knows immediately that they're looking at a werewolf without the right skills. A mongrel who can't be allowed to help make decisions or participate in the pack the way a normal wolf can."

The edges of Claire's vision went fuzzy, and her hand automatically went to her left ear, covering it. Protecting it. The twisted expressions on Katherine's and Beatrice's faces made it clear that this wasn't some sort of nice, neat operation that would involve anesthesia and pain meds—that it would be as vicious and brutal as Claire could imagine.

"But—but you wouldn't have to. I mean, couldn't you . . . ," she stammered, still holding the side of her head. Not believing that they'd really go through with it. Not her own mother. Not her own pack.

Judith's voice was smooth and rigid as steel. "It's part of our laws, Claire. Enforcing them is your mother's responsibility. If she doesn't do it, the pack will. I will. If another pack—even a *seule*—found out that we'd broken the laws just to protect an Alpha's daughter, they'd have no respect for us. We'd be targeted. Possibly even attacked. Our territory, these woods, would be considered up for grabs." She hesitated, regret fluttering across her face. "I wouldn't do it because I want to hurt you, but because there are so many threats to our pack, and they don't all come from the human world. Making exceptions weakens us."

Marie interrupted her, the crease between her eyebrows

and the lines on the sides of her mouth deepening as she spoke. "Judith is right. As much as I wish things were different, everything she has said is true." She took a step closer to Claire, lowering her voice. "All you have to do is light the fire, and you will be a Beta wolf, like the rest. Whole. Able to hunt, able to advance in the pack, someday." Marie blinked rapidly, and Claire realized that she was actually crying.

Oh, holy . . . they're going to cut off my ear. If I can't do it, they'll actually cut off my freaking ear.

Claire felt herself sway.

"What about the rest of the ceremony?" she managed to ask.

"You don't look like you're in any condition to continue," Marie said, her face smoothing as she gained control of herself, "and since we're postponing the fire lighting, I don't see why we can't do the rest later as well."

"I think that's a good idea," Beatrice offered, her kind voice wrapping around Claire like a bandage.

"Then you may go," Marie said, dismissing the other wolves with a wave. "We will not gather again until the next full moon. Unless, of course, Victoria has the baby sooner than I anticipate."

Claire shuddered. There was no way to know how long she had. She was going to have to master the fire lighting, no matter what. No more late-night phone calls with Emily. No more parties or soccer matches getting in the way. Not when the consequences for failing were so severe.

Leaving the other wolves behind, Claire and her mother walked back through the forest together, headed home.

"I am not planning to harp on tonight's failures," her mother said quietly.

Claire waited, her feet moving mechanically along the path.

"But do not *ever* keep a secret like that from me again. If I had known you were struggling, I might have been able to do something to help you. But now that the pack knows, now that it has been set in motion, my hands are tied."

Claire gritted her teeth.

She means that Judith is tying her hands—and taking my ear, if I can't light the fire.

The thought pounded through her head like an unending drumbeat of dread, growing louder and louder until it was the only thing she could hear.

Chapter Nine

SHE WAS SO late to school the next day that she went flying into her first-period class, still in her coat, her hair wet and cold against her cheeks. She hadn't seen Matthew or Emily—hadn't even stopped by her locker. Which was just as well, since that meant she still had her chem notes with her. The horror of the night before faded a little with the first bell, and with an uncomfortable thud Claire landed right back in the middle of her human life, complete with the need to pass chemistry.

She flicked through the flash cards under her desk, trying to look like she was paying attention to the history lecture at the same time. Class ended way too soon. Claire shoved the note cards back into her bag and hurried out the door, hoping she'd at least be able to ditch her coat before she had to face the test.

Matthew was waiting for her. He looked nervous and exhausted. Exactly how Claire felt. "Hey, there. Did you—" His eyes scanned her, looking for something. "Wait—have you been to your locker yet?"

Claire shook her head. "I overslept," she said, juggling her coat in her arms.

"Well, if we hurry, you'll have time." Matthew grinned at her.

She narrowed her eyes. Whatever she'd been expecting after he left the gathering, it wasn't this.

"Okay . . ." she said, turning to walk toward her locker. Playing along.

When she opened the door, her confusion rose and swirled until she was dizzy with it. Inside was exactly the sort of thing she'd expected to find yesterday. A gorgeous yellow rose, its ruffled petals filling her locker with a cloying smell. There was a little note wrapped around the stem. Slowly, Claire reached for it, unfurling the paper.

Good luck on your Chem test—not that you need it! You're too brilliant to need luck on this one.

Love,

Matthew

Claire turned to look at Matthew. She knew her disbelief showed on her face, but she didn't really care. He had completely ignored the new moon gathering, which had been massively important, but he was wishing her luck on a stupid chemistry test? Did he really think she cared that much about a school test after the disaster of the night before?

Irritation scratched its way up Claire's insides. He really couldn't deal with the fact that she was a werewolf. And she didn't know what to do about that.

But not now. I can't deal with it now—I'll just have to manage until after I figure out the fire thing.

Not having her ear mutilated had to be her priority. After the naming, she could sort out her tension with Matthew.

"What's wrong?" he asked. "Your face just went all funny."

"Oh, thanks. That's exactly what every girl wants to hear in the morning," Claire joked. Well, half-joked.

"You know what I meant," he insisted. "Are you okay?"

Swallowing hard, Claire leaned up and gave Matthew a quick kiss.

"Fine. Just tired. Thanks for the flower."

Matthew looked vaguely disappointed, which only made Claire more irritated. And nervous, since the new distance between them wasn't getting any shorter.

"Okay, I've gotta go face Mr. Gould's own special form of torture," she said.

"Huh?" Matthew looked confused.

"My chem test." Claire sighed. "I'll call you later, okay?"

With her eyes trained on the buffed gloss of the tile floor, Claire trudged down the hall.

On Wednesday afternoon, Claire and Emily walked out to the parking lot. The clouds overhead were low and gray, promising rain by nightfall. Emily unlocked the car with the key fob, and Claire sighed with jealousy.

"I know, right?" Emily said, tossing her bag into the backseat. "When is your mom going to break down and get you a car?"

"Probably never," Claire grumbled, sliding into the passenger seat. "I'll have to beg you and Matthew for rides until I'm eighty."

"Well, at least she's getting you a dress for the Autumn Ball!" Emily drove toward the edge of the school's grounds, pausing at the stop sign and wiggling her eyebrows at Claire. "And guess what? You'll never guess—I'll just tell you. I'm having an after party the night of the ball—it's going to be *the* after party, actually. It's going to be so much fun." She hesitated, just for a second. "You can come right? I mean, you and Matthew?"

Emily's excitement was contagious, and Claire started to feel the buzz of dresses and tuxes and after parties—all the normal stuff that the human side of her had been missing. "Of course we'll come," Claire said. "How on earth did you get your parents to agree to it?"

"It's their anniversary." Emily's eyes glinted wickedly. "They're going to Cabo for a couple of days, and they're leaving me with the house all to myself."

"Aren't you worried about getting caught?"

Emily shook her head. "I'll have days to clean up. And besides, it's the only way to salvage a night with Randy Steigerson."

Emily looked genuinely miserable about her date, but after so many dances when Emily had boyfriends she was crazy over and Claire sat home, Claire figured one less-than-stellar date wouldn't kill Emily.

"So, you really can't get out of that one?" she asked.

"No. First of all, Amy pointed out that he's actually a really nice guy, he's just sort of . . . awkward. But it's not like he's going to corner me in the limo or spike my drink or anything. And besides, it's getting sort of late to find another date, and I'm *not* going stag, and I'm double not missing the first-ever Autumn Ball that you're coming to! So, it's Randy Steigerson and then a kick-ass party."

"I'm . . . I'm glad you figured that out," Claire said, finally. More hurt had leaked into her voice than she'd intended.

"I called you first," Emily said quietly. "About the whole Randy thing. But you were so busy with your chem test and hanging out with your mom . . . and when Amy called to tell me she'd found a date for the ball, we just sort of hashed it out."

Emily was right—she had called, the night of the new

moon disaster. And Claire hadn't been able to call her back. How would she have explained a two-in-the-morning phone call without making Emily completely suspicious? And anyway, Amy had certainly leapt right in. It was already hard to have the same sort of relationship with Emily that they'd had before. But Amy was making it freaking impossible. For a moment, Claire was so lonely for her old life—her old friendship with Emily—that her throat closed up with the ache of it. She swallowed hard, trying to pull herself together before Emily noticed that she was on the verge of tears.

"So, who's Amy going to the dance with?" Claire asked. Her voice was almost steady.

"One of Randy's friends, Julio, asked her, mostly 'cause he knew Randy had asked me. Amy doesn't really know him, but it's not a huge deal. She told me that she mainly said yes since the guys want to double. Which is fine with me. At least I'll have one friend around, you know?"

A little puff of air flew out from between Claire's shocked lips.

Emily's eyes widened, and she put one hand up to her mouth, like she was trying to cram the words back in. "Oh my God, Claire, I totally didn't mean that the way it sounded."

Claire struggled to regain her composure. "No—I mean, I know you didn't—"

"I just figured that either you and Matthew would want to go alone, or that the two of you would end up going with the rest of the soccer guys is all. The whole reason I'm going with Randy is so that I can be at the dance with you." Emily looked so upset that Claire felt her own throat start to tighten.

She put a hand on Emily's arm. "Stop freaking out. Amy's your friend too, and I'm glad you're doubling with her. Besides, I'm guessing that I'll be stuck having dinner with Kate-Marie and Doug, and you *know* that's not going to be any fun."

Emily laughed—a short, hard, rough-edged little laugh. But it was a start.

In Claire's book bag, her cell phone started to ring. Claire bent over and dug it out of the front pocket.

"Hello?"

"Claire. I'm glad I reached you." It was her mother, and she sounded distracted. The hair on the back of Claire's neck stood up. Her mother didn't get distracted. "Are you coming home? I need to speak with you. It's important."

Claire's breath caught in her throat. It was something about the pack. It had to be. Her mother never sounded like that about anything else.

"I'm on my way now," she said. "And, um, Emily's with me."

"Well, she'll need to drop you off and go home. I'm sorry, but it can't wait."

"What do you expect me to do?" Claire asked. "We have plans!"

"Change them," her mother said sharply. "I'll see you when you arrive."

There was a click, and the line went dead.

Marie had hung up on her. Claire's anger sharpened her vision, bringing everything into intense focus. The stop sign looked like it was edged in razor blades.

Emily frowned. "What's going on?"

"My mom just canceled our plans is what," Claire fumed. "Like nothing matters except pack—" She caught herself. Right at the edge of the precipice, with nothing but blood-thirsty rocks below.

"Pack?" Emily echoed, her head craned to the left as she searched for a break in the traffic.

Claire's secret sat between them in the car, almost visible.

"Packing." Claire said, scrambling for an explanation. "Packing for a trip. Lisbeth's gone, and Mom doesn't know how to work the dryer. I'm sorry. I have to help her, and it's going to be miserable. Can we reschedule?"

Please let her buy it. Please, please, please.

Emily frowned, a faint aura of suspicion hovering around her, like a fog that wouldn't quite clear. "Will it really take that long?"

"You know my mom," Claire said simply, hoping it would be enough.

"Yeah." Emily rolled her eyes. "I do. This sucks! I wanted to look for dresses online."

"I know. We'll go shopping at an actual store soon though, okay?"

Emily grumbled, but Claire felt herself backing away from the neck-smashing ledge she'd been balanced on. Emily knew how strange Marie could be, and for once it was working in Claire's favor.

She leaned her head against the cool glass of the window and wondered if it was even safe for her to be out in public. If she was this bad at being a werewolf, maybe the pack should cut off her ear.

The thought burned, and Claire flinched away from it.

Maybe she'd just work on being a better wolf.

When Emily dropped Claire off, Claire found her mother sitting at the kitchen table, tapping her foot impatiently. There was a half-finished cup of tea in front of her and the smell of something amazing coming from the oven.

Claire sniffed. "Chicken?" she asked.

Marie nodded. "Lisbeth put it in before she left. Apparently, something will beep when it's ready to be eaten." She fiddled with the tag on the tea bag. There were circles under her eyes, and the lines on either side of her mouth were deeper than usual—twin, shadowed slashes.

Claire dropped her bag onto the floor and slid onto one of the bar stools at the kitchen island. "So? What's so urgent?"

Marie looked up at her. A muscle in her cheek twitched, a warning to Claire to watch what she said. "You know that Victoria's time is soon—that the baby is coming. Since the gathering will be almost as important for you as it is for Victoria, I wanted to tell you what will happen. And then I want to see exactly where you are with the firelighting. I do not want to be surprised like that again. After dinner, as soon as it is late enough, we will go into the woods together."

Claire clenched her teeth. She hated being micromanaged by her mother. Being ordered around like she was five. With her molars grinding against each other, she managed to nod.

"Good." Marie cleared her throat. "So, when the baby is born, we will have a ceremony to welcome her. It's done for every New One." A smile—warm, genuine, and very brief—crossed her face. "We had one for you, when you were born."

Marie's gaze was far away, seeing a memory instead of the kitchen. "I had no idea what to call you. Since there was a full moon the night after you arrived, we had a double ceremony—your naming and the full moon, combined. I was so tired that I could barely think, but then I saw the moonlight glowing against your brand-new skin. That's when I knew you would be named Claire." She blinked, her eyes clearing, seeing Claire and the kitchen again.

"It means 'light,' your name. It suited you. It still suits you." She lifted the cup of tea and took a sip. "So. We will have the same sort of celebration for Victoria's baby. I've been speaking with Beatrice about it. I didn't remember just how much was involved. It has been many years—yours was the last naming I attended. I'd forgotten much of it." The stress had returned to her mother's face, making her look older. Tired.

"Is it . . . is it bad?" Claire asked. She was worried about the expression on her mother's face. "You look sort of freaked out."

"No—not at all." Marie looked startled. "A naming is one of the most joyous ceremonies we have. It's a celebration, and when Victoria gives the baby her name—if she has picked the right name—some truly remarkable things will happen. If it is the right name. But then, I said that already, didn't I?" She sagged a little in her chair, pulling the tea mug right to the edge of the table. "It is just coming so soon after your new moon gathering. I had"—she cleared her throat—"I had underestimated the amount of effort these sorts of unusual gatherings would require. There are particular sorts of wood to be gathered, a preparation of herbs that I have to make for Victoria to drink, and it will be nearly impossible to find them in the wild with winter so close."

Her mother shut her eyes. "And, of course, I am worried about you. I'm fond of your ears." She paled, and the tea trembled in her cup as her hands shook. "I can't stand the thought of you being hurt. There is just—it is a great deal to handle at one time. And I am still new as an Alpha."

She gave Claire a wan smile. "I suppose we are both having—what is it called? A trial by fire?"

So that's why her mom had seemed so stressed lately. It made sense, and Claire was surprised she hadn't realized it sooner. *Being* a werewolf was so hard—trying to juggle the different sides of her life, to meet the demands of each without showing any strain. Claire understood why werewolves chose one side or another to favor. Judith's human life was just a thin veneer for her wolf self, with no more depth than a Halloween mask, and Katherine did the bare minimum required of her as werewolf, making the life she had to keep secret as small as possible, so it would be easier to hide.

And they were just regular, Beta wolves. Claire couldn't imagine the impossible pressure of being the Alpha. To be responsible for the whole pack had to be exponentially harder. The Alpha was the one who made sure that all the ceremonies were done when and how they were supposed to be. On top of that, the Alpha had to ensure that the pack maintained its secrecy, and she had to keep tabs on each of the wolves and watch the outside world for any signs of a threat. And though her mother had no human friends to speak of, she still had a busy and dangerously public career to manage. Just thinking about the responsibilities her mother carried was overwhelming. No wonder Marie looked like she was just barely holding things together. Of course, every time Claire thought about the punishment that waited for her if she failed to light the fire, she wanted to run shrieking into the woods and never come back. So she wasn't exactly the poster child for stress management either.

"Yeah, trial by fire. That's what it's called." The timer on the oven began to beep, and Claire slid off her stool, picking up the oven mitts that Lisbeth had thoughtfully left on the counter. She pulled the chicken out of the oven and set the pan on the stove, breathing in the smell of the roasted meat.

"So, what will I have to do?" she asked, pulling two plates out of the cabinet, shivering a little at the realization that she'd kissed Matthew in that exact spot. The heat that spread through her had nothing to do with the still-hot oven and everything to do with the ghost touch of his lips against the tender hollow beneath her ear. She could still feel his hands sliding around the small of her back, his palms pressed against her spine as he pulled her tighter against him. For one melting moment, everything else dropped away and she floated, lost in the memory.

Marie's tea mug clinked against the table, and Claire shook off the daydream, embarrassed about the burn that lingered in her cheeks.

The naming. Right. Focus.

"You will light the fire." Marie said. "After you have done that, Victoria will give the baby her name." She reached up, fiddling with the clasp of her necklace.

Claire slowly reached for a knife to cut the chicken with. "And then what?"

She slapped the hastily carved chicken breasts onto the plates and put dinner on the table.

Marie took a careful bite of her chicken, looked up at Claire, and gave her a thin smile.

"And then, if it goes well—if the fire is lit correctly and Victoria chooses the right name—the Goddess will bless the baby by putting out the fire. At least, a part of the fire. But if something goes wrong, it is like getting a bad fortune. It predicts a lifetime of difficulty for the baby. It's mostly ceremonial—the fire doesn't actually go out, but the pack searches for evidence that some bit of it has been extinguished." Her mother's face hardened. "But it can go the other way, too. I heard of a naming where a tumbleweed blew into the fire after the name was given. The fire actually grew—it was devastating for the pack."

Claire stared down at her plate, her mind racing.

Marie cleared her throat. "But I'm sure it will be fine. I believe it will. And then after that, you will demonstrate your hunting ability and your long-distance hearing." A pinched look crossed her face. "We will have to separate the ceremonies somehow. Nothing is killed at a naming. I'll have to figure that out, too, I suppose."

Claire wasn't the only one under pressure. They all had to play their roles or the baby would suffer.

But not because of me. I'm not going to have my ear cut off, and I'm not going to be responsible for dooming Victoria's baby.

She'd light the fire at the ceremony, no matter what it took.

Chapter Ten

ONCE IT WAS deeply dark, Claire followed her mother into the woods. The skin on the back of her neck stung with the embarrassment of needing her mother's help. The noise of the dried leaves beneath her feet sounded like snickering, like the forest was laughing at her ineptness.

They ended up in a small clearing, much like the one Claire usually practiced in.

"I'll go find some wood," Marie announced.

"Wait." Claire looked around. "There's plenty of stuff here already." She bent down and picked up a few small twigs, stacking them in the middle of the clearing.

"But that's nothing." Marie frowned. "The ceremonial fires are much larger than that—they take more energy, more concentration, to start."

Heat crept up into Claire's cheeks. "But if I can light the twigs, then they'll feed the larger fire," she countered.

Marie shook her head. "That is true when you are using matches or a lighter. But to do it with your mind, you must have enough power to shift the energy of the whole pile or the spark you create won't take. It will sputter and die."

Claire's shoulders slumped. "I didn't know that."

Marie smoothed back her hair. "Well, why don't you go see what branches you can find, and I will do the same. We'll make a proper pile and see what you can do with it."

It didn't take long for them to build an average-size stack of wood in the middle of the clearing. Marie stepped back, leaning against a tree. "You may begin when you are ready," she offered.

Claire crouched down in front of the branches, pushing at their heaviness with her thoughts, struggling against the cold inertia of the wood.

Nothing happened.

She tried again, but it was just like the new moon gathering. Her heart began to race with the memory of it.

"You must be calm, *chérie*, or it will not work. You must be confident and focused."

"How can I be focused when you're interrupting me?" Claire burst out.

Marie straightened, adjusting the cuffs of her shirt. "I'm only trying to help, Claire."

"Well, staring holes into my head isn't exactly helping! I was doing better on my own." Claire shoved her hair back from her face.

Marie went still as stone. "If you want to be left to practice alone, I will go. It is your ear. It is your future. I leave the responsibility in your hands." She turned to leave, looking defeated. A sharp sliver of regret pierced Claire, but she was too proud to call her mother back.

She'd just have to do it on her own. Claire listened to the near-silent retreat of her mother's footsteps and turned her attention back to the pile in front of her, trying to control her panic.

She could do this.

Except she couldn't. Hours later, even though her eyes and knees and brain ached, nothing had happened.

Exhausted and frustrated, Claire threw back her head and roared, her human voice echoing startlingly off the trees. She slumped over, her head buried in her hands.

She sat that way, listening to the stunned silence of the forest around her, wishing the trees would swallow her up.

Claire practiced on her own every night. Her fingernails were permanently dirt stained from being dug into the forest floor, and her back ached from spending so many hours hunched over like an old woman.

Her mother hadn't said anything to her about the fires since she'd left Claire in the forest, but Claire could see her aching over Claire's failure. Claire knew that Marie could read it in the set of her shoulders, in the deepening of the circles beneath eyes. It just made her practice harder, determined to save herself.

Saturday night, she stumbled home. When she made it back to the safety of her room, she called Matthew, aching for his warm voice the same way she ached for a hot shower—wanting something that would unknot her.

"Hello?" His voice was vague with sleep.

"I woke you up—I'm sorry," she said, her voice too loud in the quiet of her room.

"No—well, I mean, yes, but it's okay." She heard his sheets rustle in the background and wondered briefly if he slept shirtless. "What's going on?"

"Nothing," she spat, pacing the floor. "Really nothing. The same sort of nothing that's been going on all week."

"Oh." He cleared his throat. "You're still working on that?"

"Of course I am! I don't know how much time I have left before Victoria has the baby, and I'm getting scared, Matthew. Really scared. I still can't light the fire, and if I can't—" The words stuck in her throat. She took a ragged breath and tried again. "If I don't do it, the pack will cut off part of my ear. And there's no way around it."

There was a long, heavy pause. Claire could hear him

breathing. "I don't know what to say," he finally admitted. "It's . . . Obviously, it's awful, but there's nothing I can do about it. I mean, maybe you should just focus on doing whatever you've got to do to fix it, instead of talking to me."

It was like she'd been punched.

"You're—you're just going to abandon me?" she squeaked.

"I'm not abandoning you, Claire. I'll still be here afterward. But there's no way I can *help* you." His voice dropped. "This is a pack thing. And I'm a human."

She stood frozen in place. "You're a *gardien*," she whispered.

"Yeah. I know," he said, the words heavy as anchors. "I love you, and I'm worried for you, but talking to me doesn't change anything. *I* can't change anything. You understand, right?"

"I guess," Claire said. What she really meant was, *Of course I don't*.

"Listen, you should get some sleep. I'll talk to you tomorrow, okay?"

"Sure." She was so stunned that she could barely form the word.

"Good." Matthew sounded relieved.

Claire closed her phone, still not quite believing the conversation she'd just had. She didn't know what was making Matthew back away from pack stuff—why he acted like it was some sort of poisoned apple he'd been forced to eat. After the naming, though, she intended to find out.

* * *

The next day, she woke up under a tangled sheet of desperation. She had to do something. She needed help.

One quick call, and a very worried-sounding Victoria agreed to meet her in the clearing that night, so she just had the long, miserable rest of the day to get through.

The only thing that distracted her—that saved her—was running. She jogged for miles, until the pavement disappearing beneath her human feet was all that she could focus on, until her teeth ached with the exertion. If Victoria couldn't help her tonight, Claire didn't know what she was going to do.

When she got to the clearing late that night, Victoria was already waiting for her.

"Whoa. You look like hell." The words were out of Victoria's mouth almost before Claire was completely through the trees.

"Right back atcha," Claire retorted, looking at Victoria's puffy face and lank hair.

She laughed. "Fair enough. I take it you haven't become a fire-starting guru yet?"

Claire shook her head sadly. "No. If you can't help me tonight, I think I'm screwed. How about the name?"

Victoria shook her head. "Nothing definite yet." She sighed. "Let's focus on your problems. They seem more fixable at the moment."

"Okay," Claire said grimly. "I'll build the fire."

Mostly, she just went into the woods and pulled the same branches she'd been using back into the center of the clearing. She dumped them in pretty much the same spots each time. It didn't take long to retrieve them and put them back into a pile.

"Well, you're fast at building a fire, at least," Victoria offered.

"Yeah, but I don't think this is exactly a partial-credit situation. I have to light it," Claire said. "I'm sorry I had to drag you out here. Again."

Victoria looked at her. "I'm happy to help you. I've needed help with plenty of these things." She snorted. "I mean, look at the trouble I'm having with the naming. I *still* need help. There's no shame in that. I think that's why we have packs to begin with. If we were supposed to be completely self-sufficient, why wouldn't we all be lone wolves, *seules*?"

"I never thought about it that way," Claire said quietly.

Victoria shrugged. "I have a ton of respect for your mother. I think she's an amazing Alpha, and I wouldn't go against her. But I don't think being her daughter puts you in an easy spot."

Victoria had put Claire's tangled feelings into words so easily that it stunned her. With Matthew acting so weird and Emily needing to be kept in the dark, it had been too long since someone really understood Claire.

"You don't know how awesome it is to hear someone say that," she said.

Victoria smiled. "I've been the Alpha's daughter. It's hard

as anything. It's like nothing you do counts, but everything you do gets judged."

Claire looked over at the unlit fire, her nerves tingling uncomfortably. She knew that her own judgment was as close as the kindling. "I have to do this," she whispered.

Victoria nodded, her lower lip caught anxiously in her teeth. "Try. Don't think about it too long, just reach out for it with everything you've got."

Without even bothering to kneel down, Claire tried to push aside the wood, to find the fire, but it was like swimming with her clothes on: Everything felt impossibly heavy and wet. She shook with the effort, searched desperately for the clarity that came with being a wolf. For one second, she pushed back the heavy curtain of her humanness, and she shoved at the dull wood with her thoughts.

A flame danced along a single branch. Not deep or fast or consuming, but enough to catch. And spread.

Enough to burn.

"Yes!" Victoria did an awkward, hopping little dance toward Claire, who burst into laughter at Victoria's ridiculousness, at the giddy lightness bubbling in her own chest.

"I did it! Did you see? A real fire!"

"How could I miss it?" Victoria giggled. "Look how quickly it's taking off!"

The two of them stood, admiring the flames.

"You know you need to keep at this," Victoria warned.

"Make sure that you can do it wherever and whenever you need to."

"I know. There's too much at stake to ride on one success. But it's a start, right?"

"Better than," Victoria assured her.

The two of them sat around the fire until it had faded enough to put out.

As she walked home, Claire thought about the naming. Victoria had helped her so much. She desperately wanted to find a way to return the favor. But names weren't exactly falling out of the sky.

She slipped into the house, sifting through her thoughts like sand, searching for a solution.

The next week passed in a blur. At night, Claire slipped into the woods, lighting the fires again and again, scouring the forest for anything that would burn. Until she knew she could do it.

Until it was easy.

Halloween—and the full moon—were just a couple of days away. They would have a short gathering—quiet, late, doing only the minimum required. Doing more would be too risky. There was too great a chance that some thrill-seeking human would be wandering through the woods.

Marie's face grew even more severe as the Halloween gathering approached, and Saturday morning, for the first time,

Claire noticed threads of silver appearing in her mother's hair.

"Are you okay?" she asked, watching as the sun caught the glimmering strands while her mother stood near the window. Marie had a jeweler's loupe pressed to her eye, checking her lenses for tiny scratches and microscopic blemishes.

"Hmm?" Her mother was distracted.

"You just look sort of stressed is all." Claire wrinkled her nose at the box of cereal on the counter. She missed the days when Lisbeth cooked bacon and eggs on Saturday morning.

"I'm fine, Claire. Did you need something?" Marie snapped. Startled, Claire grabbed her cereal and slunk toward the living room.

"No. I'm going shopping with Emily. She's picking me up in an hour—I just thought I should let you know."

"Shopping?" Her mother looked up. "You hate to shop."

"It's for a dress. For the dance?" Claire prompted. She waited for understanding—recognition—to cross her mother's face. Instead, she just looked confused.

"What dance?" her mother demanded.

"The Autumn Ball. At school? I'm going with Matthew, remember?" Once again, anything that had to do with Claire's human life sailed right over Marie's head, as unnoticed as a distant airplane or a passing cloud. Claire's fingers curled around her spoon in frustration. She wasn't just a wolf. But that was the only part of her that her mother cared about. Obviously.

"Oh. Fine." Marie nodded toward the back hall. "Take the blue credit card from my purse. Don't buy anything foolish, please." She turned her attention back to the lenses lined up on the table in front of her.

Claire stomped down the hall and rummaged around in her mother's bag, pulling out the credit card and sliding it into her pocket before flopping down in the den to eat her cereal.

She wished Lisbeth was around to tell her not to spill milk on the couch or to ask her what stores she and Emily were going to. At least *she'd* be excited to see Claire's dress.

Assuming she found a dress.

Claire crunched through her breakfast. When she was finished, she stretched out on the sofa, watching TV and listening for the sound of Emily's tires against the gravel. The instant she heard it, she leapt off the couch, abandoning her cereal bowl and grabbing her jacket. She darted out the door without saying good-bye to her mother. Why should she bother? It wasn't like Marie cared where she was going or when she'd be home. Not unless it somehow involved claws and fur in the forest.

Emily looked startled to see Claire barreling out of the house.

Claire opened the passenger door and slid in. "I am so glad you're here."

"Obviously. I haven't even put the car in park yet. What's going on?"

Claire shook her head. "Just . . . my mom being my mom."

She blew out a long breath. "Okay. Sorry. I promise I'm not going to be cranky today. Besides"—she reached into her pocket and slid the blue plastic rectangle out far enough for Emily to see—"I've got her credit card. And I intend to use it."

"Well, hallelujah," Emily laughed. "Let's get you to the mall before you come to your senses."

The sun streamed in through the car window as Emily sped out of the driveway, going too fast as usual. Claire stared out at the high, clear, impossibly blue sky that meant it was going to be one of those perfect autumn days. It was hard to stay angry when the grass was still green but the leaves were painted with color, when the sun was still warm but the wind promised winter and she was with her best friend. She leaned back in the seat, feeling the last of her bad mood slip away.

"Time for music?" Emily asked with a sideways glance.

"Absolutely."

Chapter Eleven

CLAIRE WALKED INTO the mall, trailing Emily the way a hiker trails a guide through a particularly dangerous jungle. The smell of floor cleaner mixed unpleasantly with the plastic-y scent of new clothes and stale, food-court fried rice. Claire wrinkled her nose and focused on Emily, who was making a beeline for the nearest department store.

"Okay." Emily reached up, unconsciously respiking her hair. "So, first we're going to hit the sale racks at Nordstrom's, though we probably won't find anything there."

The idea of stretching out the shopping unnecessarily made Claire twitch. "Why not just go straight to the place where we're most likely to get an actual dress?" She was dying to *have* a dress, to see it hanging in her closet and be able to pet it. She just wasn't excited about the process of finding one.

Emily raised a lecturing finger, not breaking her pace. "Parental assurance. If she freaks about how much you spend, it's much better to be able to honestly say you bought the least-expensive thing you liked. Hence, the sale rack. Where you won't find anything, but after looking at it, you can shop with a clear conscience."

Claire snorted with laughter. The two of them breezed past the shoe department and up through accessories to where the formal dresses were. Claire followed Emily into the sea of clothing racks full of glimmering fabrics in a rainbow of colors, like a school of exotic fish.

After quickly rejecting the downright hideous dresses on the sale rack, Emily and Claire moved into the rest of the department and loaded their arms with dresses. Emily added two to the pile for every one that Claire picked out. When the salesladies started rolling their eyes, the two of them finally headed for the dressing room.

"Okay," said Emily. "These are the rules: As long as whatever you have on doesn't make you look like a dachshund in a tutu, you have to come out so I can see it. Deal?"

Claire sighed. With the stack of dresses she had hanging in the fitting room, it would take forever to do it Emily's way.

"What're the other rules?" she asked.

"Just one more. No whining or you're buying lunch." Emily winked and then disappeared into the little cubicle where her own massive assortment of formal wear was waiting.

Claire pulled the first dress off the hanger. It was blue, with a deep V-neck and a ruffly bottom. She slipped it over her head, looked in the mirror, and frowned. She didn't have enough of a chest for the neckline, and as a result, the tight bodice made her look thick around the middle. And the ruffles were way too fussy for her. Still . . . it wasn't *horrible*. She might as well go show it to Emily.

Claire stepped out into the aisle of the dressing rooms, being careful not to trip over the frills at her feet.

"Claire? Oh, how funny!" Claire spun around and saw Amy framed in the curve of the three-way mirror. She was wearing a blue dress. Exactly the same blue dress that Claire had on. The only difference was, it fit Amy perfectly. Sure, the hem puddled on the floor, but the ruffles balanced out her waterfall of curls, and the blue fabric made her eyes look like summer leaves. And the bodice was exactly right, the V-neck sexy without being over the top.

"Hey, Amy." Claire forced a smile, crossing her arms over her chest. "That dress looks great on you."

"You think?" Amy asked. "I've tried on about a million—I can't even tell them apart anymore."

Emily popped out of her dressing room, half-zipped into

a zebra-print gown. "Amy? Oh my God, this is so great! Are you here by yourself?"

"I was supposed to meet Yolanda here, but she bailed on me."

Emily's eyes went from Claire to Amy and back again. "You guys have on the same dress!" she exclaimed, a giggle running underneath the words.

"Yeah, I'm not getting this one," Claire said quickly. "It looks much better on Amy than it ever would on me." The compliment was honest, and Amy glowed.

"Thanks," Amy said. The sincerity in her voice made Claire want to put her guard up. Okay, so part of her wanted to be friends with Amy, but it just wasn't possible.

Amy gave Claire a grateful smile. "I'm so short. I always feel like I look like a kid playing dress-up, you know?"

"Polly Pocket goes to the prom?" Claire said, raising a joking eyebrow.

Amy snickered. "Dead on."

Bantering with Amy was like getting swept into an ocean current. It was so quick and thrilling that Claire could—for a second—ignore the danger.

"You look amazing," Emily reassured Amy. "Now we just have to find a dress for Claire. And one for me." She frowned down at the zebra-print. "I think this is too safari chic for Hanover Falls."

The fact that she'd said "we" didn't escape Claire. Apparently, their shopping trip had just turned into a shopping trip plus one. The surprised happiness that flooded her was so electric, she expected to get a shock when she reached for the dressing-room doorknob.

"I'm going to go change," she announced, stepping back into the cubicle and shutting the door. She leaned her forehead against the dusty slats and took a long, slow breath, forcing herself to calm down. To slow down.

I'm just going to focus on finding a dress.

Claire turned to face the pile of clothes in front of her. The red and black and silver fabrics passed under her gaze, but her eyes stopped when she spotted a sliver of green near the black. Dark green, the same color as the heart of the pine trees deep in the forest. Just looking at it made her feel calmer. More controlled. She reached for it instinctively.

It was long and one-shouldered—silk with a floaty piece of organza skimming down from just underneath the bust. Claire licked her lips. It was going to work. It was going to be perfect. She could tell from the little tingle in her fingers as she slid it off the hanger.

She shucked off the blue dress and stepped into the green one with the same confidence she had when she stepped into the woods.

She pulled the zipper up and turned to look in the mirror. A shiver of excitement passed through her as she stared at herself.

It was amazing. The color set off her pale skin and dark

hair, and the flow of the dress made her look strong and elegant and slender all at once. Plus, the single shoulder and gathered bust helped hide the fact that she wasn't well-endowed enough to hold up something strapless. As long as she wore heels, it wouldn't even need to be hemmed.

Barely suppressing a gleeful and hopelessly girly squeal, Claire opened the dressing room door.

"Hey, Emily! Guess what?" she crowed.

Emily poked her head around the edge of her own door. "Wha—whoa." Her eyes widened. "Oh, hell yes. That is so your dress. That is so so *so* your dress. Unfair! How did you find it so fast? You look unbelievable!"

Claire glanced over at Amy, who was standing on a little dais while a bent-backed woman slid pins into the hem of her dress. Amy's mouth had fallen open in a sort of shocked admiration.

"Claire, it's fantastic!" She shook her head happily, her curls bouncing around her shoulders.

Claire looked back at Emily and grinned. "It's pretty knockout, huh?"

"You two are already done!" Emily frowned. "Okay, let me hurry this up, and then we can all go look for shoes and stuff." She shut the door, leaving Claire and Amy smiling at each other.

Claire caught herself, dropping her smile and ducking back inside the dressing room. She caught the briefest glimpse of surprise and disappointment on Amy's face before she shut the door. Claire slid out of the dress, ignoring the twinge of sorrow in her middle. She promised herself she was going to be more careful. No more getting swept away.

I cannot juggle another friend right now.

She pulled on her jeans and looked at herself in the mirror. She had to focus on what she had already. On not risking Emily. On not losing Matthew. And on keeping her left ear whole.

The three of them stood in front of the jewelry display, the rows of fake pearls and glittering rhinestones making Claire's eyes ache. She'd already bought her dress and a pair of shoes and a purse—she was on shopping overload.

"Hey, I have the best idea!" Emily picked up a pair of crystal-studded earrings, holding them up to her ears. "Why don't you both spend the night at my house tonight? We can make it a real, old-school slumber party. We could stop and get ice cream on the way. Plus, we can talk about where we want to go to dinner before the ball and stuff."

"I'm in," Amy said, riffling through a rack of fancy hair clips. "I'm going to need a major sugar fix after all this."

Emily frowned and looked at Claire. "Oh, crap. You have a date with Matthew, don't you?"

"Yeah." Her disappointment was as sharp and unexpected as a bee sting. "I wish I could cancel and hang out with you two instead. Especially now that you've mentioned ice cream. I'll be craving it like crazy all night."

"What's with all the weird cravings?" Emily asked. "Don't think I haven't noticed that you've been eating a ton more meat than usual." Emily turned to Amy. "She's, like, an antivegetarian. Are you just doing that to piss Lisbeth off, or what?"

Amy cleared her throat. "There are lots of reasons to have weird cravings." A dark-winged shadow fluttered across her face.

"Yeah. Maybe it's a growth spurt," Claire joked, hoping the humor would ring true.

"So, do it," Emily said. "Bail on your plans and come watch bad TV with us."

"I can't." Claire sighed. "There's a bunch of stuff that I have to talk to him about." She'd meant to imply that they needed to talk about the dance, but there was a stony heaviness to her words.

Amy's eyes widened. "Is everything okay?"

"Sure," Claire said, waving a hand. "We just have some things to sort out."

Emily cocked her head to one side and opened her mouth. Claire scrambled for some new subject before Emily could start asking questions.

"So, what about this necklace?" she asked, grabbing a strand of creamy pearls with a rhinestone pendant hanging from it.

Emily closed her mouth and rolled her eyes. "It would look

great. If you were going to an old-lady lunch or something." She glanced over her shoulder. "Hang on. You wait here—I think I saw something back there that would be perfect for your dress. Stay with her, Amy, and make sure she doesn't buy anything horrible, okay?"

"I'll tie her hands behind her back," Amy said with a laugh, holding a sparkling pair of earrings up to her ears.

Claire laughed, trying to relax now that they were safely back on the subject of accessories, but everything inside her bristled. Her human side. Her wolf side. All of her was on edge.

"Hey, Claire!" Katherine popped out from behind a display of bracelets, waving wildly.

Claire froze. Was she kidding? Couldn't Katherine see that she was with other people? Other distinctly human people?

"What are you doing here?" Katherine chirped. She dropped her shopping bags and hugged Claire. "It's such a killer sale—I couldn't resist picking up a few things." She looked around, her mouth falling open when she saw Amy.

"Oh, hi."

"Hi." Amy smiled her most winning, adults-always-like-me smile. "I'm Amy Harper."

"Nice to meet you," Katherine said, looking at Claire in a way that said she was surprised Claire had friends.

"Katherine is a, uh, friend of my mom's," Claire said.

"Oh, just an acquaintance, really. It's been ages!" Katherine's whinnying laugh made Claire cringe.

"Oh, well, um, nice to meet you, too." Amy shifted awkwardly from foot to foot, giving Claire a why-is-this-so-weird sort of look. "I haven't met Claire's mom yet, but I've seen some of her pictures. They're amazing."

"Oh, right. Her pictures. I don't, um . . ." Katherine had gone bright red, and a sheen of sweat glistened at her temples.

"Here! I found it!" Emily came sprinting back, a necklace clutched victoriously in her hand.

Claire turned, and Katherine cleared her throat awkwardly. "Well, I can see I'm interrupting. I'm going to go. . . ." She scrabbled for her shopping bags. "Tell your mom I said hi, and that I'll see you guys, uh, soon."

Claire wanted to smack her. No wonder Judith stuck so close to Katherine. It was like Katherine's mouth was always three steps ahead of her brain.

Katherine swept off toward the shoe department, leaving Claire, Emily, and Amy staring after her.

"Who was that?" Emily asked.

"A friend of my mom's," Claire said simply. "Let me see the necklace you found." She held out her hand.

"I'm surprised you don't know her," Amy said. "She was all over Claire like some sort of long-lost aunt or something." She was half-joking, but there was something suspicious in her voice at the same time, and Claire struggled to get Amy talking about something else.

Emily handed her the jewelry, her gaze still trained on

Katherine and a confused, betrayed expression on her face. "No, I've . . . I've never met any of Marie's friends, I guess."

"What are you and your mom doing with her?" Amy asked, toying with a pair of earrings. "She sounded like she was really looking forward to it, whatever it was."

Emily looked over at Claire, interested. Waiting.

"I . . ." Claire scrambled for an answer. A good answer. This was why she couldn't afford to be friends with Amy. A tooth rattlingly, face slappingly great example of why it would be a horrible idea. "I think she's coming to the house to have some pictures taken. I dunno."

She held up the necklace that Emily had given her. "Oh, Emily, this is perfect!" Claire gushed in a desperate bid to get their attention off Katherine.

The necklace really was perfect. The simple rhinestone choker would be amazing with the green of the dress and her dark hair.

"It'll be great with the neckline. And it's not too fussy, either. I know you hate that." Emily looked ridiculously pleased with herself.

"Thanks." Claire reached over to hug her. "You're the best."

"What are friends for?" Emily said.

Claire looked at Emily and Amy, who were both beaming. She wished she had an answer to Emily's question, because the echoing silence hurt like hell.

Chapter Twelve

CLAIRE'S MOTHER STOPPED her as she was hurrying out of the house to meet Matthew.

"Now where are you going?" There was a frayed edge to the question that caught Claire off guard. She stared at her mother, surprised. When had Marie become such a worrier? The way she'd been looking so much older, the anxiety in her voice—she was starting to resemble Beatrice. At least, the way Beatrice had been when she was the Alpha. She'd become significantly more relaxed since she'd stepped down.

"I'm going out with Matthew," Claire said, crossing her arms defensively.

"You're not going to practice your fire lighting?"

Claire struggled to keep her face smooth. "You haven't bothered to ask me about that in ages. Why do you suddenly care now?"

Her mother slumped in on herself, looking deflated. "I could smell the smoke," she whispered. "It seemed like you were more successful when I left you alone."

Claire's head began to throb. "Actually, Victoria helped me. I've been practicing on my own since then, but it's going really well, thanks to her."

Her mother eyed her. "So, you're ready?"

Claire shrugged, her bravado fading a little bit. "I think so. I hope so. I know the pressure of having the whole pack watching—the fact that it's a test—I know that will make it harder."

Marie's expression hardened. "You must succeed. You must do whatever it takes to ensure that. Your abilities are the only thing you have to rely on, in our world."

Claire stared at her mother, amazed at the difference between her attitude and Victoria's. Wondering which one of them was right.

Outside, Matthew's car horn beeped.

"I've really got to go," Claire said. "I'll be home later."

She practically ran out of the house and into Matthew's waiting car.

"Hey, babe. How was your day?" His voice was summer

warm and rich with happiness. It sounded—he sounded—the way he had when they'd first started dating. Like things hadn't been weird and strained between them for the last few weeks. She should have been elated, but she couldn't shake off the tension that had marked the end of her shopping trip.

She groaned. "It was freaking exhausting."

"Really? I thought it was supposed to be girly, best-friend shopping stuff. What happened?" Matthew asked as she shut the door.

Claire leaned back and closed her eyes. "Amy sort of ended up tagging along with us, and things just got . . . hard. I don't know. She was asking me all these questions that weren't easy to answer. It got so bad—she started to seem sort of suspicious."

Matthew tapped the steering wheel thoughtfully. "Maybe you're being too hard on Amy. I think she's just trying to get to know you. To fit in. And you're not that easy to fit in with, you know?"

Claire stared at him, her lips parted in astonishment. Did he really mean that? And was he seriously on Amy's side? Her heart gave a painful little flip inside her chest.

He glanced over at her and took in her expression.

"You think I need to cut her more slack because I'm not easy to get along with?" she asked, keeping her words as measured as possible.

"That's not what I'm saying—I mean, you're a were-wolf. You have to be extra sensitive and careful and all that.

But maybe you're reading more into it than a normal person would."

Claire closed her mouth, turning to stare out the window. He was right, she did have to be extra careful, but just because she noticed things that other people missed didn't mean she was some sort of paranoid freak.

Matthew rubbed the bridge of his nose between two fingers. "Claire, I'm not trying to make you mad. I'm just saying there are two sides to every story. That's it."

She raised an eyebrow at him. It was the calmest response she could manage. "Fine. Let's drop it," she said.

"Yes. Let's." He looked over at her. "Okay. I'm starting this date over as of now. So, hey, babe! Are you hungry? There's a Mexican place over by Oakwood that's supposed to have killer burritos."

Claire pasted a smile on her face, playing along. "Really? That sounds good." Even though she was faking her brand-new start, she felt herself beginning to relax.

"It's over by the library, I think. I've got the address in my phone." Matthew reached for the cup holder where he always put his cell while he drove. It was empty. "It must still be on my desk." He groaned. "Do you mind if we swing by my house? It's on the way."

Claire stomach rumbled, breaking the tension in the car.

"Um, as long as you're not too hungry," he added. "We could always go to Louie's."

Claire laughed. She couldn't help it. And she was hungry. "I can wait. Let's go get your phone."

Matthew's dad was in front of the Engles' house when they pulled up, doing yard work in the dying light. He looked awkward in his sweatshirt and jeans, like he just wasn't comfortable without a tie around his neck. He had a huge pair of hedge clippers in his hands, and the sharp blades gleamed in the sunlight, making Claire shiver. It was a visual reminder of how careful she had to be around Dr. Engle—that he had the ability to destroy her. And he would, if he ever found out what she really was.

Matthew popped out of the car, and Claire followed hesitantly. It was too weird to sit in the car with his dad right there.

"Be right back," Matthew called over his shoulder, zipping past his dad and into the house, leaving the front door wide open behind him.

Dr. Engle turned to Claire. "So." He cleared his throat. "What are you and Matthew up to this evening?"

"Dinner," Claire said simply. She tried not to say much when Matthew's dad was around. It seemed safer—she'd had a few close calls over the summer when she'd very nearly revealed enough for him to guess her true identity.

A cell phone began to ring, and Dr. Engle dropped the trimmers onto the grass, digging in his back pocket for his phone and checking the screen.

"Excuse me. I'm so sorry, but I really have to take this." He gave Claire a grim smile. "Hello, Dr. Otsuke. How is everything at the lab?"

Claire froze. The Japanese researcher? Wasn't he back in Japan? The news had said he was only staying for a few days, and Matthew hadn't mentioned that he'd stayed longer.

Dr. Engle walked toward the house, too far away for her to hear the other end of the phone call. Thanks to her sharper-than-normal hearing, though, Dr. Engle's side of the conversation was still well within Claire's earshot. "The chemistry analyzer? Really? They were supposed to come to the lab to fix that last week. I had my assistant schedule it."

Claire took a step back, leaning against the reassuringly solid metal of the car.

He's still here?

Why was he still in Hanover Falls? The hair rose on the back of her neck, and she had the sudden urge to crawl into the car—or even under it. To get anywhere that wasn't so out in the open. She felt too vulnerable, too exposed, on the green expanse of the lawn.

Matthew came flying out of the house, his phone clutched in his hand. He waved at his dad, who nodded absently in response.

Claire got back into the car. Feeling a little more protected, she looked over at Matthew. "Why didn't you tell me Dr. Otsuke was still in town?" Her voice was more demanding than she'd meant it to be. But still. It was the sort of information that he should have been giving the pack, especially since he was their *gardien*. And extra especially since he was her boyfriend.

Matthew looked surprised. "I—I don't know. I guess I didn't think it was a big deal. You knew he was here, right?"

"Well, yeah—" After all, his arrival had resulted in Claire's panicked sprint through the woods to hide the evidence of her fire lighting from the press. "But I didn't know he'd *stayed*."

"He's doing some sort of test on the water around here or something. Trying to determine if it has something to do with why werewolves live where they do, to see if there are any similarities between Osaka and Hanover Falls, since they've both had at least one werewolf captured in the last couple of years." Matthew had that guarded look again—like he had his hand on a gate, ready to swing it shut as soon as she said the wrong thing.

But at least the Dr. Otsuke situation didn't seem to be too dire. Japan—and Osaka in particular—had a huge number of werewolves. If Dr. Otsuke was just here for water research, there was no reason to think that he or Dr. Engle was suspicious of Claire or any of the other wolves. She blew out a careful breath.

"Sorry. I guess I overreacted." She leaned her head against the window, vowing to shut up until they got to dinner.

On the way to the restaurant, the stars started to come out, so glimmering and thick that Matthew and Claire decided to stop by the burrito place and get dinner to go. After they got their food, they drove to the deserted library and sat in the unlit parking lot, leaning against the hood of the car and eating.

"Feeling a little better?" Matthew asked, wadding up the wrapper of his first burrito and peeling open the second.

"Yeah," Claire said around a mouthful of chicken. "Thanks." She swallowed, licking a tiny drop of guacamole off her lip. "There's just so much stuff that's up in the air right now. And now I have this naming thing hanging over me too."

"What naming thing?" Matthew asked, taking a long drink of his soda.

Claire froze midbite. That's right. She hadn't told Matthew about the ceremony for Victoria's baby yet. She chewed her food slowly, trying to figure out what to do. She wanted to talk to him about it, but the memory of how freaked out he'd been by the new moon gathering loomed like a storm cloud, warning her to be careful.

"I—when Victoria's baby is born, we'll have a special ceremony to celebrate, and that's when she'll be named. That's . . . the gathering when I *have* to light the fire."

Matthew stared down at his food. "Wow. That's a pretty serious deal, huh?" There was a flatness, a disconnectedness, to his words that made Claire want to scream.

Slowly, carefully, she put down the rest of her food and turned to look at him.

"Yeah. Actually, it's a really serious deal."

"No, I know," he said, "but there's nothing I can—"

"Do about it," Claire interrupted. "You've said that before. Actually, you've said it in one way or another every time I try to bring up stuff about the pack. Any time I mention it, you act weird." The anger built inside her, rattling her voice the way steam would rattle the lid of a boiling kettle.

"I'm not acting weird," he insisted, but Claire noticed that his eyes stayed firmly fixed on the ground next to him.

She resisted the urge to reach out and shake him—to make him look at her. "Yes, you are! I mean, you got me a flower for my damn *chemistry* test, but I practically had to drag you to the new moon gathering, and watching me try to light a fire made you absolutely reek of freaking out."

A shocked look crossed his face. "You could smell the way I felt?"

"Of course I could. I'm a werewolf, Matthew. That's what we *do*."

He crumpled up the paper bag that the food had come in, crushing it into a tiny ball.

"I know," he whispered. "I get it, I swear to God, I do. Can we just drop it, please?"

The conversation felt unfinished —like an eyeless jack-o'-lantern. But Matthew was obviously done talking, and the idea of fighting for the sake of fighting seemed stupid.

"It's getting late," she said finally. "Maybe we should get back, huh?"

Matthew threw the remains of his dinner into a nearby

trash can. "Yeah, maybe we should." He leaned in and kissed her cheek, like he was smoothing things over.

Under the touch of his lips, though, irritation still scratched at Claire. It had been a hard day, and she wasn't quite ready to soften.

That night, Claire lay in her bed and stared at the ceiling. She'd gone to bed early, exhausted, but she couldn't sleep. The day had been too much—too weird, too intense. Her mind was whirling like an out-of-control carousel, all loud music and flashing lights and freaky animals, going round and round and round without getting anywhere at all. Finally, she couldn't stand it anymore. She threw off the covers and sat up, checking the clock next to the bed. It was a little after one.

She pushed her tangled hair off her face and stared out the window at the star-flecked sky. She wondered what Emily and Amy were doing. If the strangeness of running into Katherine, with all her blabbering, had stuck with them. Of course—her breath caught—there was a way she could find out.

She could transform. Use her abilities to listen in on them.

Claire smoothed the sheets underneath her hands, hesitating. Thinking. It felt weird to eavesdrop on Emily. For one thing, it was a huge invasion of privacy. But also, it was like using her werewolf talents to do something really . . . human. Of course, if Amy weren't trying to make Emily think Claire was a bad friend, weren't planting all sorts of slightly-too-close-to-the-truth suspicions in Emily's head, then Claire wouldn't even have to be thinking about the whole thing.

What the hell. I might as well try.

She didn't want to go all the way into the woods. And she really didn't want to think about what her mother would say if she tried to explain why she was leaving the house at this hour. Claire looked around her room.

It was more than big enough. And it wasn't like there was anyone around to catch her—Lisbeth wouldn't be back until Monday morning, and Marie was down in her darkroom. If her mom happened to notice that her room smelled too much like wolf, Claire could always blame it on the stack of unwashed laundry stashed in her closet.

Slowly, Claire crept out into the open space in the middle of the room. She licked her lips. There really wasn't anything to lose. . . .

Tossing off her pajamas, she squeezed her eyes shut and reached for her wolf form. The fur. The teeth. The claws. As her lupine self swept aside her human skin, terror came crashing over Claire. She crouched on the carpet, the chemical smell of the fibers burning her nostrils. The walls were too close, the scents were too artificial. She felt penned in. Caged. There was no way to open the doorknob.

Nowhere she could run.

With her heart thudding and squeezing in her chest, Claire dug her paws into the rug and scurried backward into the corner where her nightstand met her bed. She lay there, trying to calm herself down. She'd never transformed indoors before.

There's no threat in here. Jesus, Claire, get a grip. It's your freaking room. This is all your stuff.

But the more primitive part of her brain, the one that had so much more reign when she transformed, screamed at her that it was human stuff. That anything human was dangerous. That the only safe place was a place she could leave.

That she was trapped.

It's. My. Stuff. I am not *going to lose my shit over this!*

She opened her mouth, panting. The taste of fake-lemon furniture polish and faux-floral detergent coated her tongue, but it was more bearable than breathing through her nose. Feeling like she was within clawing distance of control, she closed her eyes, shutting out the borders and barriers of the room. She focused on the security of the furniture behind her—the protection of a corner, where at least she could see a threat coming.

Her heart slowed, though her flanks and whiskers were still trembling. She had two choices: change back or try to listen to Emily and Amy. She'd already tortured herself by transforming. She might as well try to get something out of it.

Claire concentrated on her barely contained desperation to escape. She took that feeling and used it to get her hearing to stretch beyond the walls of her room.

". . . not like that. I don't know." Amy's voice was thick, like she was talking around a mouthful of something.

Probably ice cream, Claire realized. She wanted to be having a late-night sugar binge with her best friend, not listening in on one from a terrified corner of her own bedroom.

"There's only one way to find out. I mean, maybe I should give it a try? It's not like anything terrible's going to happen if I do." Emily sounded thoughtful, but sort of excited.

"Yeah. Exactly. But if you care, then why don't you just ask her? There's nothing wrong with wanting an answer either."

Claire's ears went back, pressing flat against her head. They weren't really . . . Was it possible they were talking about *her*? The fear that gripped her just brought the faraway conversation into clearer focus. She couldn't just hear Emily and Amy—she could hear the scrape of spoons against a paper carton. The tinny sound of Emily's bad speakers playing music in the background.

She was so far outside her body that she wasn't even sure she was breathing anymore.

"Well, whatever you do, I'll be behind you." Amy said.

Distantly, Claire felt something inside herself wrench. Twist. She was vaguely aware of a desire to scream.

What are they talking about? What the hell *are they talking about?*

"I mean, it's just hair." Emily said.

Claire's relief stung like a slap. The sounds from Emily's room disappeared, and she was slammed back into the confined reality of her own dark bedroom.

She shook her head and stretched out, reconnecting herself to the conversation that was happening in Emily's room.

" . . . don't need her to tell you what to do with your hair."

"No," Emily said. "I know. It's not really about that."

Claire reached to the very edges of her ability. Right out to where it frayed into nothingness. Held herself there, and waited.

"I just—I can't get used to the distance between us." Emily's voice was quiet. Hesitant. "Claire and I never used to have any secrets, but now it's like she's always hiding something." She sighed.

Oh, holy shit.

Claire forced herself to wait. To listen. Not to react. After all, she'd already known that keeping her best friend in the dark was hurting Emily as much as it was hurting her. Hearing her say it out loud made it worse somehow, but what she really cared about was finding out what Emily thought her secret was.

"Oh, Emily." Amy's voice was quiet. Sad. Unsure. "I—I can't seem to get to know her at all, even though I want to. It does seem like *something's* going on with her—some of the stuff that happened this afternoon was pretty weird. But you're the one who's really her friend. . . ."

"No, I mean, I know." Emily sounded so lost. Sorrow pooled around Claire. "It's probably just the whole her-having-a-boyfriend thing. I hope. I mean, if it's something besides that . . ."

"Then maybe you need to find out what it is," Amy suggested.

There was a pause.

"Claire will tell me if it's important," Emily said, finally. "I believe that. Anyway. Just—just forget I said anything. Let's see if there's anything good on TV, okay?"

She couldn't stand the sensation of being trapped for another second. Claire backed out of the conversation, pulling herself back into her own head. Her own room.

She transformed, relieved by the dulling of her senses that came with the return of her human form. A film of sweat covered her body, and she lay there, trembling and twitching, too exhausted to gather up her clothes and get dressed. She was elated and horrified at the same time. She'd known that Amy was making Emily suspicious, but now that she'd actually heard Emily say the words . . . they sat on her shoulders like angry birds, flapping their wings and pecking at her. The space between Claire and Emily was widening like a river in a flood. It stretched further with each passing hour, until eventually the distance between them would be insurmountable.

The thought strangled her.

Claire pushed herself up into a sitting position, wincing at the pain in her leg where her thigh had been pressed up against the sharp edge of her nightstand. One thing was for sure. She would never willingly transform indoors again.

Still shaking, she pulled on her clothes and went

downstairs to find a cup of that magic calming yoga tea Lisbeth was always drinking.

Claire had just pulled the scalding-hot mug out of the microwave when her mother appeared in the doorway, a frown tugging at the corners of her mouth. "It is very late, *chérie*. Are you all right?"

"I . . . yeah." Claire twisted the hem of her T-shirt between her fingers. "You're up late too."

The corners of Marie's mouth tugged downward, deepening her frown. "Why do you smell of wolf?" She closed her eyes for a long moment. "Do not answer that yet. I need a cup of tea first."

When Marie finally had a steaming mug in front of her, she turned to Claire.

"So? Have you been home the whole night?"

"Yes." Claire lifted her chin. She was telling the truth.

"But you have transformed. Recently." It wasn't a question. Marie had the sort of unnatural stillness about her that made Claire nervous. It was like the flatness of the sky before a storm rolled in.

"Yes," Claire said simply. She could feel the heat creeping into her face.

"Claire." There was a warning in the word. "What happened?"

Claire half-shrugged. "It was no big deal. I was just . . .

experimenting. I wanted to know what it would be like to transform indoors."

Her mother raised an eyebrow. "Why did you not check with me? I was here."

"Yeah, but you were in your darkroom and I didn't want to bug you. I just didn't think it was going to be a big deal."

"And how did you find it?"

"It was miserable," Claire admitted, her eyes glued to the floor.

Marie took a sip of her tea. "I could have told you that it would be, if you had bothered to ask." There was a laugh bubbling up underneath her words.

Claire tried to swallow, but her mouth had gone dry. She felt like she was at her breaking point—that one more thing would shatter her thin layer of control along some invisible fault lines, leaving her in a million shining pieces on the floor. And that couldn't happen. Because underneath that fragile shell, she was angry, and getting angry at her mother would mean being put on an even shorter leash. She didn't want any more orders. Any more wait-until-I-tell-you-what-to-dos. It wasn't like she'd done anything dangerous.

Claire unclenched her teeth. "Right. Of course." She stood up. "I'm pretty tired. . . ."

"Certainly." Marie waved a hand in her direction. "You should go get some sleep. We'll talk more soon."

She offered Claire a tiny smile. "I know that the desire to

test your abilities is hard to ignore. But that's why I am here. So that you don't have to learn every lesson the hard way."

"Yeah. Okay. Thanks." Claire stumbled up the stairs, scared and exhausted and stewing all at once. As soon as she tried to do one little thing on her own, her mother took over, playing her Alpha card.

Running Claire's life.

She kicked herself as she crawled into bed. After all, Marie was just being Marie. What had she thought her mother would do? At least she hadn't forced Claire to tell her about her argument with Matthew. That was something her mother hadn't managed to grab away from her.

It was a start.

On Sunday, Claire realized that she still needed to make pre-dance dinner plans with Matthew. Talking about the ball actually sounded good. After all, that was the sort of thing that was still normal between her and Matthew. Something completely anchored in her human life. Like holding hands with her in the hallway. Kissing in his car.

"Hello?" he answered, interrupting her thoughts.

"Hey—are you busy?"

"Not really, what's up?" She could hear the quiet sound of the Engles' refrigerator opening. The crack of the metal tab on a soda can.

"Well, I was talking to Emily about the Autumn Ball

yesterday, and I sort of forgot to ask you if it might be okay if she and Randy came to dinner with us."

"I don't see any reason why not," Matthew said. "I think everyone wants to go to Salvatore's, so, like, half the school is going to be there anyway. Two more won't make a difference."

Claire fidgeted in her seat. "I, um—actually, I think it'd have to be four more. Emily already promised Amy that they were going together, so . . ."

"Oh, that shouldn't be a problem. Everyone likes Amy."

Claire's chest tightened.

"I'll get Doug to tell Kate-Marie. She's sort of running the show," Matthew said.

"Really?" Sarcasm dripped from Claire's voice. "Kate-Marie running the show? There's a change of pace."

Matthew laughed. "True. But at least we have Doug for a buffer. It'll work out."

They talked for a few minutes about corsages and the restaurant and Emily's after party, which absolutely everyone was going to. By the time they hung up, Claire was feeling a little bit better. More grounded. The agony and weirdness of the night before began to fade, and Claire started to relax. In spite of being stressed about the naming, she did have some things to look forward to in the next couple of weeks. First the full moon gathering and then the ball.

As long as she could keep everything balanced, it would be the best of both worlds.

Chapter Thirteen

HALLOWEEN ARRIVED IN a rush of icy air. Winter was forcing its way into Hanover Falls, stripping the leaves off the trees with its frozen fingers and painting the ground with frost. The first snow would be falling any day, and as Lisbeth opened the door for yet another round of trick-or-treaters, Claire shivered in the cold breeze.

The kids in their masks and capes and dirty sneakers shouted their thanks as they bolted back down toward the street, clutching the prized full-size candy bars that Lisbeth handed out every year. It was the only reason anyone made the trek up the long and imposing Benoit driveway. Claire knew it made her mom uncomfortable, especially on a full moon night, when they needed all the privacy they could get. But even Marie couldn't manage to tell Lisbeth not to do it. Lisbeth looked almost as happy as the kids, beaming underneath the construction-paper circles she'd taped in a rainbow-hued vertical line to her all-white yoga clothes.

"What are you supposed to be, anyway?" Claire asked, looking up from her Spanish vocab sheet.

"I'm the chakras." Lisbeth held out her arms and looked down at herself. "You know—the energy centers of the body? It's a yoga thing."

Claire stared at her blankly. She loved Lisbeth, but she was totally weird sometimes.

"I know, you think I'm being bizarre." Lisbeth put her hands on her hips. "But this is a major holiday! *Someone* in this house needs to celebrate tonight." She peered into the candy bowl. "I'd better get some more chocolate bars out. It isn't even close to dark yet and we're already running low."

Lisbeth headed for the pantry, humming to herself. Claire followed her into the kitchen and looked out the window at the backyard, her gaze going to the edge of the property, where the woods met the lawn behind the border of the ivy-covered brick. The forest beyond looked starker, more serious, without the lush green of its summer foliage or the party-dress reds and yellows of the autumn leaves. It matched Claire's mood, and she tingled with the anticipation of the full moon gathering. Things had been tense between Claire and Emily since Saturday, and though everything seemed normal between Claire and Matthew, something didn't quite fit anymore. Like a teacup that had been broken and then glued back together. Still functional, but not as perfect as it had been before.

Tonight more than ever, Claire needed the forest and her fur and a hunt under the round, pale moon. Lisbeth might be having fun passing out her chocolate bars, but she was far from the only one in the Benoits' house who would be celebrating Halloween.

By the time she and her mother slipped out the back door, the candy was gone and the trick-or-treaters had long since gone to bed. The wintry air made Claire catch her breath—next time, she needed to wear warmer clothes. She'd be plenty warm once she transformed, but getting to the clearing was another matter. Her ears were already stinging with cold.

The two of them tiptoed into the forest without speaking, all their focus spent listening for a footfall that didn't belong. Watching for an out-of-place shadow. As they worked their way deeper into the trees, Claire's shoulders loosened. The likelihood of anyone coming this far into the forest for a Halloween thrill was pretty slim. And besides, with the rich, green scent of the plants gone, a human odor would be obvious a mile away. Claire sniffed at the breeze, catching whiffs of rabbit and deer and something intensely musky.

"What is that?" she whispered to her mother, sniffing at the air.

Marie lifted her nose briefly. "Badger," she announced.

The word tingled in Claire's ears. She'd never seen a badger before, but she'd bet they were fun to hunt.

"They're smarter than you think, and mean beyond belief," Marie said, catching wind of Claire's enthusiasm. "We may hunt it, since it is so close, but you'd be wrong to underestimate them. And we need something tonight that is easily caught. Perhaps even a rabbit, though that is an awfully poor sacrifice. . . ." Her voice trailed off as they arrived in the firelit clearing. Victoria was already there, sitting on the trunk of a recently fallen tree that lay just outside their usual circle. Her slumped shoulders and pointed-in toes told Claire instantly that Victoria didn't want to be here. That she was dreading the transformation.

"Claire, Marie. I greet you both." Her voice was flat, her eyes dull.

"I greet you, Victoria." Claire hesitated, not sure what else to say. She edged closer to the warmth of the fire.

"And I also greet you, Victoria," Marie added, walking over to place a hand on the mountain of Victoria's belly. "I know this is going to be a difficult evening for you. We will make it as easy as possible—I am planning a very simple version of the ceremonies, anyway, as a precaution."

"Thank you," Victoria whispered, hanging her head.

Claire made her way over and sat down next to her. "You okay?" she whispered.

Victoria nodded, her eyes still on the ground. "I'd say I'm desperate to be done with this pregnancy, but that would mean I'd need to have a name for the baby." She let out a long, quavering breath full of held-in tears. "But enough of my moaning. How's the fire stuff going?"

"Really well," Claire said, keeping her voice low. "I can do it every time and almost always on the first try. I'm just worried that my nerves are going to take me down—that I'll fold under pressure at the gathering, you know?"

"I know exactly," Victoria snorted. "I'm so nervous that I'm going to pick the wrong name—ugh. We're both dreading it, huh?"

Beatrice ducked into the clearing, smiling at Marie and Claire before looking worriedly at Victoria. Judith was right behind her, and they all exchanged greetings. Katherine came puffing into the clearing, all apologies as she struggled out of her voluminous fleece jacket.

"Sorry, everyone. There was a huge tree down across my normal path, so I had to cut across the gully." She put her hands on her hips, catching her breath. "How on earth did you get here so fast?" she asked Judith.

"I cut across the gully," Judith said dryly, arching an eyebrow. Katherine turned away from Judith, the scent of her embarrassment wafting through the clearing.

"Well," Katherine said, her voice quiet. "You always were the better runner."

Apparently, Claire wasn't the only one who fell short in

Judith's extremely judgmental eyes, though after what had happened at the mall, Claire sort of didn't blame Judith for how she treated Katherine.

Marie glanced up at the sky, which was more visible than ever through the naked branches of the trees. "Everyone's here. That's all that matters right now. Let's begin." There was an unusual sharpness in her voice that made something deep inside Claire snap to attention. From the way the other wolves scrambled into place around the fire, Claire guessed she wasn't the only one. She drew in a deep breath, her lungs aching from the combination of the cold air and the wood smoke.

Marie raised her arms and began the opening chant. Her voice was quieter than usual, touching the edges of the clearing but going no farther. Casting no echo. Still, the words flowed over Claire, and her muscles loosened in response. She rose up on her toes and bounced, feeling relaxed and excited at the same time. For the first time in weeks, she was surrounded by people who were just like her. And even though she got along with plenty of people—human people—better than she did with Judith, there was still a comfort that came from knowing they didn't have to keep secrets from each other. That Judith didn't love her or hate her just because she was a werewolf—and neither did any of the other women around the fire.

Marie lowered her arms, a smile spreading across her face. "You may transform." The smile faded. "But quietly. Caution is required tonight."

The rustle of fabric and the thud of paws hitting the ground were the only noises in the clearing. Victoria let out a thin and impossibly high whine. The noise would have been inaudible to any ears less sensitive than a werewolf's.

It's the last time. It has to be the last time, Beatrice soothed.

Claire snapped at the chill air, her teeth closing over the metallic taste in the wind that promised snow. She wanted to run. Was dying to run.

We'll bring you back something good, she promised.

You'd better. Victoria twitched her tail in a pained sort of amusement.

Those who are able—Marie's ears flicked in the direction of the deepest part of the forest—*let us go and hunt.*

Everyone except Victoria swept into the woods behind Marie, though Claire could see the reluctance weighing down Beatrice's tail and flattening her ears as she ran.

The pack veered to the left, following a scent that Claire had been too distracted by Beatrice to catch. It was just a rabbit. Disappointment coursed through Claire. She'd really wanted to go after the badger. A rabbit was barely even a catch.

She forced herself to let it go—there would be plenty of full moons in the future, when the pack wasn't so worried about babies and Halloween pranks. She'd make sure they hunted a badger then. A streak of fear-scented heat raced past Claire's left side, catching her off guard and nearly causing her to stumble over a tree root.

The rabbit. Crap. She'd been so focused on the animal she wasn't hunting that she'd missed the one they actually had a chance to get. She broke from the pack and wheeled around, following the hop-skip run of the rabbit. The rest of the pack was close behind her, and Claire reveled in the brief sense of being in the lead—nothing between her and her prey.

Soon enough, though, Marie tore past Claire and took her rightful place at the front of the pack. Claire fell back, just a pace or two, and Marie snatched the rabbit a slim moment before he disappeared into a hole in the ground. She killed him quickly and efficiently.

The other wolves skidded to a halt, and Katherine raised her head, the beginnings of a howl pouring from her throat. Claire cringed, knowing full well that this was exactly the sort of thing her mother had told them not to do. Judith turned and rammed her head into Katherine's shoulder, cutting off the sound as Katherine wobbled in surprise.

Marie said to be quiet! Judith sat and scratched her ear.

Sorry. Katherine hung her head. *I wasn't thinking. I—*

You put us all at risk with your thoughtlessness. Marie put down the rabbit and paced over to Katherine.

It won't happen again. Katherine sank down onto the carpet of dead leaves, her nose buried between her paws.

Claire's heart began to pound. She'd seen that look—that posture—on her mother before. Not in her wolf form but in her human form. And it meant one thing. Marie wasn't going to let this go.

It certainly won't happen again tonight. You are no longer welcome at the feast. You will go get your things. You will speak to no one, and you will go home. Marie stood over Katherine, who lay on the ground looking up at the Alpha wolf.

Katherine whined a pathetic, apologetic whine.

Marie leaned down and caught the soft flesh at the side of Katherine's neck in her mouth. Not hard enough to hurt— Claire could see the space between her teeth—but enough to make Katherine's eyes widen.

I will not be disobeyed. Marie left Katherine shaking on the forest floor. She scooped up the rabbit and began trotting back in the direction of the fire, with Beatrice close behind her. Claire hesitated, staring for a moment at Katherine's pleading expression aimed at the retreating forms of Beatrice and Marie.

Judith brushed past her, following the others. *Get used to it. There is no law except pack law. Let's go.*

A sudden anger flared inside Claire. What Katherine did was wrong—stupid, even. This was no game—she'd seen that last summer. Every time they were in the woods it was a life-and-death risk, but tonight they had good reason to be extra cautious. Her anger grew as she considered Katherine's recklessness. And over a stupid rabbit.

This was, she realized, exactly the sort of thing that made

her mother think she had to control every inch of what happened in the pack. Which meant that Claire would suffer the consequences of Katherine's actions. There would be more rules, more commands, because it was the only way Marie knew how to keep them all safe.

Claire turned to go with the others, leaving Katherine alone in the heart of the woods.

They finished the rest of the ceremony quickly, the mood in the clearing gray and muted as a cloud.

Claire walked alongside her mother as they made their way back toward the house. Marie looked more tired than usual, the circles under her eyes shadowed nearly black by the moon, but she seemed as calm as ever. Claire watched out of the corner of her eye as her mother stepped carefully over tree roots and ducked under the low, leafless branches that reached for her hair like thin-fingered hands.

There was no scent of anger in the air. No reminder of what had passed between her mother and Katherine.

"Mom?" she ventured, too curious to stay silent. "Are you still—I mean, the thing with Katherine—" Claire fumbled around for the right words.

"The thing with Katherine is finished. There is no need to dwell on it." Marie's voice was quiet. Steady.

"So, you're not angry?"

"No. That is not our way. And it is especially not my way. She erred, and as the Alpha it was my duty to correct her. So

I did. One cannot lead the pack by carrying grudges or playing favorites. That path only ends in chaos." Marie shrugged. "There is the law, and it must be followed. It is my job to ensure that. My feelings for Katherine—who has been a loyal and faithful member of our pack for many years—have nothing to do with it."

It was so similar to what Judith had said that Claire shivered. But it made sense. There was no room for error in a werewolf's life. The kindest thing a pack leader could do was to keep those mistakes from happening—to keep all the wolves alive. Even when it meant being strict. Even when it meant being merciless. Even when it made the wrinkles in Marie's forehead deeper and made her eyes look tired.

Lost in thought, Claire trailed behind her mother, reluctant to leave the forest. Things were harder underneath the trees. More dangerous. Even brutal.

But at least they were honest, which was a lot more than she could say for her human life.

Chapter Fourteen

THE CHILL THAT had been in the air turned into a true, aching cold over the next two weeks. The day before the dance, a bank of heavy, iron-gray clouds rolled in, and the weathermen excitedly predicted a few inches of snow by the weekend.

After school that Friday, Claire headed outside into the swirl of huge, feathery flakes. She bent her head against the falling snow. She stomped through the inch or so that was already on the ground, hurrying toward the parking lot and Emily's car. This weekend was going to be the most human, the most normal, that she'd had in ages, and she was going to enjoy every second of it. She and Emily were doing pre-ball pedicures, just the two of them.

The windows of Emily's car had been cleared off, and she could see Emily inside, her head bent over her phone as she texted furiously. Claire opened the back door and threw her book bag in.

"What's up?" she asked.

"Kate-Marie *Brown* is what," Emily griped. "She's ridiculous."

"Well, we agree on that." Claire shut the back door and opened the front, crawling into the passenger seat. No matter how long she dated Matthew or how many of the same parties they went to, Kate-Marie Brown and her inner circle of haute couture handmaidens still looked at Claire like she was as disposable as a paper cup.

"What'd she do now?" Claire asked.

"Okay, you know how I ended up getting that really fab black and silver dress?"

"Of course. It's amazing."

"Right. Well, somehow it came up in trig, and Kate-Marie freaked. I mean fuh-reaked. I guess she's wearing black jewelry and a silver dress, and she is not amused that I'm—and I quote—'jacking her color scheme.' How can anyone call dibs on a *color*? And why does she care, anyway? It's not like we're going to be posing for yearbook photos together."

"It's Kate-Marie," Claire said. "She thinks she can have whatever she wants. Do you want to go find a different dress, or do you want to suffer her wrath?"

Emily raised an eyebrow. "Are you joking? Kate-Marie

might run some sort of high school empire in her head, but I don't give a crap what she thinks. And I hope you don't, either."

Claire shook her head. "Nope."

"Good. Then, let's go back to my house and do the mani-pedi thing."

Claire leaned back in her seat, feeling better about things with Emily than she had in ages. "Well, your house it is, then," she said happily.

By the time Claire got home, it was well after dark, and even the tips of the browning grass had disappeared under the snow. Emily had invited her to stay the night, but Claire hadn't wanted to push her luck quite that far.

She climbed the stairs and glanced down the hall at her mother's room. The door was shut, and Claire could hear her mother talking on the phone, though she couldn't make out what was being said. She turned and headed for her room. She wanted to try on her dress one more time, take a ridiculously long shower, and watch the *Late Show* in bed.

Her dress hung in the front of her closet, and just see-ing the garment bag made Claire want to twirl around the room. She pulled it out, breathing in the crisp smell of silk and organza.

She yanked off the jeans and sweater she'd worn to school and slipped the dress over her head, shivering as the fabric slithered over her skin. The dress came to the floor, covering all but the tips of her shoes. She turned in the mirror, admiring the way the silk peeked through the overlay in the back. It was so *girly*.

With a sigh, she wriggled out of the dress and hung it back in its protective bag. She kicked her dirty clothes toward the laundry basket, wandered into her bathroom, and turned on the shower. Tomorrow night was going to be fabulous, and as far as she was concerned, it couldn't come fast enough.

When she got out of the shower, Claire heard her mother pacing the hall outside her room. She opened the door and stuck her head out.

"Mom? What's going on?"

Marie looked at her, and the expression on her mother's face startled Claire. Marie looked almost ecstatic. The dark circles under her eyes had faded, and there was a soft flush of pink in her normally bone-pale cheeks.

"Victoria has just had her baby," Marie announced. The excitement was coming off her in waves. "They are both fine, and Beatrice is as happy as I've ever heard her." She smiled broadly.

"That's great," Claire said, still mystified by the sudden change in her mother.

"I knew you'd want to know right away, since we'll be gathering tomorrow night for the naming. I assume you're ready to light the fire?"

Claire froze. Tomorrow night.

Oh, crap. No. This is not happening.

Her fingertips tingled unpleasantly as she tried to wrap her head around this sudden change in plans. She couldn't skip the ball to go to a gathering—it would look too suspicious. Not to mention how badly she'd be disappointing Matthew. The dance—the normal, human dance—was pretty much the only thing left holding them together. They'd both been looking forward to the ball for weeks. She wouldn't take that away from him. She couldn't.

"Is something wrong, *chérie*? You look . . . shocked." Marie cocked her head to the side, studying Claire.

"It's . . . I thought there would be a little more time." She bit her lip. "The dance is tomorrow night. I can't . . . There's no way I can miss it. Everyone will talk."

Marie lifted her eyebrows. "This should not be coming as a surprise, Claire. You knew Victoria's baby could arrive at any time. The gathering is not optional. And part of being a werewolf is learning how to make humans believe unbelievable things. This is a very important moment for our pack—a little party with your human friends is no comparison."

Claire leaned against the door frame. Emily's party. Oh god, she was going to miss Emily's after party. Her stomach churned.

"What time is the gathering?" she whispered.

"We will meet just before midnight—the ceremony begins on the stroke of a new day." Marie crossed her arms. "And you will not be late. I am sorry that the timing is bad for you. Truly."

Just before midnight. That would give her time to go to the dance, at least. She'd just have to come up with a way to bail on the after party without ruining her relationship with her best friend.

Claire looked up at her mother. Marie's expression was firm, final. There was no point in arguing with her when she looked like that.

"Fine. I'll be there."

"Good. I will be looking forward to seeing you succeed." Her mother padded back down the hall to her room.

Claire walked back into her room and stared out the window at the woods. She sent Matthew a text, telling him to call her as soon as he could. If she was going to have any chance of pulling off the dance and the naming in the same night, she was going to need his help.

Like, a lot of his help.

While she waited for him to call, she thought about Victoria. Wondered if she'd manage to pick a name—if she was still as nervous as Claire was about the gathering. Claire wished she had some sort of special skill for naming, the way Victoria did with the fire lighting. . . .

The puzzle pieces slid together in her mind.

Maybe there was something she could try. If she could somehow hear the baby, maybe she would give her some sort of clue. And this time, at least, she'd be using her extra abilities for the right reasons—to help the pack.

Claire dug up some warm clothes and crept down the stairs. Sneaking out was risky, but she didn't have much choice. There was no way she was transforming in the house again.

Ever.

The freezing air slipped inside the collar of her fleece, giving Claire goose bumps. The forest was quiet in the snow. It took forever to get anywhere, since she'd had to cover the footprints she'd made in the powdery white blanket covering the lawn. Halfway to the woods, she realized that she'd left her phone on her bedside table, where she'd plugged it in to charge.

Damn. If she missed Matthew's call—or if her mom heard the phone ringing and got suspicious about Claire not answering . . .

Damn.

She stood for a moment, the icy air pinching her ears with its sharp-nailed fingers, and weighed the risk of going back against her abandoned phone. She had already taken a huge chance by coming out at all—if she went back now, she might not be able to get out here again. She might as well go see what she could find out. That way, she'd at least have something to show for it if she got caught.

She bent her head over the path of her footprints and focused on getting herself into the safety of the forest as fast as she could.

In her practice clearing, she tossed off her clothes and

transformed in a rush, trying to get into her wolf form before the cold seized her completely. As soon as she was changed, she focused on getting warm, using the wolf trick of holding the illusion of heat between her two forms. She thought about sunlight and about the hot sand of a white beach burning the soles of her feet. Slowly, her shivering stopped. Claire glanced down at her paws, which were tipped with deep-rose-colored claws. The nail polish had looked fantastic in her human form, but it looked ridiculous now that she was a wolf.

She shook herself. There was no time to waste. The longer she was gone, the bigger the chance that Marie would notice she had left. Claire sat down, her thick fur protecting her from the damp cold of the snow. She shook her head, hard, making her wolf ears flap and fluffing out the fur on her neck.

Feeling more relaxed, she shut her eyes and focused. She listened for Victoria first, since she was sure to be wherever the baby was. Claire tried to picture the little house where Beatrice and Victoria lived—the hospital would have meant too many hard questions, so Victoria had given birth at home. After a few moments, Claire heard a weary voice. It sounded as though it were filling the clearing, but Claire knew it was only in her head.

"She's so perfect," Victoria cooed. "Look at her little eyelashes! They're so curly."

"You're keeping her awake," Beatrice cautioned. "You should both be getting some rest."

"I know, I know. I just want to *look* at her."

Claire focused harder, heard the small grunting breaths of the baby. She concentrated on the sound. Listened for something. Anything. There was a pause, a tiny gasp, and then a mewling wail as the baby began to cry.

Startled, Claire lost focus and was suddenly very alone in the silence of the clearing.

Crap.

By the time she managed to hear Victoria again, the crying had stopped. The baby was still breathing a hitching sort of breath that sounded less than calm, though.

"Maybe she's hungry?"

Claire could hear Victoria's voice, but it sounded fainter, farther away. The baby's breath rang in her ears, so new, so full of meaning, even though she was still wordless. It was as though she was nothing more than the air that puffed in and out of her just-born body.

As the sound surrounded Claire, an idea drifted into her mind.

If her breath was all the baby had, why not name her after it?

The rightness of it settled over her. Victoria couldn't just use the word "breath." It wasn't even a name. It was something Lisbeth would name a kid. But she could look up some name meanings, find something that fit.

Suddenly excited about the possibility of actually being

able to help Victoria, Claire changed back into her human form, gasping as the cold air caught at her before she managed to get her clothes back on. As quickly as she could, she walked back to the house, carefully erasing her tracks as she went.

She slipped in the back door and stood leaning against it, listening hard to the noises of the house. She didn't hear anything at first, but then the furnace kicked off and there was a soft *click-tap* from the depths of the house, somewhere in the vicinity of Marie's darkroom.

Claire squeezed her eyes shut and made a silent run for her room.

When the door was safely closed behind her and she'd changed her clothes to get rid of the snow smell, Claire grabbed her phone.

One missed call. *Crap.*

Matthew'd left a short, call-me-back sort of message, but it was already nearly one o'clock in the morning—she'd been in the woods longer than she'd intended, and it was way too late to call him back now. She'd have to try him back in the morning. Kicking herself again for forgetting her phone, Claire sat down in front of her computer. At least she could finish the stuff for the naming. She pulled up a couple of baby-name websites.

In no time at all, she found exactly what she was looking for. The name hummed at the tip of her tongue, begging her to say it.

Chapter Fifteen

IN SPITE OF her late night, Claire woke early the next morning, too excited and edgy to sleep in. Emily and Amy would be at her house after lunch, along with Lisbeth, who'd been all too happy to agree to run the pre-dance hair-and-makeup show.

But it was only a matter of hours until everyone showed up, and Claire had a lot to do before they got there. She'd need clothes to change into after the dance, since she couldn't exactly go traipsing into the woods in a gown. She dug through her closet, scrounged up an old duffel bag, and stuck some dark sweats and running shoes into it.

Marie knocked on her open door just as Claire was tugging the zipper closed.

"What is that for?" she asked, looking at the bag.

"It's clothes for the gathering. I can't wear my dress in the woods." Claire stared at the confused look on her mother's face. She couldn't quite figure out what Marie was thinking—why she seemed so mystified. A horrible feeling gathered in her throat. It was like stepping into a lake that was vastly colder and infinitely deeper than she'd expected it to be.

"You are still going to the dance?" her mother asked. "I thought we'd discussed that. The naming is tonight." An odd little frown puckered her lips.

Claire could barely hear over the pounding in her ears. "I know. But not until later. I have time to do both."

Marie crossed her arms. "The naming is extremely important."

So is the Autumn Ball.

Not that her mother seemed to notice—not that she seemed to care.

"There is much to set up for tonight. I still need to find some ginseng, the wood is not ready for your fire—"

The mention of the fire was enough to send a tingle through Claire's still-whole left ear. She knew how to light it—could do it like breathing—but there was so much at stake. . . .

Marie shook her head. "I had hoped you might help me, but if you cannot or will not abandon this"—she paused—

"*event*, then I will do it on my own." Her mother sighed. "Lisbeth is coming over, I suppose?"

Claire swallowed. "Yes. She's going to help me and Emily and Amy get ready."

"Fine. I'll leave her a camera—I suppose you might want to take some photographs. I'll be leaving in a few hours to start the preparations. If you need anything, I'll be available by cell phone. Otherwise, I guess I will see you in the woods." Marie reached up and straightened the collar of her shirt.

"You're . . . You're leaving?" Claire's cheeks stung like she'd been slapped. It had been obvious that her human life was becoming less and less important to her mother, but her mother knew how much this dance meant to her—or at least, she *should* know. But she was already halfway out the door.

It wasn't as though Claire expected her mother to be like the other moms she knew—for one thing, her mother had always been distant. And when Claire discovered what secrets Marie had to keep, she'd begun to understand why. Still, when they'd grown closer in their wolf lives, she'd thought at least some of that might trickle down into the human parts of their lives. Instead, it seemed like Marie barely even noticed Claire when she wasn't covered in fur.

Her mother twitched a shoulder in Claire's direction. "I have much to do in order to fulfill my responsibilities to the pack. It has to come first. For all of us. Always."

Claire sat down on the bed, the air punched out of her lungs by the force of her mother's words.

Concern flitted across Marie's face. "I am not leaving in order to hurt you, *chérie*. I must do it, in spite of the fact that you feel wounded. I must do it because I love you, and I want to keep you safe. Putting the pack first is the best way to keep you safe. You understand that?"

Claire nodded painfully. Wounded, as her mother had so ably observed. She understood perfectly, but that didn't make it hurt even a little bit less.

"Good. Call me if you need me. I will be waiting for you in the forest with much anticipation." With a quick little smile, Marie disappeared down the hall, leaving Claire aching at the foot of the bed.

Her cell phone rang, breaking the wringing sadness that had seeped through her, as dark and silent as ink.

It was Matthew.

"Hello?" she answered, her voice dull.

"Claire? You sound weird. Are you sick?"

His words came out in a rush, but as soon as Claire heard them, an idea sprang up in front of her. A way to make it all work—and maybe without infuriating Emily.

"No, not yet," she replied. "But I'm going to be."

"Huh?" he asked, confused.

"Some stuff happened last night, and things are going to be a little more . . . complicated than they were before."

Matthew sighed. "Story of your life, right?"

"Pretty much," Claire confessed, though it stung a little bit to admit that in the face of what had just happened with her mother. "So, here's what's happening."

She gave him the brief version—that Victoria had had her baby and that the naming, the absolutely mandatory naming, would happen just after the dance. When she was supposed to be at Emily's crowning-glory-of-her-high-school-years after party. But his questions about how she was feeling had given her the perfect idea for a way out.

She would have a great time at dinner, a fabulous time at the dance, and then, just as things were drawing to a close, she would bring on a fake . . . something. Stomach flu. Migraine. Broken bone. Whatever it took to get her out of Emily's party. Matthew could drop her off by the woods, and then she'd be home free.

"Do you mind?" she asked, twisting a loose thread from her comforter between her fingers.

"Not really," he said. "That's part of the job, I guess."

He sounded like she'd just asked him to come with her while she bought tampons.

"Do you"—he paused—"need me to stay or just to drop you off?"

The worry in his voice made Claire grimace, and she was glad he couldn't see her face. The tension between them bobbed to the surface of their conversation like ice. But the last thing she wanted was to have a big fight with him now, when she needed his help so badly.

"No—I mean, thanks, but I think the best thing is if you go to the party. You know, make a big deal to Emily about how sick I got and how really upset I am that I'm not at the party. You could even tell her that I tried to come but you and Lisbeth wouldn't let me." The more she talked about it, the more she convinced herself that it was the right plan.

"Oh." Matthew sounded relieved, but Claire ignored it. "Yeah, I guess I can see that it would work better that way." He paused. "Wow. It really has gotten complicated, hasn't it?"

"Like you said, story of my life." She thought of what Marie had said just before she'd left. "And it doesn't look like it's going to be getting any simpler, either." She was half-talking to herself, but the heaviness of the silence on the other end of the phone caught her attention.

"I'm beginning to see that," he said slowly. "But anyway"— he perked up—"at least we can go to the dance, right? It's going to be great."

"I can't wait," said Claire. She glanced at the clock. "Speaking of which, Emily and Amy and Lisbeth are going to be here *soon*."

"And I have a corsage to get." Matthew's voice was getting more excited by the second, and Claire knew she'd made the right choice by refusing to bail on the dance completely. "I'll see you at five thirty, okay?"

"I'll be ready," Claire promised.

An hour and a half later, Lisbeth came crashing into the house, armed with a bag full of curling irons and hot rollers and wicked-looking bobby pins. Panting, she dumped them onto Claire's bed.

"Please tell me you have makeup," she begged Claire.

"Yep," said Claire. "All lined up and waiting." She pointed to the cosmetics on her vanity.

"Oh, thank God. Well, let me get this stuff plugged in, and you can start with your makeup while it heats up. When are Emily and Amy getting here?"

Claire shrugged. "Any time. And the guys are picking us up at five thirty."

Lisbeth's jaw dropped. "Three heads of hair need to be done by five thirty? Yikes. I'm not exactly a pro at this, Claire. More like a well-equipped amateur. Interested bystander, even."

Claire picked up an eyeliner pencil. "Yeah, but Emily's hair's short, so it won't take long, and Amy's hair will probably look perfect when she gets here, anyway." Claire knew she sounded pathetic, but she didn't care.

Lisbeth froze, a curling iron in each hand. "Whoa. I thought you two were friends."

Claire focused on tracing the edge of her eyelid in the mirror. "She wants to be friends. She's friends with Emily, but it's just . . . complicated."

Lisbeth came up behind her and squeezed Claire's

shoulder. "I'd love to tell you that it gets less complicated as you get older"—she wrinkled her nose—"but it really doesn't. Whatever happens, though, however it works out, I'm always on your side."

Downstairs, the front door banged open.

"Claire? Helloooo! We're here!" Emily's voice climbed the stairs ahead of her. She came into the room, even more loaded down with bags and boxes than Lisbeth had been. Amy trundled in behind her, half-hidden behind an enormous garment bag. Emily dropped her stuff and practically fluttered over to Claire.

"I'm so excited—can you believe it's finally *today* and we're actually going to a dance together? I could barely sleep last night. Oooh—is that the eyeshadow you're wearing? I love it!"

Lisbeth laughed, shaking her head at Emily's usual no-one-gets-a-word-in-edgewise entrance. Still, Emily's excitement was contagious, and Claire felt her own anticipation rising.

"Hi, Claire," Amy said. There was a sort of thrilled hesitation in her voice, like she was reaching for something hot—like she was afraid she might get burned. "Thanks for having us over to get ready."

"No problem," Claire said, toying with her mascara. "We'd better get started, though, or we'll still be half-done when the guys get here."

"Amen," said Lisbeth, swooping over to Emily with a handful of rhinestone-studded hairpins.

After nearly an hour, Lisbeth escaped downstairs, claiming she'd earned a tea break, though Claire could tell that she was just trying to give the three of them a little time alone.

"So, is everything ready for the party?" Claire asked Emily.

A pleased and proud look swept across Emily's face. Claire felt herself shrivel just a little bit. Even if she managed to get Emily to believe her fictional illness, she would still be missing the most wild and exciting thing Emily had ever done. No matter how amazing the naming ended up being, it was going to cost Claire to be there. It was going to take something from her human life.

"Oh, it's ready all right. The breakables and valuables are stashed in the back of my mom's closet, the kitchen's full of plastic cups, and the freezer is full of ice." She dropped her voice. "I got a couple of the football players to agree to bring the keg—I mean, I am woman, hear me roar and all that, but those things are freaking *heavy*."

Amy laughed, her tumble of blond curls shaking around her shoulders. She'd asked Lisbeth to keep her hair down, and it looked gorgeous—Lisbeth hadn't done much more than smooth her curls and put some shiny stuff on the ends. But it was still amazing. Jealousy dropped a mean-eyed veil over Claire as she stared at the gleaming ringlets.

"Well," she said, wrenching her attention back to Emily, "I'm sure it's going to be amazing."

"It better, because if—" Emily raised a warning finger, and

in the process she bumped her makeup bag on Claire's nightstand, sending tubes and brushes everywhere. "Oh, damn!" She scooped up the ones that were still on the nightstand and then disappeared, rustling the bedskirt as she dug around for whatever might have rolled under the bed.

"Hey, Claire, did you get a dog that you haven't told me about?" Emily's voice was muffled.

Terror shot through Claire, making her cold to the tips of her fingers. She'd been so careful—what had she forgotten? Amy looked up, an interested expression glowing in her eyes.

"Nope—why?" Claire kept her voice as calm as she could, but there was a tiny tremor in it that she couldn't quite hide. Thoughts whisked through her as quickly as clouds tearing across a stormy sky. How bad was it going to be? Could she fix it? But the one thought that wouldn't go away was the idea—the knowledge—that Emily was standing at the edge of a life-or-death cliff, and Claire was the one who'd led her there.

The guilt was grinding. Crushing. Claire's lungs burned in her chest.

"Well, this was under your bed." Emily emerged from underneath the bedskirt, a tube of concealer in one hand and a tuft of shadowy-gray wolf hair in the other.

Immediately, Claire remembered the night she'd transformed in her room—backed herself up to the bed, terrified by the boxed-in feeling. She'd probably been shedding like crazy, and though she thought she'd cleaned up any evidence she might have left, she hadn't bothered to vacuum under the bed.

"Oh, yeah. That's from Lisbeth and Mark's dog, probably. Didn't I tell you? They got a chow. They named it Karma, which I think is freaking ridiculous, but he's really cute. She brought him over one day. When mom was out, obviously."

The lies dripped from her lips without any effort—as easily as snow fluttering down from the sky. Of course, the moment the words had left her mouth, she realized the error she'd made. Lisbeth was *at the house*. If Emily asked about the stupid, non-existent dog that Claire had just created, she'd be in even hotter water than she already was. She held her breath. Prayed that Emily would buy it and then drop it.

Out of the corner of her eye, she saw Amy staring at her. Actually, it was more like Amy was trying to bore holes through Claire's head so that she could see what Claire was hiding inside it.

Shit.

Emily dropped the tuft of wolf fur, wrinkling her nose. "Ew. I hate chows. They're so mean!"

Claire searched for a new subject. Fast. Something safe, something nonsuspicious, something like . . .

"So, did you get Randy a boutonniere?" It was lame, but it worked.

"What? No way. That's just for prom." Emily looked scandalized. "You didn't get one for Matthew, did you?"

Claire shook her head. "No. I think he got me a corsage, though."

"Of course! He's supposed to. It's, like, an unwritten rule. The guys do corsages for Autumn Ball and prom, but boutonniere's are only for prom." Emily was off and running, filling Claire in on all the crucial-but-totally-not-obvious rules of the dances.

Claire wasn't listening. She didn't care—she was too relieved to care. All that mattered was that Emily had completely forgotten about the "dog" that had been in Claire's room.

Still, the back of Claire's neck was still tingling unpleasantly. What just happened—it had been ugly, but it was a good reminder that she was going to have to be on her toes even more than usual tonight. There could be no mistakes.

Amy was chatting with Emily about the traditional pre-dance restaurants, and she turned to Claire with a conspiratorial smile on her face.

"I'm glad I'm not the only one who doesn't know what I'm doing," she said. "We're both so lucky to have Emily." It was an innocent enough comment. Friendly, even. But it made Claire shiver.

Lisbeth knocked and elbowed her way in through the door, carrying a tray laden with sodas, a bowl of pretzels, and a lone tea mug.

"Fortifications," she announced. She turned to Claire and

gave her a devilish little grin as Emily dove for a Diet Coke. "Get your butt in front of that vanity, missy. It's time to do your hair."

Amy stood up. "If you guys don't mind, I'm ready to get dressed. Is there somewhere . . ." Claire could smell the powdery scent of shyness, coming from Amy.

"Sure. Guest room—two doors down on the right," Lisbeth said.

"Thanks." Amy looked relieved and grabbed her dress. "You coming with?" she asked Emily, who was finished with her hair and makeup, too.

Emily looked back and forth between Claire and Amy, hesitating. "Um . . . yeah, I guess." She turned to Claire. "Come down when your hair's done?"

"Yep."

Emily and Amy headed down the hall, and Claire felt her shoulders slump with the sudden lack of tension.

"Is everything going okay?" Lisbeth asked, her voice quiet as a sigh. She began pulling the hot rollers out of Claire's hair and dropping them onto the top of the vanity.

Claire shrugged. "I don't really know." It was true enough. And also vague enough that it might keep Lisbeth from asking any more questions. Claire's palms were starting to sweat from the effort of keeping everyone happily—and safely—ignorant.

Lisbeth put a row of the pins in her mouth and started piling Claire's curls on top of her head.

Claire winced as Lisbeth scraped a hairpin against her scalp. "Ow. Do you have to pin those things into my actual skull?"

"Sorry," Lisbeth said around a mouthful of metal spikes. "Almost done." She tacked in a few more bobby pins and then shellacked everything in place with a cloud of hair spray.

When the stinging chemical spray had finally settled, Claire opened her eyes and looked in the mirror. With her hair up and the subtle-but-glamorous makeup she'd put on earlier sharpening her cheekbones and darkening her eyes, she looked older. More sophisticated. And very much like her mother. Claire's heart fluttered in her chest.

"Just look at you. You're all grown up." Lisbeth's lip quivered.

That was all it took to break the spell. Claire groaned and stood up from the vanity. "Okay, thanks for the primping and all, but there's no crying allowed. It's just a dance, Lisbeth."

"Yeah, but it's your first one, and—"

"That's it! Out!"

Lisbeth looked hurt.

"Oh, c'mon." Claire sighed. "At least let me get my dress on before you get all weepy, okay?"

"Deal." Lisbeth sniffed, heading for the door.

Alone in her room at last, Claire closed her eyes and took a long, slow breath. So far, so good.

I can do this. It's one night. With one lie at the end of it. I. Can. Do. This.

She really didn't have that much time before the guys were due to arrive. She hurried over to her closet and slipped on her dress before stepping into the heels that looked so cute but pinched her toes like hell.

After a last, satisfied glance in the mirror, Claire picked up her duffel bag and headed down the hall. Emily opened the door to the guest room before Claire was even halfway there, and came tearing out into the hall, all shrieking smiles and sparkling dress.

"Oh my freaking God, Claire, you look *amazing*!"

"Thanks." Claire felt her cheeks getting warm. "You look great too. Very punk-rock glam."

Amy stepped out behind Emily, and Claire's joy evaporated. Amy looked innocent and sexy and approachable all at once. She looked like the perfect human girl who was going to the perfect human dance and who was worrying about exactly nothing more than that. She reeked of anticipation, and jealousy snaked through Claire. She'd spent a whole day plotting and scheming just to go to the dance, and she was still going to disappoint Emily terribly before the night was over.

"Oooh—is that what you're wearing to my house?" Emily stared at the bag, practically rubbing her hands together with anticipation.

Claire resisted the urge to slip the duffel behind her back, out of Emily's reach. "Yep," she said. "I can't wear these heels all night," she added, hating herself for stretching her lies an extra inch.

The doorbell rang, and Amy's face broke into a wide grin. "They're here."

The three of them flounced downstairs, their high heels clicking onto the marble floor of the front hall just as Lisbeth opened the door.

Chapter Sixteen

MATTHEW STOOD ON the porch, glancing over his shoulder at Randy and Julio, who were just climbing out of Randy's Suburban. Underneath a charcoal gray overcoat, Matthew had on a crisp white shirt and onyx black tuxedo. He looked amazing. Claire watched him as he stepped into the house and took in her hair, her dress, her overall way-more-glamorous-than-the-usual-Claire ensemble. A muscle in his jaw tightened and he swallowed hard.

"Claire. You look absolutely gorgeous. No—stunning. That's the word I want. I'm stunned," Matthew said, as the other guys crept in behind him, muttering compliments to Emily and Amy.

Claire grinned at Matthew, the glow of his attention throwing everything else into shadow. "You look pretty fabulous yourself."

"Thanks," he said, a little stiffly. "It's pretty different from my usual outfits, I guess."

Lisbeth cleared her throat. "Okay, you guys. Go over in front of the fireplace. I'm no Marie Benoit, but I'm still capable of taking a pre-dance photo, I think."

Lisbeth arranged them in front of the mantle like living statues, rearranged them, then struggled with the lens and the flash. Claire's throat tightened as Lisbeth fought with the camera. It should have been her mother who was there. Taking the photos. Joking with everyone. Pretending she wasn't getting choked up.

On top of the sadness coiling around her, Claire noticed that Matthew had moved over by the couch, joking with Amy about something while Lisbeth took a "look at my corsage" photo of Claire.

The corsage was gorgeous—a wristlet that curved around her arm with clusters of tiny white and pale green orchids. It set off Claire's dress and the creamy skin of her hands.

Julio had brought Amy a hideous pin-on number, with one giant, vaguely wilted rose surrounded by a nest of sparkly teal ribbon. Claire noticed Amy's disappointment as soon as Julio had opened the box. But now she and Matthew were joking about it—at least, Claire hoped they were. That's the only reason that Claire could think of that his eyes would keep coming back to the bustline of Amy's dress. Or, rather, it was the only reason she wanted to think he would keep looking there. She shifted for Lisbeth, smiled, held up her wrist, all the while acutely aware that she and Matthew were no longer on the same sure footing they had been a few months ago.

After Lisbeth had gotten all the photos she wanted and shoved forty dollars "for emergencies" into Claire's hand, the six of them finally made it out of the house. Claire had borrowed a thin, lacy silver wrap from her mother's closet, but it did pretty much nothing to protect her from the biting wind. Matthew grabbed her duffel bag, slid an arm around her, and hustled her out to his car.

The six of them piled into the cars and headed for Salvatore's, a little Italian restaurant with lots of candles, crisp tablecloths, and overpriced pasta. They walked in the door, and the smell of simmering tomato sauce tickled Claire's nostrils. She glanced around the room. She knew Salvatore's was a pretty common pre-dance place to eat, but everywhere she looked, Claire saw someone she knew.

As the hostess led them to their table—two down from Yolanda and her date—Matthew looked over at Claire.

"You okay?" he asked.

"It's just so . . ." she trailed off.

"So popular? So crowded? So much like the cafeteria at noon?" Matthew offered.

Claire laughed nervously. "Something like that," she said.

The two of them slid into their seats at a long table—Amy, Emily, and their dates on one side, and Doug Kingman, Kate-Marie Brown, and assorted other soccer-players-plus-dates on the other. Kate-Marie was already throwing evil looks at Emily's dress while she smoothed her own silver gown. Emily lifted her chin and stared right back at Kate-Marie. Claire sighed, her head beginning to ache. If things kept going this way, she wouldn't have to fake being sick at the end of the night.

She reached for one of the oversize menus that the hostess had slapped down in front of them and buried her head in it.

"Wow, Emily, I like your shoes. They really bring out the *tacky* in your dress." Kate-Marie's voice was singsongy and dangerous at the same time. Hypnotic. Like a cobra weaving before it strikes.

A red-hot flush swept across Emily's cheeks, and she opened her mouth, but before she could respond, Kate-Marie leaned in. "Oh, don't *blush*," she whispered. "It absolutely *ruins* your color scheme."

Horrified, Claire turned to stare at Kate-Marie. Her silver dress dipped too low at the neckline, and she was absolutely dripping in jewelry.

"Well, you look absolutely perfect," Emily shot back. "The silver really sets off your bitchiness."

From the way Kate-Marie was holding her fork, Claire was pretty sure she was ready to skewer Emily.

Emily stood and flounced down to the far end of the table, dragging Randy behind her. He was staring at Emily like she was the lottery and he'd just won.

"You'd think they'd be *grateful* that I invited them along to dinner in the first place," Kate-Marie grumbled to Doug.

Without even looking up from the menu, Matthew said, "Oh, come on. Without Amy, there wouldn't even be a dance to go to tonight." There was a warmth in his voice that made Claire want to grind her teeth.

Kate-Marie stopped, leaning toward Amy like she was some kind of blond life preserver. "That's right. You were on the decorating committee, weren't you?"

Amy nodded, smiling. "Wait until you see it. We spent all morning putting it together, and the ballroom looks amazing! Claire and Emily helped make the leaves and stuff too."

Emily looked defiantly at Kate-Marie, but Claire just sank down into her seat, staring too intently at the description of the rigatoni Bolognese.

"Are you okay?" Matthew whispered.

"I think so," Claire said, trying to look worried. "I have a weird headache. I'm probably just hungry and excited." She did feel weird. The spat between Emily and Kate-Marie had made her ridiculously tense. She might as well use it to her advantage. Start sowing the seeds of the I'm-getting-sick plant early.

Matthew's lips pressed together, like he was steeling

himself against the lie. "Well, let's get some food in you and see if that helps," he said, his voice a fraction too loud.

The hovering waiter perked up, slouching over to their table like an innocent man going to his execution.

"Are you ready to order?" he asked.

As everyone put in their requests, Claire managed to pull herself together. She talked to Doug, who made her laugh, and Randy, who turned out to be surprisingly nice and easy to talk to. In fact, when Claire looked at Emily, she realized that Emily looked pleased and maybe even a little bit giddy.

Huh. How about that.

Feeling more excited for Emily than she wanted to let on, Claire took a bite of the pasta that had been put in front of her. She tried to remember not to look so healthy that she couldn't seem sick later.

When everyone had eaten and the bill had been sorted out, the couples trailed out of the restaurant. Matthew and Claire walked out behind one of the other soccer players and his date.

Claire grabbed Matthew's hand and squeezed.

"I can't believe we're actually going to the dance," she whispered, staring up at him.

He glanced down at her, a surprised, wanting sort of look flickering across his face. "I've been looking forward to it for a long time," he whispered back.

With their hands firmly linked, they hurried toward his car and the waiting ballroom.

After giving their tickets to Mrs. Pratchett, the English teacher standing guard by the door, Claire and Matthew ducked under the bronze-painted branches and into the ball.

It was gorgeous.

Fairy lights and the glittery leaves that Claire had sort of helped Emily and Amy with hung everywhere. Piles of miniature pumpkins and sparkly acorns decorated the tables. In the corner was a DJ, his computer wired into several sets of enormous speakers. A few couples were already on the dance floor, and Claire noticed with a selfish sort of pleasure that her dress was much prettier than any of the others she could see.

"Looks nice this year. Last year was such a flop—that stupid trick-or-treat theme was really pathetic." Matthew rolled his eyes.

"I think it looks fantastic," Claire said. She sounded like a little kid at her first carnival, and it made her grimace. There was no need to remind everyone in earshot that she'd never been to a dance before.

Emily came tearing up behind her, dragging Randy along by the hand. "Sorry—I couldn't find the tickets! I forgot that I put them in the dumb secret pocket of my bag. It's, like, five inches wide! I didn't think it would be that hard to remember where they were." She rolled her eyes at herself.

Next to her, Randy smiled, looking amused and pleased at the same time. Claire tried to shoot Emily a hey-this-looks-like-it's-going-really-well glance, but Emily wasn't paying attention. Amy had come up behind her and was whispering something in her ear.

Emily shook her head, her gaze shifting in Claire's direction.

"C'mon." Emily grabbed Randy's hand and jerked her head in the direction of the dance floor. "Let's go dance."

Claire grinned. This was what she had come for. What she'd been so jealous of all those times that Emily had gone to the dances while Claire sat home and ate Lisbeth's brownies. She wrapped her arm around Matthew's waist and leaned into him.

"Right behind you," she said.

Matthew put his arm around Claire's shoulders, and the two of them followed in Emily's wake.

The DJ was actually decent. Amy and Claire and Emily ended up in their own little corner of the dance floor, with their dates hovering nearby. The three of them made a perfect circle, dancing like they were at their own private party. It was like they'd been hanging out for years, and Claire let herself enjoy it. It was like sneaking a drink out of someone's mom's liquor cabinet—thrilling and forbidden and probably a little bit stupid. But right then, she was having too much fun trading hip-checks with Emily and singing along to all the songs with Amy to worry about it.

The pounding bass gave way to the sweet hum of a slow

song, and Matthew caught her shoulder, spinning her around to face him.

"Hey, you," he said. "How about a dance?"

"Are you kidding?" She grinned. "I thought you'd never ask."

He slid his arm around Claire's waist and spun her away from the girls. She held onto his shoulder as he twirled her, her dress fluttering behind her like a butterfly wing. Matthew smiled down at her. It was a sweet-as-cider moment.

As they danced, the heat from his skin radiated through the thin fabric of her dress. It poured across her middle and wrapped around her waist where his hand rested against her. Claire's skin felt starved inside the green silk.

She tilted her face up as Matthew bent to kiss her, while the fairy lights twinkled overhead. His mouth begged hers for more, and the press of his fingers against her hips made Claire ache to be alone with him.

He pulled back from the kiss, just a fraction of an inch, the length of his body still crushed against hers.

"Oh, God," he whispered. "I don't want you to go tonight. There's got to be some way for you to get out of it—just this once." His lips grazed her ear and she trembled.

"I can't. I want to. I—oh, Jesus," she breathed, as he tugged her into the darkness behind a glitter-flecked tree, running his fingertips across her bare collarbone. She caught his hand and held it, not capable of thinking while he was lighting a fire beneath her skin. "Matthew, it's not something I can just make go away. I would if I could, but you know how serious this naming thing is." In spite of the molten look in his eyes, Claire's desire went cold—an ember turning to ash. He knew she couldn't give him what he was asking for—he knew the pack came first tonight.

Does he even get how much it took for me to be here at all?

"I know." He looked hard at her expression, his own face falling in response. "I shouldn't have asked you to do that."

"I don't want it to be like this either, but the baby's *here* and there's nothing I can do about it."

"I didn't say it was your fault. I'm sorry—I just got so caught up with wanting you. I didn't mean to make things hard."

Claire leaned into him, closing the distance between them. "It's not your fault, either," she said. She'd gotten just as caught up in the moment as he had.

He backed away from her with a sigh. "And I'm guessing you're going to tell me it's not fair to blame the baby."

Claire swatted him. "Now you're being ridiculous."

He flinched like she'd stung him.

"Come on," she said. "I didn't mean it like that."

"Okay. I mean, I get it."

Amy peeked around the paper-mâchè tree. "Well, *there* you are." Her voice was louder than it needed to be, and her eyes looked funny.

Are they drinking already? And if they are, why hasn't some-one at least offered *me some?*

Not that she really wanted to be drunk, but her insides were all knots and edges, and it was getting worse by the minute.

"Come on." Amy reached out and caught Claire's hand, pulling her past Matthew. Out on the dance floor, the sweet strains of the ballad had long since died away, replaced by a fast song. "My feet haven't gone numb yet, which means it's still time to dance!"

Claire followed Amy's bouncing curls, infected by her good mood. They danced until Claire's neck was damp with sweat and her toes thrummed from the pain of her pinching shoes. It seemed like only a few minutes later when Matthew dragged her over to the side of the room and told her they should think about leaving.

"Why?" Claire asked.

He pulled his phone out of his pocket and showed her the time. It was already a little after ten. The naming was less than two hours away, and by the time they said good-bye to every-one and got to the woods, it would be at least eleven thirty. With a disappointed sigh, Claire nodded and looked around for Emily, who'd disappeared a good twenty minutes earlier.

"I'm going to go find Emily and tell her I'm sick," she said.

"Good luck with that," Matthew said, shifting back. Behind them, Claire spotted Amy frozen in place, watching them intently. There was something sharp in her eyes. Something . . . almost vindicated.

Claire gave her a pitiful smile—an I'm-feeling-really-crappy smile. Amy's expression turned to concern, and Claire waved her off. With a shrug, Amy went back to the dance floor.

Claire put a hand over her middle and faked a stomach cramp. She hoped her dance sweat would pass for sickness sweat. She finally saw Emily in the far corner, talking intently with Randy. Claire limped over to her.

Emily immediately frowned when she saw Claire. "What's going on? Why do you look weird? Are you okay?"

Claire bit her lip. "I-I don't know." She swallowed. "I think dinner might have . . . it's not sitting right. My stomach is really funky. Matthew and I are going to take off so that I can rest for a little bit." She didn't want to bail on Emily right away—it would be easier to pretend that she needed to be sick enough to rest and then claim that it just got worse, once she was out from under so many watching pairs of eyes.

"But you're still coming to my house, right?" Emily's face had gone tight. Desperate. It hurt Claire to look at her. It took the shine off her perfect evening. Lying to Emily—hurting Emily, even if it was only to protect her—was everything that Claire hated about living a double life.

"Are you kidding? Of course. I'm sure I'll be fine in an hour, but the idea of beer right now . . ." Claire twisted her mouth, hoping it looked as though she was fighting back a wave of nausea. "I just need to go get some fresh air and rest for a few minutes." She reached out and grabbed Emily. "You know I'm dying to come to your party," she said. It was true, and her voice rang with the honesty of it. Of course, she wouldn't go to the party—couldn't go to the party—but she desperately wished that she could.

"Okay," said Emily, her face brightening. "Go and rest and I'll see you there. Tell Matthew I said he'd better nurse you back to health hella quick or he's going to have me to answer to."

Claire laughed, hoping Emily couldn't hear the nerves in the sound. She didn't need a reminder of the sort of awkward position she was putting Matthew in.

"I'll tell him," she said, heading back through the dance floor with her arm still wrapped around her middle.

She and Matthew worked their way back through the crowd. Claire did her best to look sort of tired and ill as they said their good-byes. When they finally made it out into the parking lot, the November air felt fantastic against Claire's skin.

Chapter Seventeen

"DAMN WAS IT hot in there," she said as she limped toward Matthew's car. Her feet were killing her, and she hoped it wasn't going to slow her down when she ran to the gathering. Maybe wearing the cute-but-deadly shoes hadn't been the best idea after all. At least she had her bag of comfortable clothes—complete with running shoes—waiting for her in the car.

"Yeah, it was." Matthew unlocked the doors and Claire slid into the passenger seat, kicking off her heels and pressing her feet against the cold floor of the car with a moan of happiness. Matthew got in and started the car. "So, did you have a good time?"

"Nope." Claire leaned back in the seat, closing her eyes.

Matthew stopped the car halfway through backing out of the parking spot. "Really?" He sounded stunned.

"Of course not. A 'good time.' Please! I had a great time." Claire turned her head so that her cheek was resting against the headrest, and she looked at Matthew. "Though I am surprised that we've been dating for almost six months and you still haven't figured out that I'm a smart-ass."

Matthew half-smiled, but it was mixed with a grimace that made Claire freeze. "Well, in my defense, there's a lot we've both had to figure out. It hasn't exactly been easy, right?" He turned to look over his shoulder as he backed the rest of the way out into the parking lot.

She didn't respond. She couldn't. The comment had cut her, slicing bone deep.

Slowly, Claire reached up and started the process of unpinning her hair. She wasn't going to blow up at Matthew. She wasn't. She was just going to focus on turning off her human side and getting to the naming. And step one was her hair. There was no way she was trekking into the woods in an updo. She'd look ridiculous. She dropped the pins into an ever-growing pile in her lap, trying to ignore the wounded feeling that throbbed in her chest.

Matthew stopped at a red light. He looked over at her and took a deep breath. "Are you pissed at me?" he asked.

Claire felt the words bubbling up inside her and struggled

to keep herself from saying them. But it was no use. She'd never been able to lie to Matthew, and in spite of the crappy timing, her habitual honesty took over.

"I'm not . . . 'pissed' isn't the right word," she said, gathering up the pile of pins and dropping them into the cup holder.

"Well, then, what is? Something's going on with you." His voice was heated, and it was more than Claire could take.

She exploded. "Of course something's going on with me! I'm a werewolf, Matthew, something's always going on with me. And for whatever reason, you don't seem to want to deal with that part of my life."

His eyes widened. "What are you talking about? I've never asked you to hide what you are."

"Yeah, but it's like you have to hold your nose every time you mention it. This is major stuff that's happening. It's not a game or some club I joined. It's my life, and it's not normal. Deal with it." Claire flicked a stray hairpin off her lap.

"You're right—it's not normal, and I haven't complained about that at all. But there's no handbook for being your boyfriend. Did it ever occur to you that I'm doing the best I can?" His voice was as rough as a gravel road. "The human stuff is easy—"

"You can't just have my human side," she interrupted. "Not when you're a *gardien*. Not when you're supposed to be my boyfriend."

He cut her off. "What do you mean, 'supposed to be' your boyfriend? I've done everything you—or the pack—has asked me to do. Didn't we just leave the dance early? Didn't I tell you I'd cover for you at Emily's party so that you could do your wolf stuff?" He sounded as frustrated as Claire felt.

The woods appeared at the side of the road as he turned the corner, driving just fast enough that Claire reached out and caught the door handle.

"Yes," she said, her voice surgically precise and scalpel sharp. "You've done everything I asked you to. But that's it. It's like my werewolf side is some kind of obstacle you have to get past." She was gathering momentum, her anger swelling with each word. She barreled on, not giving Matthew a chance to interrupt her again.

"I'm not some sort of girlfriend buffet—you can't just pick the parts you want. I know that my being a werewolf makes things hard, but you constantly treat it like some sort of burden, and it's not. It's *who I am*. And quite frankly, I think I'm handling it pretty goddamn well. It would be nice if you'd give me a little credit." They were almost to her drop-off spot, and Claire reached behind her, snatching her duffel bag of clothes off the backseat.

The hot-pepper scent of anger wafted up from Matthew's skin.

He stopped the car near the abandoned little ranger's hut at the edge of the forest, where she'd planned to change. The road was empty—desolate. "Give you a little credit? Why? You're not giving me any."

Claire's mouth fell open. She threw open the car door so hard that the hinges creaked in protest. "Are you kidding? I have told you *everything*. If you don't think that's 'credit' . . ." She shook her head, swinging her legs out of the car. Her gorgeous dress suddenly felt ridiculous. She got out and stood in the November wind, clutching the duffel bag in one hand. With her back to the car and her mouth so full of acid words that she could barely swallow, she stepped toward the woods. Her heels sank into the half-frozen mud, and she stumbled, cursing.

"Claire!" Matthew called after her.

Unable to stop herself, she turned and saw him leaning across the passenger seat. The moonlight glowed against the white of his tux shirt, reflecting up onto his frustrated, worried face.

"What?" she asked, her voice trembling.

Damn it. I am not going to cry right now. Damn it!

"Just be careful, all right?" There was plenty of exhaustion in his voice, but not a lot of love.

"You too," she warned, and then turned and strode into the woods with as much dignity as she could—which wasn't much, with the cold making her shudder, the wind whipping her hair into her eyes, and her shoes sticking in the mud.

The ground beneath her blurred as the tears she struggled against filled her eyes, clinging to her mascara-blackened lashes. She sniffed, trying desperately to get ahold of herself.

She couldn't show up to the naming like this. As soon as the trees behind her were thick enough that she couldn't see the road, couldn't smell the blacktop, she yanked off her clothes and shoved them into the bag. She'd meant to change into her sweats—take an easy jog through the woods. But she wanted out of her human skin every bit as badly as she wanted to ditch her heels.

The second she'd pulled the duffel's zipper shut, she transformed. Her wolf form wrapped around her like an embrace—her sure paws on the ground, her warm fur. Claire's unbelievably sharp senses laid the world bare in front of her. She lifted her head and took several deep breaths. The scent of the cold was thrilling and exotic—it smelled like the icy sparkle of the stars. Metallic. Hard. Pure. It calmed her.

Her human life wasn't critical right this second. She'd sort things out with Matthew later, but she had something important to do first. The naming would start soon, and she had no intention of ruining it by being distracted or upset.

Or late.

She looked up at the moon, realizing that she needed to start running if she was going to make it on time. She snatched up the bursting-full duffel bag, held it between her teeth, and headed for the clearing.

When she could see the first glimpse of the clearing through the trees, she stopped and dropped the bag, licking her whiskers to try and get the artificial taste of the nylon web-bing out of her mouth.

She'd rather have stayed wolf, but she had a fire to light and she needed to be smooth skinned while she did it. As quickly as she could, Claire changed back into her human form and hurried into her clothes. A sheen of sweat dampened her skin, and the cold air licked at it, chilling her instantly. Shivering hard, Claire burst into the clearing. Her mother, Katherine, and Judith were already there. Near the waiting firewood—but not too close—there was a little bedlike nest of leaves and dry grass.

"M-m-marie, I greet you," she chattered. It still felt weird to call her mother by her first name, but the pack laws required her to greet everyone that way.

"And I greet you, Claire. Thank you for being on time, in spite of your other . . . engagements."

Katherine perked up. "I greet you, Claire. What other engagements?"

"I greet you, too, Katherine. I was at the Autumn Ball. A dance."

"Oooh." Katherine sighed. "How fun! And you're probably missing the end of it for this. You must be so disappointed."

Across the clearing, Claire noticed Judith staring at her and Katherine with a contemptuous sneer on her face. Marie might have been uninterested in Claire's human life, but Judith seemed almost offended by it. Claire's fight with

Matthew swelled in her thoughts, and her anger flared back to life. What was with everyone only wanting part of her? She was never going to be all human or all wolf. That was the *point*. And the people who should have understood that the most were the ones who were making it the hardest.

"I greet you, Claire," Judith said, interrupting her thoughts.

Claire returned her greeting.

"You're lucky to have such an important role tonight. You are ready to light the fire, right?" There was an ugly sneer on Judith's face. A disbelieving sneer. Like she had a scalpel at the ready.

Claire's pulse quickened, her tongue suddenly sticking to the roof of her mouth. "Of course."

Before Judith could even open her mouth, Beatrice and Victoria appeared at the edge of the trees. Victoria held a bundle in her arms. There were violet blue shadows under her eyes, but she looked radiantly happy. Claire saw a flicker of nervousness in her expression, but for the most part, she was hiding it well.

Everyone rushed over to see the baby, who was nothing more than a tiny face in a mound of blankets. They greeted Beatrice and Victoria almost without looking at them, too busy cooing over the baby's tiny pink cheeks.

"Won't she be cold?" Claire whispered to her mother.

"No—or rather, she may feel the cold on her face, but infants of our kind are not susceptible to the temperature the way human babies are. It is the wolf blood in them." Marie wrapped an arm around Claire in a rare and unexpected gesture. "She is so very small. It reminds me of your naming. Though it was hot that night. Unbearably hot."

Claire stared at the baby, trying to imagine herself that small, to imagine a younger Marie holding her in the woods, waiting for her naming.

"We'll begin shortly—I hope both of you are ready. Beatrice? May I speak with you for a moment?" Marie stepped away, and Beatrice followed her.

Judith and Katherine drifted away, leaving Victoria and Claire alone.

"She's pretty," Claire said sincerely.

"Thanks." Victoria beamed. "You ready?"

"I guess so." Claire leaned in. "So, I was thinking about the name thing last night. Please don't be mad—I . . . I listened to her. From the woods. Just to see if anything came to me. I would have asked you first, but I only thought of it last night, and there wasn't time. . . ."

Victoria's eyes widened. "Did you—did anything happen?" She didn't look like she minded having been listened in on. Actually, she looked like she was desperate for an answer.

"Her breath was so loud—so . . . *clear*." Claire hesitated. "I looked it up, and the name Aura—it means 'breath' in Latin."

Victoria froze and Claire panicked, worried that she'd offended her, that she'd ruined the closeness they'd built over the last couple of weeks by taking things too far with her suggestions.

"If you think it's not right, I'll totally understand, and I wouldn't want you to use it, but you did so much to help me, I just thought—"

"It's perfect," Victoria whispered. "Look at her. It's *perfect*. Oh my Goddess, Claire, I was going to name her after my great-grandmother, because I couldn't think of anything else that was right, but it still didn't really fit her. She doesn't look like a Rose. But Aura—" She looked up at Claire, her eyes damp. "Thank you."

Claire nodded, hoping she hadn't picked the wrong name—that the ceremony didn't go wrong somehow because of her idea. The realization crashed over her that she suddenly stood to fail twice tonight. If she was mistaken about the name, she'd have doomed herself and the baby both. But she couldn't leave Victoria all on her own. Not after Victoria had done so much to help with the fire lighting.

"Well." Marie cleared her throat. "Let's not keep Victoria out any longer than we need to. I am sure she is exhausted. Claire? Are you ready to begin?"

Claire looked over at the enormous pile of wood. She had maybe lit something close to that size, but it seemed to loom over her. Daring her to try and light it.

It was only a few feet from where she stood, but her nerves were so electrified that her limbs felt numb. Each step took an eternity. It was like wading through syrup. Her blood was humming with adrenaline, and she stared at the limbs.

She closed her eyes for a moment, searching for an island of calm in her sea of panic. She couldn't do this if she was freaking out. She thought of Matthew, and in one sharp moment her anger laid bare everything she'd had trapped inside her. The worry and insecurity and trying to be perfect for everyone, all the time, stared back at her like glass-eyed dolls.

What the hell had she been *doing*?

The things she'd told Matthew earlier had been true.

This is who I am. No more balancing acts. No more werewolf side and human side. From now on, it's just me.

Confidence tore through her with a sound like ripping fabric. With everything inside her, she pushed back the veil of her human form—the thick, heavy, sticky web of it, seeing the fire as clearly as she'd just seen herself. What it was. What it could be. The heat that the branches held trapped inside, that could so easily be . . .

Released.

A hot yellow flame grabbed onto one of the branches deep in the middle, spreading itself out along the bark like a flag unfurling. There was a crackling. A pop. And then the heat poured out. It washed over Claire, unlocked her knees, and sent her tumbling to the ground.

"Claire!" Her mother exclaimed. "Are you all right?"

Claire lifted her head, staring at the roaring fire, and shook with joy and relief. It was over. She'd succeeded.

"I'm great," she whispered.

"Well. We've all seen that you can light the fire." A smile carved its way across Marie's face, and Claire could see her work to contain her happiness.

Victoria let out a little cheer, which startled the baby, who started to cry. Victoria glanced down, shushing her back to sleep.

Claire looked over at her and grinned, though the sight of the baby took a little of the glow off her elation. There was more at stake than just her, and she'd planted herself right in the middle of it.

Voluntarily.

She bit her lip, praying she'd done the right thing by trying to help Victoria.

"Let's proceed with the rest of the naming before the baby wakes again," Marie said. The women all scrambled into a circle around the fire. Victoria positioned herself in front of the carefully piled leaves, covering them with a flannel blanket before laying the baby on it. The baby was sound asleep again, her lips pursed and her lashes curling against her pink cheek.

Marie raised her arms, smiling at them all. "And now we begin. A beginning for this baby, a new beginning for Victoria, and a continuation of our pack. Victoria, please drink this." Marie handed her a container of something that wafted an herbaceous-smelling steam into the clearing. "The herbs will help you to heal from the birth and give you the strength to complete tonight's ceremony."

Victoria took a cautious sip. A little smile spread across her face. "It's good," she said.

"Of course it is," Marie said. She looked like a hen ruffling its feathers. "Your body knows what it needs. Now drink up."

Victoria drained the container, her cheeks flushing pink with the heat of the tea. "Done," she announced. Her eyes looked brighter, and with her rosy skin, she looked better—healthier—than she had in months.

"Excellent."

Marie turned to the group and began to chant, calling all their names.

"You may transform," Marie announced.

The women became wolves in the blink of an eye, and there was a great deal of prancing and yipping—the excitement they were all feeling brought with it the instinctive urge to move. Claire paced restlessly, anxious about what was coming. The only two wolves who were completely still were Marie, who sat with her head cocked in amusement, and Victoria, who lay curled around the baby, who slept.

All right. Let us continue before anyone gets too carried away. Marie stood, pacing closer to Victoria and the baby.

First, we will each give the baby our blessing—a wish for her future. Katherine? Perhaps you would like to begin. Marie withdrew slightly, still overseeing but giving the other wolves room to move closer to the baby.

Katherine walked forward, nuzzling the tiny bundle the

slightest bit. Her nose left a wet mark on the pink blanket. *I wish you health, Little One. I bless you with it.*

She turned to Victoria. *She's beautiful.*

Victoria thumped her tail on the ground wearily. *Thank you. And thank you for your blessing.*

Katherine went back to her place in the circle, looking pleased.

Judith came and stood near the baby, her posture serious, almost severe. *I wish you patience. You will need much of it in your life. I bless you with it.*

She turned and retreated without saying anything to Victoria—without waiting for a response.

Claire hung back, trying to figure out what to bless Victoria's daughter with. She didn't want to say something stupid. She wished she'd had more time to think about it, that her mother had told her about this part, too, and not just the giving-the-name stuff. She sighed.

While Claire was lost in thought, Marie bent over the baby and blessed her with strength, followed by Beatrice, who lay down close beside the baby and Victoria and very quietly offered her a blessing of love.

Seeing Beatrice and Victoria wrapped around the tiny baby made a wistful sort of longing rise in Claire's throat, half-choking her. The feeling smelled so strong, she could taste it, like the bitter peel of an orange mixed with darkly sweet chocolate. The three of them looked so happy. Claire wanted what they had—wanted it desperately. That contentment. No one wanting the others to be more or less than they were.

She stepped forward, and Beatrice got to her feet, grimacing as one of her knees popped.

Your turn, Not-the-Littlest-One.

Claire crouched near the baby, breathing in the milky pure smell of her breath, the scent of her skin.

I bless you with happiness. She closed her eyes briefly, and when she opened them, she saw Victoria nuzzled in close to the baby, who had awoken.

Thank you. Thank you all for such amazing gifts. I'm sure she will be all of those things—have all of those things—and more.

Claire backed away, watching Victoria and her daughter stare at each other, the infant's slate blue eyes studying the enormous wolf in front of her.

It is time for the naming. Marie nudged Victoria gently. *Are you ready?*

Claire's heart began to thud again, her chest aching from so much stress in one night.

Victoria lowered her head. *I guess so. What . . . what do I . . .* She hesitated.

Marie sat down. *Tell her the name you have chosen. The rest will sort itself out.*

Claire didn't like the sound of the second part. Forcing herself not to worry, not to think, she watched as Victoria bent low over her daughter. The movement drew the baby's attention, and she turned to look at her mother. There was a serious, determined expression on her little face, and her tiny rosebud lips sucked hungrily at the air.

Victoria's nose nearly brushed the earth.

Hi, Little One. You have good friends here. They have helped me, and they will help you. And when they do, they will call you by your name. And your name, my daughter, is Aura.

From deep in the forest came the roaring howl of an approaching wind thundering through the pines like an enormous animal. Victoria threw herself over Aura, and Claire braced herself instinctively just as the gale whipped into the clearing. It slammed into her side, rocking her. Fear and elation raced through her. Whatever was happening was either very good or very bad, but she had a clear sense that the naming had somehow made it happen.

The wind tore through the center of the clearing. Claire worried it would fan the flames of the ceremonial fire, scatter the sparks into the flailing, fluttering undergrowth, but it didn't. The fire simply died, blown out like a candle.

As quickly as it had come, the gust stopped, leaving the wolves shaken. They crouched in the dark clearing, their fur full of leaves and twigs. Stunned. Silent.

Marie shook out her coat, padding quickly over to Victoria. *Is Aura all right?*

Victoria hesitated. *I think so. She seems to be.*

On the ground, still swaddled in her blankets, the baby

began to fuss in an empty, pathetic sort of way.

I would like to pick her up. To be sure. She sounds as though she may be hungry. Victoria looked from Aura to Marie and back, her ears flicking wildly.

Of course. I would normally say a few closing words, but the ceremony is—obviously—over. I have never—she stopped. *Well. Let us transform. We can discuss it then, before Claire finishes demonstrating her skills. We will have to relight the fire, but that's as good a way as any to separate the two ceremonies.*

Marie turned to the rest of the wolves. Claire eased out of her defensive stance, her muscles shaking in protest.

You may transform, Marie announced.

Victoria was the only one who immediately changed form. She scooped Aura up and hurried off to find her clothes. The rest of the wolves ranged into the woods, searching for the clothes that had been scattered by the wind. It didn't take Claire long—the scents of detergent and human skin stood out in the forest. She transformed among the trees, dressing quickly and then reaching up to retrieve a last sock that had been caught in the low branches of a scrubby tree.

She hurried back to the gathering, wrapping her arms around herself against the cold, trying to shut out her confusion about what had just happened. She wasn't sure if she should be expecting celebration or condemnation in the clearing—she had either seriously helped Victoria or seriously misled her. The other wolves were already in the clearing, huddled close for warmth. Victoria sat on a fallen log, nursing Aura.

"Claire's back," Katherine said.

The others turned to look at Claire. She waited, her heart pounding—pouncing—in her chest.

"You should be very pleased," Marie said to Victoria, pride glittering in her eyes.

"I didn't do it alone," Victoria said. "Claire helped me."

"Really?" Marie looked startled.

"I tried to," Claire said. "Victoria helped me so much with the fire—I was just trying to do the same for her." The frenetic beat of her heart let up the tiniest bit. "So—that was supposed to happen?"

Beatrice said "more or less" at the same moment that Judith said "Yes."

Beatrice snorted. "Come on, Judith, be fair. At every naming I've ever been to, we've watched the fire—and hard—for any sign that even a little part of it had gone out. Once, years ago, my mother spoke of a naming where a branch fell out of the fire, putting out its flames as it rolled."

Katherine shivered. "I've never seen anything even remotely like that."

Marie smiled. "You see, Claire, the Goddess takes part of the fire as her tithe—it is the sacrifice we make for the name. The story goes that the more fitting the name that is chosen, the greater the sacrifice—the larger the portion of the fire that is extinguished."

Claire turned the words over in her mind, happiness

stretching inside her like a bent-winged bird. "So, since the whole fire went out—"

"Not just 'went out,'" Beatrice crowed. "It was *blown out*, Young One."

"Yes," Marie said. "It means what you think it means. That the name was exactly right."

Victoria glowed. She stared down at Aura, and her whole body was suffused with light and happiness. Claire felt her throat tighten. There would be no bad luck for this baby. Not with all the blessings they'd given her. Not with a name that had gotten *that* sort of reaction.

"All right, everyone," Marie said. "It is getting late, and there is still much to be done. Victoria, perhaps you should take Aura. There is no need to drag her through any more tonight, and you cannot take her on the hunt, anyway."

Irritation briefly creased Victoria's features, but her face smoothed out when she looked down at Aura, who was such a tiny bundle in the black enormity of the forest.

"Yes," she murmured. "I think I will take her home." She looked up at Claire. "If you need me, you call. I'll come. You know that, right? You did so much for Aura—there's nothing I wouldn't do for you. *Nothing.*" Her gaze burned brightly enough to blind Claire to everything else.

"Thank you," Claire said softly.

Victoria nodded, standing up carefully so that Aura wouldn't be jostled.

When the two of them had left, Judith and Beatrice quickly built another pile of wood in the center of the clearing.

Marie turned to Claire. "You've already lit the fire. Do you want to do it again? You do not have to. Not tonight."

Judith's expression turned to flint, but Claire was still burning from the success of the naming and from Victoria's loyalty. She was scorching with it.

"I'll light it." She stepped close to the pile.

Marie lifted an eyebrow. She looked surprised.

She also looked very much like she approved.

Claire glanced at the wood, feeling the fire so strongly that it flared to life effortlessly. She could almost see the sparks leaping from her fingertips. The force of the sudden blaze created a breeze in the clearing, and Claire's hair drifted across her cheek.

She didn't even bother to look over at Judith. She didn't care what her reaction was. Her mother's square-shouldered pride was enough.

"Well, you've obviously mastered that skill," Marie said quietly. "Let's transform."

Claire's four paws hit the ground before anyone else's. Next to her, Beatrice let out a wolfy version of a chuckle.

Marie gave a silencing grumble.

Since you are transformed, you may show us your far-reaching ability to hear.

Pleased at the surprised expression that lit Judith's eyes,

Claire turned to face the fire, wrapped her tail close around her body, and let out a long, whistling breath through her nose. She shook out her fur, trying to relax her body enough that the other wolves would be able to read the voices she heard in her head in her posture and scent.

She decided to listen for Matthew—he was easy for her to hear. She imagined the sound of his voice, all warm, round vowels and the way his laugh rumbled in his chest.

"No, 's not like that. You don' *understand*."

Claire could hear a voice answering Matthew, but she couldn't quite make out what it was saying, and she couldn't figure out why his voice sounded slurred. She focused harder.

"Jus' drop it. Please. I'm going to get 'nother beer." Matthew again.

He was slurring because he was drunk.

The realization sent such a wave of embarrassment through Claire that she was sure the others could smell it. Judith sniffed the air and gave a quiet, amused bark.

Claire's concentration fell, and she was snapped back into the clearing, the fire hot on her face, the other wolves staring at her, their ears laid back. She looked around at the pack.

Uh, maybe I should try to listen for Victoria instead.

Judith cocked her head to one side. *Is this ability failing you, too?*

A growl rose in Claire's throat before she could stop it. How dare Judith question her? After she'd worked so hard, done so much, was it really possible that she hadn't proved herself to this stupid she-wolf who would never come close to being as powerful as Claire's mother was, as powerful as Claire herself intended to become? She felt her lips pulling back into a snarl.

Claire! Enough! Marie barked.

The ring of her mother's bark—the Alpha's bark—in Claire's ears was enough to shake her out of her angry display. She hung her head, arching her back in an effort to look as sorry as she suddenly felt. She hadn't meant to explode like that. It had just been too much—to be questioned, doubted, after she'd finally succeeded.

Beatrice sat back down, turned to Marie. *May I?*

Marie dipped her head in assent. *Of course.*

I can also listen to the speech of those who are far away. Beatrice stared hard at Judith, who lowered herself to the ground. *I heard Matthew's voice, though perhaps not as well as Claire did.*

Beatrice glanced at Claire and tossed her head.

To be honest, everything that Claire has just shown us would have been beyond my reach at her age. I know she is younger than you, Judith, and that she hasn't experienced all the things you have. But that is no reason to doubt her word. It is no reason to treat her like she has nothing to offer our pack. Her pack. To which she belongs every bit as much as you do.

Judith pawed at her nose in apology, but Claire could see her ears pulling back in suspicion, just the tiniest bit, when her eyes turned in Claire's direction.

Thank you, Beatrice. Marie stood and shook herself hard from head to tail.

Katherine edged over and nudged Judith with her nose, urging her up.

So, all that is left is the hunt. Marie stared hard at Claire. *Are you ready?*

Claire's paws twitched against the ground in answer. Hell, yes, she was ready. There was no pressure for her in leading the hunt. Beneath her pelt, her muscles strained toward the woods, desperate for the release of running through the skeletal trees. Hungry for the single-minded focus of tracking prey.

Let's go. She stood and padded purposefully into the woods, nose lifted, scenting the air. Smelling small animals, warm in their burrows. Fat birds roosting high in the trees. And somewhere to the west, far away, the faint scent of something big and warm.

Without hesitating, Claire began to run, her nose working frantically to keep from losing the scent. She wove through the forest, her paws barely whispering against the leaves that littered the ground. The others trailed behind her, Marie close to her, the others farther away. There was no sign of their sprint through the woods, except for the tiny animals that fell silent as they passed. When they were only a few yards from her quarry, Claire circled around, flushing the deer from its hiding place and sending it scampering through the woods.

Oh! We lost it. Katherine whimpered, panting hard.

Of course we didn't. Claire bumped Katherine's flank with her hip as she raced back by the rest of the pack. *It's headed for the clearing. C'mon, it's easier this way.*

There was no time to explain. Claire focused on the scented air in front of her, the faint snapping of twigs and bracken beneath the deer's hooves. Carefully, she drove the deer back toward the clearing, until they were only a few yards from the fire. Breathing hard, Claire put on a burst of careless speed, not caring how much noise she made. It didn't matter— the deer knew she was coming.

Midstride, Claire crouched low and then leapt, landing on the deer's back and sending them both tumbling to the ground. Marie and Judith joined her at once, and in another minute, the deer lay dead on the forest floor. Claire tossed back her head and yipped. It was over.

Judith stood over the deer's nut brown back, her shoulders hunched, panting hard.

Well, you managed it, but Goddess, that was a long way to run.

Claire stopped her prancing and stared straight into Judith's eyes, not bothered that the other wolf ranked higher in the pack than she did. She was so over this.

It's easier to run a long way than it is to drag a dead deer a half mile through the forest with our teeth, she pointed out.

Marie stepped between them. *Enough. Judith, Katherine, help Claire and me bring the body into the clearing.*

The feast went by in a blur. Claire was half-elated that she'd done everything with no missteps and half-exhausted from the effort of trying so hard. By the time the remains of the deer were buried deep in the forest, Claire was more than ready to change back into her human skin and crawl into her bed.

Marie sat in front of the fire, and the other wolves followed suit.

Let us return to our human forms.

There was a flutter of activity as the wolves transformed, dressing in an instant and then fussing around with tying shoes and tucking in shirts.

Marie stood in front of them, already dressed, down to the last button on her shirt. "This has truly been a remarkable night. Not only has Claire proved that she is a complete wolf, but our pack has grown, and we have had the most successful naming in our remembered history. Thank you, all of you, for your efforts this evening. Go home. Go home and be happy, and I will see all of you when the moon is full again."

Go home and be happy. Right. Claire's mood deflated like a pin-struck balloon. Going home meant going back into her human world, and her human world was a mess. There was nothing to do about Emily and the party except cross her fingers and hope that Matthew had come through—and that Emily had believed their lies.

But Matthew . . . she didn't like the way she'd left things

with him. She needed to talk to him—figure out a way to smooth things over.

Once he'd sobered up.

The women went their separate ways through the woods. Claire trailed a few paces behind her mother, carrying her bag in silence.

"Why so quiet, *chérie*?" Her mother's tone was light, but there was an undertone of concern. Uncertainty.

"I'm just tired is all," Claire said. "There's been a lot today."

"Of course." Marie smiled. "I am sure that's true." She was all too happy to believe Claire—Claire could see her mother's desire to keep the moment unspoiled. To revel in her victory.

"I am proud of you, Claire. You have made me very happy to be your mother."

The words wrapped around Claire like a coat, warming her. Protecting her. She snuggled down inside the praise. If she could do something as impossible as making her mother proud, then maybe she could straighten out the tangle she'd made of her human life.

Chapter Eighteen

BACK AT THE house, Claire headed straight for her room. She grabbed her phone to send Matthew a text, and found a half-dozen unread messages. They were all from Emily. The first three were all variations of RU OK??? The first one sounded irritated, but the other two were pure worry. Claire wondered exactly what Matthew had told Emily.

The next one said, WHAT HAPPENED BTWN U AND MATTHEW? Claire's fingertips went tingly. Holding her breath, she clicked through the next two messages.

TEXT ME BACK AS SOON AS U CAN.

ARE YOU DEAD OR WHAT??? CALL ME ASAP!

The three messages went through Claire like an electric shock. What had Matthew said to Emily that could make her freak out like that? She stood, rooted to the spot, staring down at the phone.

She could feel her fingers twitching toward Emily's number, desperate to know. It was just a little after two—Emily might still be awake, surveying the mess . . . but probably not. And Claire was supposed to be so sick that she'd had to miss the party. If she called, it might look suspicious.

She knew she'd have to wait until tomorrow. There was no other way.

Damn.

Unable to stop herself, Claire opened a new message.

To Matthew.

I think we need 2 talk. Call me tomorrow.

She flipped the phone shut and buried her head in her hands. She'd been looking forward to the dance and the naming for so long, and the night had turned into a total disaster.

Well, not a total disaster. The naming had been amazing. Trying to hold on to that one bright spot, Claire did the only thing she could think to do. She headed for the bathroom and a hot shower.

Claire spent the night tossing and turning, alternately too hot and too cold, slipping in and out of anxious dreams. When morning finally came, she dragged herself out of bed. It was a little after nine thirty. It was too early to call Emily, but she picked up the phone anyway. After the messages Emily had left her last night, it wasn't like she could be mad at Claire for waking her up at the crack of dawn.

It went to voice mail.

Claire hesitated. All sorts of horrible things were running through her mind, most of them involving Emily realizing that Claire had never been sick—that there was some other reason she'd skipped the party.

She got dressed and threw her hair into a ponytail, trying to find a way to make the time pass. She made her bed. She flipped through the channels on the TV. Eventually, she sat on the edge of the bed and watched the clock crawl toward eleven o'clock. She got more and more tense with each minute that passed.

At two minutes past eleven, she couldn't stand it anymore. She dialed Emily again. This time, Emily answered it.

"Hello?" Her rough, pained voice reminded Claire that she was supposed to be sick.

"Sorry," she said, trying to sound as pathetic as possible. It wasn't that hard. She just pretended that the ache in her chest was really in her stomach. "I know it's early. But I woke up and saw your texts and I'm freaking out. What happened?"

"Oh, God," Emily groaned. "It was—wait. Are you okay? Why didn't you call?"

"I think it was dinner," Claire lied. "I started feeling bad at the dance, and it got so awful that I had Matthew take me home. I was—it was gross." Even Emily was likely to let her off the hook when it came to details about throwing up. "Eventually, I just sort of passed out. I'm sorry I wasn't there. I really, really am."

"Me too," said Emily. Claire could hear her rustling around. "It was really fun, except . . ."

Claire's heart started thudding in her chest. "Except what?" she prompted.

"Matthew was—I don't know exactly what happened. He was drunk and talking about how the two of you had a fight. A couple of times Amy tried to pull him aside and talk to him, but I think he sort of brushed her off. She was really worried the rest of the night, but she wouldn't tell me why. She said it was private. Which pissed me off a little, 'cause it's not like I'm some stranger to her, but whatever. Anyway, long story short, there was definitely drama, and you probably want to sort that crap out with Matthew before the rumor mill grinds you to a pulp."

Claire doubled over, feeling like she'd been punched. What had Matthew told Amy that would make her so upset? If he'd let on that she wasn't really sick and Amy told Emily, it would shatter their friendship from the inside out.

In the background a door clicked and a voice—a guy's voice—rumbled.

"Okay, I'll be there in a second," Emily said to him.

"Who's that?" Claire demanded.

"Randy," Emily admitted. "He was really sweet last night. A bunch of people stayed over, and even though he could have driven home, he slept on the couch so that he could help clean up this morning."

Claire had heard that same, wistful-excited sound in Emily's voice before. The one that meant she really, really liked a guy.

"Listen, I'm sorry, Claire. I've gotta go deal with things here. Just . . . talk to Matthew and then call me back."

"Okay," Claire whispered. "Thanks."

"I'm sorry. I'll talk to you soon." Emily's voice was worried, and Claire hung up with a knot of tension growing like wings between her shoulder blades.

With a stomach-churning chorus of self-doubt pounding in her head, she called Matthew. It went straight to voice mail.

"It's Claire. Call me. We need to talk." She tried to sound calm, but part of her didn't care if he knew she was freaking out.

She flipped the phone shut and sat down on the edge of her bed, running her fingers through her tangled ponytail, trying to figure out what to do. She needed coffee. And she needed to get out of the house. If she paced her room any more, she was going to be insane before noon.

The only place she could think to go was The Cloister, but it was better than nothing. She grabbed her history book and threw on a pair of shoes. Downstairs, her mother was in the darkroom, working. Claire knocked on the door.

"Yes?" her mother called. "What is it?" She sounded irritated.

"I want to take the car," Claire said. "To go to the coffee shop." It wasn't exactly a question. But it was the best Claire could manage, as upset as she was.

There was a pause from the other side of the door.

"Fine," her mother said. "The keys are on the hook. Be careful." The 'be careful' was a dismissal.

Claire scurried up the stairs, snatched up the keys, and hurried out to the car.

The Cloister was far from empty, but the late-Sunday-morning crowd didn't involve anyone Claire knew. She ordered an enormous coffee and automatically headed for the little table by the window where she and Emily always sat. With the familiar cup in her hand, the comforting buzz of the coffee grinder, and the sugary smell of the pastries in the glass-fronted case, Claire felt herself calm down the smallest bit.

Something had happened. Okay. But maybe it wasn't as bad as she thought. After all, maybe Emily was exaggerating. What had happened between Matthew and Amy might not have been any big deal. Maybe Amy wasn't suspicious.

She checked her phone. Still no call from Matthew. No message. The blank screen smirked at her, and she shoved it back into her pocket.

She stood up, heading for the pastry case. Maybe an

almond croissant would help take her mind off the waiting. The line was insanely long, and she decided to head to the bathroom first. It was a tiny, one-stall bathroom with a faucet that dripped and a mirror that had a chipped gilt frame. Claire stood in front of the sink, adjusting her ponytail.

The door swung open and Claire moved aside, glancing up to see who was squeezing into the bathroom with her.

In a halo of blond curls and ginger perfume, Amy walked through the door.

Claire froze, her hands still wrapped around her ponytail.

Amy's eyes widened as she recognized Claire, and her automatic sort of smile slipped off her face. Claire watched her glance around the bathroom, checking to see if they were alone.

"Hey, Claire. You're . . . here. Are you okay?" Amy looked worried. In more ways than one.

Claire's breath came in quick, shallow little puffs, and the skin along her spine crawled with an adrenaline-filled warning.

"I'm feeling a lot better," Claire said carefully, letting go of her ponytail. "I talked to Emily this morning."

Amy winced, and Claire could see her think about lying, but then she squared her shoulders and took a step toward Claire, her eyebrows settling in a determined line.

"What did she tell you?"

Claire swallowed hard, her pulse pounding against the

too-delicate walls of her veins. "I heard about what happened at the party."

Amy's determined expression gave way to sorrow. "I'm sorry. I—I can't imagine how hard all of this is for you, but I can't just keep my mouth shut. After that stuff that happened at the mall and then last night and . . . I wasn't trying to listen in, but I heard you and Matthew talking at the dance. . . ." She took a step forward, holding out her hand like she meant to touch Claire but she couldn't figure out how. "I know what's going on with you. Why you're always hiding. I figured it out, Claire, and I want you to know that it's okay. I understand."

Claire's fear gave way to shock with such speed that she reached out to steady herself on the wall. It was like plunging down the first big hill on a roller coaster without any warning.

"You . . . know?" she choked out.

Amy gave her a sad little smile. "Yeah. There was a girl back in Philadelphia—well, I mean, I wasn't *sure* about her in the beginning, but now that I know what to look for . . . it wasn't that hard to see what you"—she glanced at the thin bathroom door and dropped her voice—"what was making you act so strange. Claire, I *know*, and I'm worried. You can't hide it much longer. I won't stand by and let you try to cover this up," she finished, her words lead-weighted with meaning.

The air around them was suddenly too thick to breathe. Claire's lungs had seized in her chest. Spots danced in front of her eyes.

"Claire? Are you okay?"

She slumped against the wall, ignoring the cool, slightly sticky tiles. A breath burned its way though her chest. She couldn't think—her mind was nothing but a seething mass of panic and anger and betrayal. Because Amy knew.

Amy knew.

Amy knew.

Amy knew.

"I have to go," Claire whispered.

In one swift motion she turned, whipped open the door, and ran into the coffee shop.

As quickly as she could without looking inhuman, Claire hurried over to her table, snatched up her history book, and tore out to the parking lot without even looking to see if Amy was behind her.

She tossed her things into the Mercedes and drove home, running all the yellow lights and rolling through the stop signs on the way. With every second that passed, Claire's fear grew, shredding her from the inside out, howling inside her head until it was impossible to hear, to think. If Amy knew, it put everyone in danger.

There was no difference between the humans in Claire's life and the werewolves. One word from Amy's lips could destroy them all.

Chapter Nineteen

THE DRIVEWAY WAS empty when Claire pulled up. She left the car in front of the house and raced inside, tossing the keys onto the hall table. Assuming her mother would still be in her darkroom, Claire tore downstairs and pounded frantically at the door.

"Just a moment!" Claire heard her mother moving through the little anteroom before swinging open the door that stood between them. "What on earth is wrong, *chérie*? Please tell me you haven't wrecked the car."

Claire gripped the door frame, her fingers white as marble.

"I haven't wrecked the car," she whispered. "It's much, much worse than that."

Marie's expression shifted from irritation to genuine concern. "Come in and sit down," she told Claire, pulling her into the little cubicle of a room that stood between the hallway and her darkroom. Claire felt the tears gathering in her eyes, trembling at the edge of her lashes and making the world around her quavery and insubstantial. She let herself be dragged along by her mother, who pushed her onto one of the high stools around her work table. Marie bent down just slightly, so that she and Claire were eye to eye.

"Tell me what happened. Whatever it is, Claire, it will be okay. I will fix it." Her mother's voice was quiet and smooth and dark—an inky ribbon. As her words whisked over Claire's skin, she shivered, seeing Judith's disapproving face.

She knew, with absolute certainty, that she couldn't tell her mother. Not like this. Because Marie would try to fix it, and Claire would look like a guilty little sniveling brat of a kid who had gone running to mommy-in-charge to get her out of a scrape.

But this was much more than a scrape.

And Claire was much more than a well-connected kid. She had to take responsibility for what had happened. If she didn't tell the whole pack, she'd never be able to live with herself.

"I need to tell everyone. Please—can you call a meeting? For tonight?"

Marie frowned. "Claire, there's no need for that. If I feel the rest of the pack needs to be involved, I will call them. But I'm sure we can work out whatever has happened."

Claire shook her head, thinking of her thread-thin relationship with Emily and the scalding argument she'd had with Matthew the night before. "I'm sorry," she whispered. "I've already ruined so much in my human life—I can't ruin things with the pack, too." She looked up at her mother. "Don't you understand? If you try to fix this, I'll look horrible." The tears that had been threatening spilled onto her cheeks. "I—I can't. I have to own up to what happened. I have to tell the whole pack. Please."

Her mother closed her eyes for a brief moment and took a deep breath. Gathering herself.

"I can see that you are serious about this. I still think it is unnecessary, but I am not blind to the way that . . . certain members of the pack view you. I will not force you to tell me. I will call the meeting. Is—" She hesitated. "Whatever it is—are you sure it can wait until tonight?"

Claire rubbed the bridge of her nose between two fingers. "I think so." Amy hadn't seemed like she was in any great hurry to reveal Claire's identity. If all she wanted was to turn Claire in, Claire would already be in a cage somewhere. The idea laced her thoughts with panic.

"I mean, I hope so," she whispered.

"I will go make the calls." Marie hurried out of the darkroom.

The adrenaline leaked out of Claire's body. She slumped against the table, still terrified but also exhausted. She didn't know what the pack would say when she told them her identity had been compromised, but she knew what it meant for Amy.

Shaking with the uncertainty of it all, Claire stumbled up to her room and lay down on her bed, checking her phone one more time, not quite able to believe that Matthew still hadn't called her back. She pulled the pillow tight over her head and lay in the smothering darkness, trying not to think.

Sometime later, Marie knocked on Claire's door.

"Yeah?" Claire called, her head still stuffed under the pillow.

"It is arranged. We will meet tonight, early. I have told everyone that we will begin at ten o'clock." Marie's voice was muffled by the down of the pillow, but Claire couldn't bring herself to look at her mother.

"Thank you," she said.

There was a wooden thump—something hitting the top of her vanity table. "I brought you some food. Do you—can I do anything for you?"

"No." Claire's voice was miserable. She was miserable. Every word her mother spoke made it harder to keep from thinking. When she heard the door click shut, she reached for her headphones, jamming them into her ears and turning the music up until it seared through her head, obliterating everything else.

Ten o' clock. It was already late afternoon. She just had to wait a few hours.

The few hours passed with a fossilizing slowness. She lay there, wondering what they would say. If the pack would kick her out and what, exactly, they would do with Amy. She still seemed to want to be friends with Claire. Maybe there was some other solution they could come up with. Maybe it wouldn't be an automatic death sentence.

Eventually, the dark slipped down her windowpane and covered the lawn and forest, broken only by the lights from the house and the pinpricks of the stars in the velvet black sky. After the sun had completely disappeared, taking with it the faint light that had crept underneath her pillow, Claire lay in the gloom until she couldn't stand it anymore. She sat up and swung her legs over the side of the bed, watching as the moon rose over the tops of the trees. It was a fat crescent moon, rising points-first into the blackness, like a cup. Or something with horns.

She watched as it traced its path across the sky. She just wanted to get to the gathering. Everything felt out of control—her fight with Matthew, the bizarre intensity of the naming, and now Amy. The only thing she was certain about was that telling the pack—the whole pack—was the right thing to do. It was the only way she could get her hands around the situation.

Behind her, Marie opened the door.

Without knocking.

"It's time to go, *chérie*. Are you ready?"

"Yes. Let's go." Claire stood up and turned to face her mother. Marie looked her over, almost clinically, her face growing more alarmed as she took in Claire's posture and expression. "Claire, just tell me what happened. I am your Alpha. I can command you, if necessary."

"Please," Claire whispered. "Please don't do that. I have to do it this way. You know I do. When we get there, I promise I'll tell everyone what happened. Just as soon as we get there."

"Then let's go. And quickly."

The fact that her mother had not commanded her to reveal what she knew gave Claire the strength to walk out of the room. If her mother was willing to wait—to respect Claire's desire to face the pack—then she really must be doing the right thing.

Outside, the November air cleared her head. Stripped of the cocoon of numbness that Claire had spun around herself, her panic returned, threatening to overtake her. She and her mother hurried toward the woods. The two of them scurried beneath the protective arms of the trees, following the invisible but well-remembered path to the clearing. Claire kept her eyes on the leaf-strewn ground, watching the shifting patterns of the splintered moonlight on the forest floor.

In the distance, the flicker of a fire caught Claire's eye. Someone had gotten there before them. She began to run, the secret burning her mouth from the inside out.

In the clearing, Beatrice sat close to the fire, her face a mask of worry.

"Victoria's not with her," Claire whispered. She'd been hoping to see at least one supportive face around the fire.

"No," her mother said. "She won't be. The baby is still too little to be away from Victoria. She will have a few months before she is required to attend to her pack responsibilities." She grimaced. "No matter how dire they may be."

Guilt sluiced through Claire in an icy rush.

She slunk into the clearing ahead of her mother, and Beatrice immediately hurried over to her, wrapping her arms around Claire.

"Oh, Young One. What happened?"

"No use asking," said Marie. "She won't tell me—not until the pack is gathered."

Judith stepped out of the trees, her eyebrows raised in surprise. "Which is as it should be. If something happens that affects the whole pack, then we should deal with it as a pack."

She'd clearly heard the last part of the conversation, but though she was looking at Claire with irritation, she didn't have her usual, dismissive stare.

Katherine stepped into the clearing behind Judith. "Sorry. I was trying to DVR a show and I couldn't get it set up. So. We're all here?"

Marie shot Katherine a withering look. "Yes. We're all here. Please be seated, and we will hear what Claire has to say."

The other women sank down around the fire. Standing in front of their expectant faces, Claire suddenly wondered if maybe she should have told Marie after all. She didn't want to see the looks on their faces when she told them what had happened.

But it was too late now. Whether or not she wanted to know, she was about to find out.

She stared into the depths of the fire, unable to meet their eyes as she spoke.

"There's a girl—Amy Harper. She's a . . . a friend of a friend. And apparently, she got suspicious about me for some reason." Claire swallowed hard. "And last night, she overheard me talking and somehow, she figured out what I am. That I'm a werewolf. She told me this morning that she knows. Amy Harper knows I'm a werewolf." The words hung in the clearing, heavy and electric as a storm cloud. Claire felt her legs quivering underneath her, and she sat down in front of the fire before she collapsed.

There was a moment of stunned silence. The sort of silence that said it was just as bad as they'd been afraid it would be. Claire stared into the heart of the fire, the broken pieces of her life strewn around her. Beatrice shuffled over and put an arm around her shoulders.

"Okay. Claire. Listen. This is bad. But it *happens*. That's why we have laws for it—ways to handle it." Her low voice was full of spiderweb cracks.

"Beatrice is right." Marie stood up, and Claire looked at her. Her mother's expression was neutral, but pain flared in her eyes. "We will simply do what we have to—the same way we have for hundreds of years."

Just when Claire felt the freezing ache inside her start to melt, Judith jumped in. "But we just had that . . . that *incident* this summer. . . ."

Zahlia.

Though they were not allowed to speak her name ever again, they all thought it. Beatrice pulled her arm away.

Judith shook her head. "Killing another human right now is more dangerous than it has ever been. The town is still on edge. That other researcher—the Japanese man—is still here."

Claire felt everything around her swim, like the air had gone liquid and slow. She'd been so worried about herself and the pack, but she didn't want to think about what saving themselves would mean for Amy. The thought of her lying somewhere— dead, broken—was more than Claire could stomach.

"Isn't there some other way?" she whispered. The eyes around the fire all immediately came to rest on her as she spoke. "I mean, she seems to want to be friends with me, even though she knows. She seems *worried* about me."

The thought of Emily, red-eyed and sniffling, crossed Claire's mind. Killing Amy meant hurting Emily, too. She wrapped her arms around her middle, feeling like she was on the edge of falling apart. "We don't always have to kill a human who finds out, right? I mean, look at Matthew."

Marie shook her head. "Too many humans who know is dangerous for the pack. There will be no more *gardiens*."

"It sounds like maybe one human who knows has been dangerous," Judith said. She looked over at Claire. "Are you sure Matthew has been loyal? Do you know why Amy became suspicious in the first place?"

Panic beat wildly in Claire's chest, like a caged animal throwing itself against the bars. The pack was talking so calmly—so certainly—about killing Amy. She didn't want to sacrifice herself, but if it kept Matthew out of this, she would do it.

"She said that there were things I said—things that she pieced together. And then she overheard Matthew and me at the dance last night, talking about coming to the naming. She said between that and some stuff that happened while we were shopping, she figured it out."

Katherine drew in a sharp breath, and the pack's attention turned away from Claire as they all focused on Katherine's shocked, horrified face. "It wasn't the time I ran into you at the mall, was it?"

Claire laced her fingers, twisting them together until they hurt. She didn't want to lay the blame at anyone else's feet. While she hesitated, Katherine's mouth fell open.

"But I didn't even *say* anything," Katherine protested.

Marie turned to Claire with a question in her eyes.

"I don't know exactly what made her suspicious," Claire said simply.

Katherine balled her hands up into fists, pressing them into the sides of her totally impractical khakis. She stared at Claire, her mouth pursed into an ugly little circle. "How can you—"

"Just stop it," Judith snapped at her. "You're the one who leapt in and told us you were at the mall—Claire didn't say anything. And I'm not surprised to hear that you were indiscreet. It's just like the Halloween gathering, when you started to howl in spite of the danger. You don't *think*—"

"Enough!" Marie interrupted.

Claire stood, aching. Frozen. Waiting.

Her mother sighed. "Amy must be killed. I will not take that sort of a chance with the pack's safety." She turned her sad gaze to Claire. "Or with yours."

"We don't have to kill her," Claire protested, scrambling wildly for an alternative. Kidnapping her. Somehow erasing her memory. Something. Anything.

"You're right." Judith stepped forward smoothly. "We don't have to kill her. Pack law dictates that it is the responsibility of the wolf whose identity has been compromised to eliminate the human who knows. *We* don't have to kill Amy. *You* do."

The words slammed into Claire like a series of hammer blows. The urge to throw up swirled inside her, making the inside of her mouth taste sour. She tried to see herself lunging after a screaming Amy. Or twisting her fragile neck. But she couldn't. Couldn't imagine it. Couldn't do it. Not ever.

"You *can* do it, Claire." Her mother sank down in front of her, between Claire and the fire. Looking at her. Reading her thoughts in her posture. Her scent. "The laws are very clear on this." Marie's voice grew quiet, tinged with an ancient, knowing sort of sadness. "Living with the horror of killing a human is the price that you pay for being compromised in this way. For the danger that you have brought to the pack. I am sorry," she whispered, her eyes wet.

Claire's breath caught in her throat, constricting into a sob. She couldn't stop the tears that raced down her cheeks, and she didn't bother to hide them.

"There has to be another way—a better way," she begged.

Marie shook her head firmly but not unkindly. "The best way is to plan it carefully and do it quickly." She reached for Claire's hand. "And the planning —we are allowed to help you with that. We will make it as easy as we can, *chérie*. For you and Amy both."

"I can't—"

"You have to. Or the whole pack is at risk. A human death is terrible, but there are six of us—and, of course, Aura. It may be your identity that Amy has discovered, but it puts all of us in danger. Your whole wolf family. And so you will do this to save all of us. Do you understand?"

The memory of her half-starved mother cowering in Dr. Engle's cage last summer rose in Claire's mind. Behind it came a vision of Victoria dead at the hands of vengeful hunters and Aura crying for a mother she would never know. And then there were Judith, Katherine, and Beatrice ... and none of this was their fault.

Claire huddled into herself, closing her eyes against the awfulness of what was happening. "Okay," she whispered.

Her mother released her hand and stood.

"So, we have little time to waste. Let us begin. Judith? I know you have some ... experience in this area. Perhaps you would like to start."

Claire's eyes flew open, and she stared at Judith's stony face. Judith returned her gaze. She nodded, slowly, a crack of vulnerability appearing in her masklike expression. "It's true. It was years ago. But someone found out what I really am."

"But you couldn't have killed someone. Until Zahl—" Claire caught herself just in time. "Until last summer, there hadn't been a werewolf attack in Hanover Falls for over a hundred years."

"No recorded attacks," Judith countered. "No one knew that it was a werewolf who killed him. No one was even sure he'd been killed at all. It looked very much like an accident." She turned her face up toward the sky. "I was—" Her voice faltered, and she cleared her throat, still studying the stars that speckled the patch of sky above the clearing. "I was dating him. He came one night, to surprise me, and saw me leave to go for a run in the woods. He saw me transform." Her fingers trembled in her lap. "He panicked—there was no time for a good plan. I caught him and broke his neck. And left him at the bottom of the ravine. He was dressed like someone who might have been walking in the woods. Everyone assumed he'd fallen." Her eyes glittered in the reflected starlight, tears gathering in the corners. She scrubbed her hands across her face and cleared her throat, the vulnerability disappearing from her voice.

"That's how it must be done or the hunt for us simply begins again." She looked thoughtfully at Claire. "Perhaps you can make it look like a suicide. There's nothing wrong with that. Can you think of any reason why she would be depressed?"

Claire shook her head. "Everyone likes her. She's ridiculously happy. She's practically the poster-girl for well-adjusted people."

"Okay, so, some other sort of accident." Judith was being so matter-of-fact. Like she was picking out paint colors. Or talking about which restaurant to try. But there were lines at the corners of her mouth that were telling their own story. Hoping that Claire couldn't tell just how bad it was going to be.

But Claire could tell. And it was terrifying.

Judith leaned back against the fallen tree. "A car accident is pretty hard to stage—it would be better if we could think of something that was just her. Electricity? Water?"

Claire blinked as a memory—welcome, unwelcome—

stepped out of her subconscious. "She can't swim," she whispered. "Amy can't swim."

"So drowning, then . . ." Judith said, a faraway look in her eyes. "It would be easy. Not a lot of evidence. Not as easy for Amy, maybe. But it sounds like the best option."

"But where?" Katherine interrupted. "It couldn't be anywhere with people around—I mean, imagine how horrible it would be for them to see her die like that." A disgusted expression distorted her features, like a squeamish girl being forced to pick up a dead mouse. The pain in Claire's chest swelled, stretching against her ribs.

Judith shot Claire a sorrowful look before turning to Katherine. "What it would do to some random human bystander? What about what it will do to Claire? I don't think I've ever heard you be quite so insensitive, Katherine. And that's saying something." Her words dripped with venom, and it was like she had pulled aside a curtain. Claire could suddenly see where her anger and distrust came from. The wound that killing a human had left on Judith kept her walled off from everyone and everything.

While she felt a sympathy for Judith that she'd never expected, at the same time, a fierce determination bloomed in Claire.

She was not going to let that happen. She was not going to end up like Judith, cut off from the world. Angry. Afraid.

She was a werewolf. She would do whatever it took to fix

things—to keep herself safe. If that meant taking the life of a human, then she would find a way to do it. To live with it.

Amy knows. She might as well be pointing a loaded gun at us—all of us. I'm just going to stop her before she pulls the trigger.

What Amy knew might be invisible, but it was as deadly as any weapon. Claire dug her fingernails into her palms, focusing on the pain in her hands instead of the ache that wrapped around her heart. She'd harden herself somehow. And then she'd work like hell to bring herself back—to keep from living the sort of half-empty life that Judith had made for herself.

But before she could figure out how she was going to survive it, she had to figure out exactly how she was going to do it—how she was going to kill Amy.

Chapter Twenty

THE PACK—MINUS VICTORIA—talked well into the small hours of the morning. Discussing whether a pool or a natural body of water would be best. Where there were bridges with low sides. Whether Claire could wait a few days or if it needed to be the next night.

"The sooner it's done, the better it will be for everyone." Marie said. There was decision, rather than discussion, in her voice. "It must be done tomorrow night."

Claire quailed, her resolve wavering.

"I need time to get it set up—I mean, to find a reason to

get her alone without looking suspicious." She barely managed to choke out the words.

Her mother nodded, her lips set in a hard line. "I know. But you *must* be quick. With every day that passes, the risk that she will tell—that she has told—increases. Spend tomorrow arranging what you must, and then find a way to get her alone. Any longer than that and the danger is too great. As your Alpha, I am commanding you to finish it by tomorrow night."

Claire squeezed her eyes shut. "Fine." It was more like a breath than a word, but it satisfied her mother.

"What about all those arty shops by the river? There are a couple of old footbridges around there," Beatrice suggested.

Claire sucked in a breath. Amy was a pottery fanatic. If she could convince her that one of those little galleries wanted to see her stuff, Amy would probably be thrilled to go down and meet with them.

Even alone.

Even after dark.

"What?" Judith asked, watching the emotions scroll across Claire's face.

"I think I know how to do it," Claire whispered. She didn't want to say the words, because then it would be true.

But, really, it was already true.

As simply as she could, she explained things to the rest of the pack.

"It's a good plan," Beatrice said.

Judith tilted her head from side to side. "It's only pass-able," she said, "but it's all we've got."

"For now, it will have to do. It has been a very long day. Let's go home." Marie stood up and looked around the circle at the other women. "Thank you for coming—for your help and suggestions. We will come through this as we have before. Scarred, perhaps, but surviving all the same."

Katherine stood up, nodding to Marie and casting a curiously blank look in Claire's direction before slipping off into the woods. Beatrice shook her head at Katherine's retreating form and came over to Claire, wrapping her arms around her in a firm hug.

"It will be okay. You'll see. Remember what I told you at the new moon gathering? When I gave you the necklace? You are still stronger than you know." She pressed her dry lips to Claire's cheek. "Be careful. The last few months, watching you grow . . . I love you too much to stand anything bad happening to you."

Claire curved her lips into a smile, but there was nothing genuine about it. Still, it seemed to please Beatrice. With a final squeeze, she turned to go, patting Marie on the arm as she went past.

When she'd left, Judith stepped close to Claire. Marie moved over to put out the fire, discreetly giving them space to talk.

Judith didn't hug Claire. She didn't touch her or smile at her. She simply held Claire's gaze with her blue-gray eyes, which were exactly the color of a February morning.

"Beatrice isn't telling you the truth. She's trying to be nice, but if you treat this like it's no big deal, it will just make things worse for you in the end."

The words were painful, but the honesty of the hurt felt better than the lying smile she'd put on for Beatrice.

"I know," Claire whispered.

"No, you don't," Judith said quietly. "This will break you. The same way that the surface of the moon has been broken by the meteors that smash against it. But this doesn't have to destroy you. The shattered moon still glows. You will still *be*. And from there you will have to find your own way through."

It was the worst thing anyone had said to Claire all night. But, somehow, it gave her the courage to face the next twenty-four hours. And she was determined to do exactly what Judith had said—to find her own way through.

Claire didn't go to school the next day. She couldn't. It was easy to extend the sickness she'd faked on Saturday night—it probably made the whole thing more believable, anyway. The dance seemed like a lifetime ago. Her dress was still stuffed into the duffel bag she'd carried into the woods, tossed into a corner of her room. There were texts from Emily piling up on her phone, and downstairs her mother was hovering uncomfortably.

She reached for her phone, texting Emily back. If something had gone . . . wrong, then Emily would know about it— Emily would tell her.

Still feel like crap. Everything okay with you?

Claire sent the text and then held her breath, waiting for a response. A few minutes later, her phone beeped, which meant that Emily was texting midclass.

Sorry! Boring day here—everyone's still hungover. Amy's acting weird, too, but she won't say why.

Emily's message was reassuring and worrying at the same time. Amy still hadn't said anything, which was good, but Emily was probably employing the "pester them until they tell you what's going on" tactic. Claire knew how persuasive Emily could be when she wanted to know something.

She couldn't let Emily find out. As much as she wanted to pretend things were fine, that Amy wasn't living her last day, she couldn't afford to wait.

She looked out at the woods and begged the Goddess to help her.

Claire swung herself out of bed and pulled on a ratty pair of jeans and one of Matthew's old sweatshirts. She'd just go to his house. School would be out in a couple of hours, and if she was there—waiting for him—then he'd *have* to talk to her.

She thundered down the stairs and into the kitchen, where her mother was pretending to be busy reading a catalog.

"Where's Lisbeth?" she demanded.

"I gave her the day off," Marie said, as though it were the most natural thing in the world.

Claire blinked, thinking through her options. Her very limited options.

"I'm taking the car," she announced. "I have to go to Matthew's."

Marie looked up at her sharply. "I don't think so. I'm not letting you drive the Mercedes while you have so much on your mind—you'll be too distracted. I'll take you over to the Engles'."

Claire's shoulders slumped. "Fine," she said. She didn't care how she got there. She just needed to go.

The two of them rode in silence most of the way. A few blocks from the Engles' house, Marie turned to her. "I know you have not asked for my advice."

Claire looked back at her mother. "Didn't you give me your advice last night? If I don't have any choice, then what words of wisdom do I need?" Her voice was cold and hard as hail.

Irritation flashed across Marie's face, erased in a moment by an understanding that made Claire's stomach sink. Marie was treating her like a cancer patient. Like she was terminal.

"I would not have you do this if there were any other way, Claire. But the law is immutable on this point. And so I would advise you to do it without thinking. The less you dwell on it now, the easier it may be to tuck away later. So that it does not define you, the way it defined Judith. I do not wish to see you . . ."

"Shattered?" Claire offered, thinking of Judith's description of the rock-battered moon.

"Exactly," Marie agreed, turning onto the Engles' street.

Claire stared at the passing houses. She didn't know how to tell her mother that it was already too late. That nothing was ever going to be the same again. Something had changed in her when she'd agreed to kill Amy, even if she hadn't done it yet. It was like watching a dropped glass fall toward the floor, knowing that it was going to break but not knowing how badly. Just knowing that it couldn't be saved.

The Engles' driveway was empty, and Claire was grateful. She'd figured that Dr. Engle would be at the lab, but Matthew's mom might have been home.

"Where will you—do you want me to wait with you? It's rather cold."

Claire shook her head. "I'll be okay. He'll be home in an hour or so." She slipped out of the car and went to sit on the biting concrete of the porch step. Her mother drove away slowly. Claire could see her watching in the rearview mirror. She put her hands in her pockets, tucked herself down into her coat, and waited.

When Matthew pulled into the driveway, the wind had numbed her nose, and her hips ached from sitting on the concrete.

When he stepped out of the car and saw her, a smile skittered across his face and then his lips went flat as a closed door.

"Claire? What are you doing here?"

She stood up. "I have to talk to you. Please."

He nodded. "I know. I need to talk to you, too."

Her heart hiccuped in her chest. Something about the way he said the words made it sound like he was breaking up with her.

"Let's go inside," he said.

The two of them ended up at the kitchen table.

The ticking of the old-fashioned wall clock above the stove pounded against Claire's ears, reminding her that she didn't have time to waste. Still, she couldn't find the words to tell him—especially not when things seemed so uncertain between them.

"Listen," he said, jumping in ahead of Claire. "I don't know what you heard happened at Emily's on Saturday night, and I know we haven't talked, but it all started with the fight we had in the car—"

She spoke over top of him, not wanting to rehash their argument right then. "I have something to tell you, and I don't . . ." She bit her lip. "I *need* to tell you. But it's wolf stuff, and it's bad. And if you can't handle it—"

He held up a hand, stopping her. "Wait. I don't want to have this fight again. I'm *not* freaked out by the werewolf stuff. I never have been."

She made a face. "But when I was tested, you didn't even want to be there. It's like you're trying to ignore the werewolf side of my life. I mean, what about what happened after Yolanda's party?" She paused, remembering the rough wood of the utility shed against her fur. Remembering how badly

Matthew had lied when Emily had almost found her and how tense and horrible things had been between them afterward.

The memory made her too edgy to sit still. She pushed the chair back from the table and paced in front of the counter.

Matthew shook his head disbelievingly. "You told me to leave you alone so many times. . . . It's not exactly easy to figure out how involved I'm supposed to be—when I'm being a *gardien* and when I'm being your boyfriend."

Claire ground the heel of her hand into the bridge of her nose, squeezing her eyes shut. "But there's no *difference* between the two."

"Of course there is!" he said, standing up. "They're both things I am, but they're not the same."

"Right," she said, dropping her hands and stepping toward him. "And I'm two things too. A wolf and a human. But you know both. I just want to be myself with you—all of myself, not just the human part and not just the wolf. I thought that's what was so great about you being a *gardien* in the first place. Until you started acting like you only wanted to date the one version of me."

"I'm not saying that! *You're* the one who keeps saying it. Yes, it's hard. I mean, when Doug doesn't get something that's going on in Kate-Marie's life, he ruins the lunch conversation by pestering all of us until we tell him what the hell we think he should do. And then he does it and things are fixed. I don't have that option. I'm not allowed to talk to any of my friends about your life, and I don't exactly love the idea of having a heart-to-heart with your mother about it. You're all I have, but instead of telling me what you want me to do, you spend all your time being mad that I'm not perfect."

"It's not like I have some secret werewolf dating guide that I'm not showing you," she fumed. "I want us to be together, but I want to be *with* you. Not in charge of you. You can't just lurk around at the edge of everything, waiting for me to tell you to jump. I don't know what I'm doing, either, and you're not the only one who can't get advice from your friends." Her words were coming fast and faster, and she felt the conversation spinning away from her.

He reached out and caught her wrist. "Stop. Listen to me. I love you. All of you. I'm not trying to ignore the fact that you're a werewolf." Misery creased his forehead, crinkled the corners of his eyes. "Our relationship is never going to be easy. And I won't lie—sometimes, I wish it was. I look at what Kate-Marie and Doug have, and it's so simple."

She pulled her wrist out of his lax grip. "I can't help that."

"I know." He stepped in and wrapped his arms around her. "And I don't *want* what those two have. I want you. No matter how complicated it is. But you can't expect me to have some magic way to make it easy."

She stared at him mutely, her lips parted. Thinking about what he'd said. Turning it over in her mind.

He waited a moment, watching her, and then—without

waiting for her to make the first move—he pulled her close. She leaned her head onto the warm, familiar curve of his shoulder. A firefly flash of relief shone through her then disappeared as quickly as it had come. In the dark that followed, there was nothing but despair.

She and Matthew were finally sorting things out, and she was going to have to ruin it by telling him the worst thing imaginable.

"You might not think that when you hear how complicated it is," she said.

"I already know—"

She lifted her head from his shoulder and looked into his eyes. At the confidence and love and relief that were glowing there, like hot coals.

"No, you don't," she said. "Something happened. It's—it's horrible. And I have to tell you." The words were coming faster, tripping over one another as they rushed out. "And I need you to help me and I'm sorry because it's going to ruin everything we just talked about—"

The light in his eyes turned to worry. He lifted a hand to cup the side of her face. "Claire. Stop. Just tell me. What happened?"

"Amy knows," she said simply, needing to get it out. Like ripping off a Band-Aid.

Matthew's eyes widened. "That must be what she wanted to talk to me about at Emily's. I said we'd had a fight and she got all concerned, but I didn't want to talk to her about it and . . . Oh God, she knows you're a werewolf?" he whispered.

"Yes. She—we—ran into Katherine at the mall, and I guess Amy got suspicious, and then she overheard you and me at the dance and figured it out somehow. She was acting like she still wanted to be friends, like—like she thought she could help me, almost." Claire hung her head. "But the bottom line is that she knows. I told the pack—I had to." Even though it was warm in the Engles' kitchen, her teeth started to chatter.

"Of course you did. What did they say? What are they going to do?" He looked at her with a mixture of dread and hope.

"They aren't going to do anything," she said.

"Really?" His eyebrows shot up. "But no matter how nice Amy is, that can't be safe—"

She interrupted him. "No, it's not, and that's why they've said I have to kill her." Her voice rose with each word, quavering and half-hysterical.

He sat down heavily on one of the kitchen chairs, which creaked in protest. He stared at her and she said nothing. She watched him thinking. Saw him swallow.

"They won't make an exception?" His voice was little more than a croak.

Claire shook her head.

"But when I found out, they made me a *gardien*. Why can't they do the same thing for Amy?" His face was pale as milk.

"A *gardien* is a really rare thing, Matthew. Before you became a secret-keeper, you'd already been kind to my mom, and then you helped me get her out of your dad's lab. This situation is different, and the pack's already said that having any more *gardiens* is too dangerous. When humans discover us, we don't just make them part of our world. We do everything we can to keep the worlds apart." It sounded like something Marie would say, but Claire could hear the truth in her own words. It murmured to her, ugly and undeniable.

"Why do *you* have to do it?" he whispered.

"Because I'm the one who was found out. It's—it's sort of a punishment." It felt like the words were too big for her throat.

Matthew stared down at his hands for a long time. Claire dug her fingernails into her thighs, bracing herself. She wouldn't be surprised if he took back everything he'd just said about not minding that she was a werewolf.

Finally, he looked up at her. "Is there any way around it? Some sort of loophole or something?"

She stared at him. Hard. "Do you really think I haven't twisted the whole thing inside out and upside down looking for a way out? It's the law. And beyond that, my mother—my Alpha—ordered me to do it. To have her dead by tonight."

"You really don't have a choice, do you?" Something about the defeated way he said it shook Claire to the core.

"No, I don't." She paused. "But you do. You can't walk away

from the pack, but you don't actually have to help me do this." Her voice was almost inaudible. "I would understand. I would walk away from it if I could."

"I'm not letting you go through this alone." His anguished gaze held hers, and grief and relief trampled through Claire, crushing everything else.

"You would really do that?" she asked, still not quite able to believe it.

He held out a hand to her. "For you. And no other reason. How can I help? What—what needs to be done?" He swallowed hard.

"I need an alibi," Claire whispered, "and also an untraceable e-mail address."

Chapter Twenty-One

BACK IN HER room, Claire sat in front of the computer, her hands poised above the keys.

"I don't want to do this." Her voice was flat.

"I know." Matthew reached over and brushed her hair away from her face, his thumb tracing the angle of her cheekbone. "Is there—I . . ." He sighed. "Nothing I say is going to make this any better, is it?"

Claire shook her head. She stared down at the keyboard, thinking only about what she needed to do next, instead of why she was doing it in the first place. In less than five minutes, she'd figured out how to set up an untraceable e-mail account, complete with a professional-looking signature.

Claire clicked open a new message and started to type out an e-mail. She tried to keep from using any sort of abbreviations, so that she'd sound older. She'd seen Lisbeth's e-mails—anyone over the age of twenty-two wrote messages like an English teacher was going to read them.

> Hi! I'm Lynn - I own the Potter's Wheel, on River Glen Drive. I saw some of your work when I was in Philadelphia last month, and I was really impressed. Kelly from Thrown Gallery gave me your e-mail address. I'm looking for some young artists in Hanover Falls for a new show I'm setting up. Would you be interested in meeting?

She sent the message and waited, watching the minutes tick past on her computer, praying that this wasn't the one afternoon that Amy decided not to check her e-mail. Everything inside her burned. It hurt to breathe.

Half an hour later, the computer pinged, and an e-mail popped into her inbox. Claire clicked open the message.

> Hey, Lynn - Thanks for the message. I'm very interested! I'm glad Kelly gave u my e-mail addy.

With her fingers shaking over the keys, Claire sent a response.

> Great! Can you come by around eight tonight? If you
> could bring some samples of your work, we can see
> where it might fit in the gallery. We're down on River Bend
> Drive. Just park in the lot and walk across the bridge,
> and we'll be on your right.

She had to close her eyes when she pressed send. It was like handing someone a noose and asking them to check if it would fit around their neck.

Amy responded faster than a kid grabbing an ice cream cone.

> That would be great! I'll be there right at eight - I'm so
> excited!

It was done.

Claire crumpled into herself like a wadded-up piece of paper, wishing she could shrink herself down until she was small enough to disappear.

Matthew wrapped his arms around her, scooting her over into his lap.

"I'm staying with you until it's time. I'll drive you there," he announced.

Claire shook her head. "No," she whispered. "You have to go home."

"Claire, let me stay with you. Let me *help* you."

She leaned into him.

"I wish you could," she said, "but you have to go home. You're sure your parents won't be there?"

"I'm sure," he said.

"I'll come straight there, after—" She couldn't bring herself to say the words. "I'll come over when it's done." She shuddered, and Matthew tightened his arms around her.

"Be careful." His voice was urgent, pleading, in her ear. "I couldn't stand it if anything happened to you. I love you, Claire. And I'm so sor—"

"Don't say it," she begged. "It just makes it worse." She turned her head so that her forehead was pressed against the side of his neck. "Just tell me one more time that you still love me."

"I do love you," he said. "I love you now, and I'll love you tomorrow, no matter what you have to do tonight. You're not choosing this, Claire. You're not responsible for things you don't choose."

His kind words fell flat inside Claire. She didn't believe him. Amy's death might have been an order, but she was still the one who was going to reach out and take her life. Pushing away the thought, she straightened enough to kiss him.

"I'll see you soon," she said.

He slipped out of the room, and the click of the door closing behind him was the loneliest sound Claire had ever heard.

When darkness fell, Claire dragged herself downstairs, so wrapped up in adrenaline and disbelief that she didn't even feel the stairs beneath her feet.

Her mother looked up at her.

"I'm going," Claire said simply.

"So soon?" Marie seemed surprised, but she recovered quickly. Smoothly.

"Yep." Claire's voice was crisp as an apple but not nearly as sweet. "It's worked out. She fell—she bought it." She was going to say, 'She fell for it,' but it was too close to the truth of what was going to happen.

What she was going to do.

Marie turned to her.

"Claire—just . . . be careful. Please. I do not wish to see you broken by this. Not in body and not in mind."

Claire shrugged. There was nothing she could say. She had little enough hope for herself—there wasn't any left over to offer her mother.

"I'll call you when it's done." She grabbed a dark-colored coat, and looked longingly at the car keys hanging on the hook. It would be nice to have the warmth and protection of her mother's Mercedes, but it was just too damn recognizable. Besides, she didn't deserve anything nice—not with what she was about to do. Claire shrugged on her jacket, stepped out into the cold, and walked away.

She did not look back.

Claire found a spot next to the bridge, behind some prickly-leaved holly bushes. Below her, the sound of the river, icy and dark and swift, roared endlessly.

The waiting was torture, but Claire reveled in it. The awfulness of the anticipation was the only thing that made her believe she hadn't turned into a monster yet.

There was a tiny part of her that hoped if she could hold enough hurt, bear enough pain, then she could do this one horrible thing without shattering.

But it still seemed like an unbelievably big maybe.

She shivered in the cold, thinking how much easier it would be to do this if she were in her wolf form. The bridge rail was too high, though. There was no way to throw Amy over without using her arms, and besides, even in her human form, Claire was more than strong enough to lift Amy. To drop her over the side, into the wide, deep, hungry river below.

At four minutes past eight, she heard the sound of a car pulling into the lot. A door slamming. And then a creaking complaint from the boards at the other end of the bridge. Claire's gaze swept over the scene—the road was deserted except for Amy's car. Claire could barely make out Amy's blond curls bouncing in the darkness. She'd be practically invisible to anyone without the sort of acute senses that Claire had.

This was the moment. Claire just had to stand up and walk to the center of the bridge.

Then it would all be over. Claire would be safe and the pack would be protected and they could all start to put the whole ugly thing behind them.

Except that Amy would be dead.

On the bridge, Amy started to whistle. A thready, faint whistle that was hopeful and scared all at once.

The sound of it—so very human and so very alive—broke Claire. She felt it deep inside herself as she cracked under the strain of it all. The shock of the fracture traveled through her. She jumped, recoiling, filled with the sort of near-miss fear that came with slamming on a car's breaks the moment before a crash. As Claire stood, shaking from the jolt, one shining realization stared back at her.

She couldn't kill Amy. She wouldn't. No matter what it meant.

There was no time to think about the decision. Every second brought Amy farther along the bridge—closer to where Claire was waiting. She snuck out of her hiding spot before Amy was close enough to see her, and then she ran. Fast and hard and as far away from Amy as she could get.

* * *

She tore through the streets, running as fast as she could in her human form, trusting the darkness to hide her unnatural speed.

The Engles' driveway was empty, and Claire was grateful. She slipped around to the back door, and Matthew opened it before she even had a chance to knock.

His face was worried and relieved as he pulled her into the house and shut the door behind her.

"Is it . . . done?" he whispered.

Claire's legs shook. "No. I couldn't do it. She's down at some pottery store that never asked to see her work in the first place, probably confused as hell. But she's alive." Her knees started to buckle. "I have to sit down." She staggered over to a kitchen chair and collapsed into it.

Leaving Amy alive might get Claire killed, but she knew with absolute certainty that it was the only way. If she took Amy's life, it would destroy her. It would be worse than dying.

"What are we going to do?" Matthew asked.

"I don't know," Claire admitted. Between the fingers of terror that squeezed her, a leaping sort of joy slipped through, like a fish flashing through a net. It was the exhilaration of being right. Of being almost *whole*.

Almost.

She'd been able to accept the idea of killing Amy, even if she hadn't been able to do it. And it had cracked something inside her. She would have to live with that—and she could.

Because deciding not to go through with it had taken the pressure off her broken places.

She might be cracked, but she wasn't going to shatter.

"I have to talk to her," Claire said, thinking furiously. "Maybe you can, too. She likes you, so maybe she'll listen to you. She can't be a *gardien*—my mother already rejected that idea—but there must be some humans who know and just don't say anything because they *understand*. Maybe if I get her to understand, she'll keep her mouth shut."

Matthew gripped her shoulders. "Claire, it's too big a risk. If she tells, you'll be caught. Or worse."

"I know," she said grimly.

He licked his lips. "And what about the pack? What about your mother? What are they going to do? You disobeyed them by not killing her tonight. Claire, it's their law. *Your* law."

She closed her eyes. She didn't want to disobey an order. Break the law. But there had to be a way. She just needed some time. . . . Her eyes flew open.

"Right. Right! And the law says I have to kill her."

Matthew nodded, looking like he'd just pulled her off a ledge. Like she was finally talking sense. "Okay. So let's just figure out—"

"But it doesn't say when," she interrupted. "I could do it in five years. Ten years. When we're eighty."

"Claire. That's a technicality. Your mom ordered you to do it tonight. Do you really think they'll just let that go?"

"Probably not. It would at least give me time to try and convince Amy not to say anything—that if she keeps her mouth shut, we'll both be okay. The pack might not make her a *gardien*, but maybe I can get her to keep the secret anyway. If I can find a way to fix things without killing her, they might just force me to become a *seule*. They might not kill me, as long as the pack's not at risk."

"They'll make you leave the pack?" His mouth fell open.

Claire closed her eyes, trying to stay calm—to hold on to the glimmering, butterfly-winged feeling she'd had when she realized she couldn't push Amy over the bridge.

The doorbell rang, and Claire's eyes flew open.

Matthew stepped over to the door and peered through the peephole.

Claire watched as the color drained from his face.

"Who is it?" she asked, fear tugging at her voice.

He edged back into the kitchen, his eyes wild. "It's Amy," he whispered. "Shit."

"Perfect," Claire said. The edges of her vision had gone fuzzy, and she had an elated, half-crazed feeling that was out beyond the limits of panic. "No time like the present. Let's talk to her."

Matthew moved toward Claire, brushing the hair off her forehead. "Please. Not yet. Let—let me talk to her. Go hide somewhere, and let me see if I can figure out what happened. Why she's *here*. Please, Claire. Let me try first."

She looked at his anguished face and knew that she loved him too much to say no.

Besides, there was time now.

There was plenty of time.

"Okay," she agreed.

"Oh, thank God. Okay"—he stared around the room—"you can't go upstairs—she might see you go past the front window. It'll have to be the basement. It's the only place."

"Fine," she said, stretching up to kiss him. She'd meant it to be a quick, reassuring kiss, but the chaos and frenzy of the last few hours turned into need. Matthew's arms wrapped around her waist, pulling her against him with a force that made her gasp. His mouth pressed against hers. The current that passed between them was dizzying. Claire wound her hands around his neck, tracing a path with her fingertips from his hairline down below his collar.

Amy knocked on the front door. Panting, he pulled away from her.

"Downstairs," he reminded her. "Please. Wait for me."

"Okay," she said, breathless. She turned and headed for the door, darting down the stairs. Standing in the shadows that pooled on the basement floor, Claire strained to listen to what was going on above her.

She heard the click of the latch and Matthew sounding surprised.

"Hey, Amy—what are you doing here?"

It was hard to hear Amy's response. The wind carried her voice away from the house.

"Really? That's weird. Maybe they forgot," Matthew said. Claire could hear his footsteps. "Come on in."

They moved into the living room, and one of them—Amy or Matthew, she couldn't tell which—swung the door shut behind them. Claire found her fingers curling unconsciously into fists. Amy and Matthew were too far away. Even her hearing wasn't good enough to get through that many closed doors. Cursing the fact that the basement didn't extend below the living room, she slipped back around to the bottom of the stairs, trying to hear.

"So, what, uh, what brings you by?" Matthew's voice was tense. Claire could practically see him sitting on the arm of his mother's chintz-covered chair anxiously bouncing his knee.

"It's about Claire, actually." Amy's voice was still faint, and Claire crept up a few steps. "I'm really worried that I've made a huge mess of the whole situation, and I don't know what to do about it." She sounded genuinely miserable, and Claire blinked in surprise.

"Okay . . ." Matthew's voice was slow, careful, and suspicious. Claire squeezed her eyes shut. He really was a terrible liar.

Amy said something, but her voice had gotten so soft that Claire couldn't hear.

Crap.

She didn't want to go any farther up the stairs—they creaked terribly, and besides, she'd be completely exposed if someone opened the basement door. But the only other way she'd be able to hear—really hear—was if she was in her wolf form.

She bit her lip. She'd be able to change back long before anyone saw her, but she'd sworn she'd never transform inside again. And Matthew's basement, with all the lycanthropy books that reeked of Dr. Engle, was even worse than her bedroom.

She hesitated, trying to decide if she could stand the terror of being trapped inside. But whatever Amy was saying up there, Claire needed to hear it.

Fine. It can't get any worse than it already is, right?

Her decision made, Claire ducked back into the darkest corner of the basement, where she'd have the most time to get back into her human shape if anyone came downstairs. Bracing herself, she transformed. There was a soft thud as her tail hit the wall behind her, and Claire held her breath as the shock of the noise and the oppression of the walls shot through her at the same time.

It wasn't quite as bad as she'd feared. She still felt the knife-edged panic of being trapped indoors, but it didn't shock her the way it had the first time. She flattened her ears to her head and focused on Matthew's voice. There was a faint smell of him lingering in the basement, and she used it to help her concentrate.

"...you can tell me. Really." Matthew's voice was reassuring.

Claire held her breath and listened hard for Amy's response.

"But you're involved too, and that makes it so hard." There was a tiny catch in her breath, as if she was crying.

"Just because I'm loyal to Claire doesn't mean you can't talk to me," Matthew said.

"Listen, I think it's great that you're standing by her. Really. That's one thing that's completely different from what happened to the girl I knew in Philadelphia—one reason this is a little bit less awful. It's a terrible secret to keep alone, but it's not exactly something most people want to spread around. I totally get why Claire is always so distant. Why she won't open up to me, no matter how nice I try to be."

The words pricked at Claire, needle-pointed and painful. Amy saw her exactly the way the rest of the world saw Marie. Which was everything she'd never wanted to be.

"That's very . . . understanding of you," Matthew said. He sounded confused.

"So, anyway, on Saturday, I heard the two of you talking at the ball, and I finally put all the pieces together. The way she was too nauseous to go to the party, the cravings Claire was talking about at the mall, the way she was worried about a growth spurt . . . Plus, she was always so tired and stressed, and a couple of times she mentioned something complicated going on with the two of you. But when I heard her talking about the baby, it just all made sense. It was same stuff that happened to Samantha, the girl I knew in Philadelphia who got pregnant. She tried to get rid of the baby on her own, and she nearly died."

Claire's insides froze. *Get rid of the baby?*

Amy thought she was *pregnant?* A sick feeling spread through her.

Upstairs, Amy barreled on. "I just got scared that Claire would try something like that, and so, when I saw her on Sunday, I finally said something to her, and she freaked."

There was a brief pause, and Matthew took a huge breath. "Amy, I think there's been a really massive misunderstanding."

"What do you mean?"

Claire closed her eyes, remembering their encounter in the bathroom.

"Amy, Claire's not pregnant." The words were blunt as a hammer.

Claire listened so hard for Amy's response that her ears twitched.

"She's—oh. Oh my God. Are you sure? I mean, you don't think she's just hiding it from you?"

"I don't really want to get into the specifics with you, but believe me, there is *no way* that Claire's pregnant." Claire could practically hear him gritting his teeth when he said it.

"Holy crap. Matthew, I told her I wouldn't stand by and watch her try to cover it up. I thought she might try to get rid of the baby on her own or something, and . . . *crap.* What if she thinks I told someone? She'll never forgive me!"

Claire shuddered. Amy didn't know how close to the truth she was—how close Claire had come to killing her. A completely innocent human.

"Please, Matthew. I don't think she'll listen to me after what I said to her yesterday. Will you help me talk to her?"

"Sure." Claire heard Matthew's voice shift as he stood up. "I'm actually going over there in a little while. I'll tell her you want to talk to her, and I'll make sure she'll listen."

"Could I go with you?" Amy asked hopefully. "I'd love to just get this fixed."

"Ah . . . she's, um . . ."

Oh, come on! One good lie! I'm sick, remember?

Claire's nose twitched.

"I think she might not be in the best mood to talk," Matthew said. "Let me try first. I'll make her see that you really just meant to help—that it was all a big mistake—and then I'll have her call you later tonight, okay?"

"That would be fantastic," said Amy. Their footsteps moved toward the front door. "And Matthew? Thanks. I can't tell you how much I appreciate your help. Claire's really lucky to have you, you know?"

"Trust me, I'm the lucky one," Matthew said. The sincerity in his voice made Claire ache. She shrank back against the wall and transformed, pulling on her clothes. She knelt on the carpet, leaning against the paneling with her hands over her eyes. Shaking with the relief of what she didn't have to do.

Sick with the thought of what might have happened if she had decided to go through with it. If she'd been obedient to the pack.

The pack, who would demand that she explain why she hadn't killed Amy and why she'd been wrong about Amy knowing in the first place. The idea of telling them what had happened loomed over her, all teeth and claws, and Claire trembled. She heard Matthew coming down the stairs, but she couldn't bring herself to pull her hands away from her face.

Matthew knelt down and wrapped his arms around her, pulling her into his chest and tucking her head under his chin.

"I know," he whispered. "I know. But it's okay—everything's going to be fine now. She doesn't know anything."

"Exactly," she gasped, pressing herself against him. "She was going to *die*, Matthew. I was going to kill her, and she doesn't know *anything*."

"No." He leaned back and pulled her hands away from her face, forcing her to look at him. "You were told to kill her. And you decided you couldn't. That's what matters—the fact that you didn't go through with it."

"But I was going to," she whispered. "Doesn't that make me . . . I have to be some sort of broken person, to be able to even think about doing that."

"I don't think you're defined by the things you're capable of doing. I think the things you actually do have a hell of a lot more to say about who you are."

There was truth in what he was saying, but Claire still hesitated.

"I love you," he said. "It's going to be okay. You're going to be okay."

"I hope so," she whispered, burying her face in his chest. "I really, really hope so."

Chapter Twenty-Two

CLAIRE LET HERSELF into the house, as worn out and used up as the dead leaves that skittered across the driveway behind her. Marie stood up as soon as she saw Claire. "Oh! You're back. Thank goodness. I expected you hours ago—why didn't you call? Did something go wrong? Amy—you finished it, yes? Is Matthew okay?"

The rush of words was so unlike Marie that Claire knew how truly horrified her mother was by the situation. She hadn't sounded like this when Claire rescued her from Dr. Engle, and she had been her usual collected self even when they were killing Zahlia. But everyone had their limits, and Marie had clearly reached hers.

Claire slid onto one of the stools in front of the kitchen island. "I was just at Matthew's, and he's fine," she said, choosing her words carefully. "He talked to Amy. She came over while I was there."

"Talked to her about what? Did she see you?" Marie's eyes narrowed, and she stared at Claire. Little worried lines appeared at the corners of her eyes.

"No, she didn't see me. He was—" She hesitated. She might be able to play it off as a happy coincidence, act like she was absolutely behind the plan to kill Amy until she realized that Amy didn't know anything.

But she didn't want to. Even if it meant suffering pack consequences. She had too few chances to be honest about who she was—she wasn't going to turn everything into a lie. Hoping that her voice wasn't shaking, she started to explain.

"He was going to find out what she knew, what she was thinking. And then I was going to talk to her. Because when I saw her on the bridge, I couldn't do it. I realized that I couldn't kill her."

"You have to kill her, Claire. I commanded you. It is the *law*, and you are in danger." Marie spread her hands on the granite counter, her fingertips clawing at the smooth surface.

Claire swallowed hard. "First of all, the law says I have to kill her, but it doesn't specify when. It wouldn't be breaking the law to wait, and I wanted to see if there was some way that I could save us both."

"Claire, that's a technicality. No one is kept safe if you put off the inevitable, and living in dread is as bad as living with the consequences—"

"Wait," Claire interrupted.

Marie drew in a sharp breath through her nose, her eyes glittering with the rage of a challenged Alpha. Before she could explode, Claire rushed to explain.

"She doesn't know."

"What?" Marie whispered.

"Amy." Claire put her shaking hands in her lap, hiding them from her mother's view. "She doesn't know. When she said she knew what I was, that her suspicions had been confirmed and she was going to tell, she meant . . ." Claire hesitated, not wanting to get into a conversation about whether or not she'd gone all the way with Matthew. "She thought something else was going on with me, but she was wrong. She told Matthew everything, and I was listening. She wants to be *friends*." The last word came out in a disbelieving squeak.

"How do you know she's not just hiding what she knows?" Marie demanded. "She might not have wanted to reveal things to Matthew—she knows you're dating. What she said before—you seemed so certain. There's still too much risk. . . . in spite of what you heard, you must still kill her."

Anger flared in Claire. She shook her head. "Not if she's innocent. And she doesn't know."

"Claire, you can't—"

Claire laid her head on the table, not willing to look her mother in the eye. "She thought I was pregnant. She noticed some weird stuff was going on with me, but she thought it was because I was pregnant. She believes I'm human."

"Oh. And you—oh, my Goddess."

Claire lifted her head and stared at her mother, not caring that she out-ranked Claire in her human life as well as in the werewolf world. "And the thing is, I only know that because I didn't rush to take her life. I made a horrible mistake when I told the pack that she knew my secret. I had misunderstood her in the worst possible way, and I will take responsibility for that. If there are consequences, I will suffer them. But what happened today—the chance I took, that Matthew took, to find another way—that wasn't wrong. It saved Amy. And it saved me, too. I didn't want to end up like Judith." She stared down at the floor. "I *couldn't* end up like Judith. I'd rather be a *seule*. I'd rather be dead."

"Don't say that." Marie's voice was low, warning. "Judith has created a difficult life for herself. But she's no worse off than Katherine, who's doing her best to convince herself that she's really a human. Everyone has to make choices they don't like—do things they don't want to do. They live with it as best they can, and it's better than not living at all."

Claire shook her head. "I don't believe that. I want a better life than either of them, and I think I can find one. I know that the pack laws have been created for good reasons—that they're meant to keep us safe. But twice now I've done what I knew was right, even when the pack told me it was wrong. When I saved you last summer, and now, when I saved Amy."

Claire looked up at her mother. "I don't regret doing those things. You can punish me if you need to, but you can't make me regret it."

Marie ran a hand over her face, looking haggard in a way that she never had before. "I admit that when you have gone against the pack, it has worked in your favor. That your decisions have been sound. But you must work within our laws or you cannot be a member of the pack."

It wasn't an out-and-out threat to make Claire a *seule*, but it was enough to make Claire's stomach go liquid. She couldn't quit now, though. If she backed down, she'd just be sealing her fate.

"I've only ever tried to do what was right," she said.

Marie stared at her, looking deflated. "I know. And, though you have gone about it in a less than ideal way, you have proved that you are able to think through situations." She squared her shoulders. "But you have tried to circumvent both our laws and my commands, which is a direct affront to the entire pack. The consequences you face could be extremely serious. I will not lose control of this pack. Not even to save you." Her expression shadowed. "Not because I wish to sacrifice you." Her voice had gone hoarse. "But some things are bigger than our relationship. I wish you would understand that. It would save both of us a great deal of pain if you understood that."

Claire looked at her mother in silence for a long moment. "I think I do understand," she said slowly. "That's why I couldn't kill Amy. Even if it meant something terrible for me."

Marie stared back at her. "I see your point, but I am not yet sure that you see mine. Now, go upstairs and go to bed." Marie turned and reached for the phone.

"Are you really sending me to my room?" Claire asked, astonished.

"Yes. You're so exhausted, you look positively gray. Go take a nap. I will call the rest of the pack and tell them what has happened. We will likely meet tonight, and whatever happens, you might as well be rested." Her mother looked like her old self as she barked the order at Claire. And as soon as she heard the words, Claire felt stunned by her exhaustion.

In spite of the anxiety swirling inside her, she climbed the stairs and fell into bed.

When her mother shook her awake, it was dark in Claire's room.

"Come. We are gathering soon, and you need to get ready," Marie whispered.

The mention of a gathering jolted her awake.

"I'll meet you downstairs," Marie said.

Claire rolled out of bed, yanked a brush through her

nap-snarled hair, and looked into the dark mirror. She'd told her mother that she was willing to face the pack. That she would accept whatever punishment they decided was appropriate. She'd meant it.

But that didn't mean she wasn't scared. There was a shining sphere of nerves spinning inside her with enough speed to make Claire feel unbalanced. She shook herself and went downstairs to meet her mother.

The two of them traveled the familiar path through the forest in silence. In spite of the fear that stroked her, there was a tiny glimmer of something solid, something good, that nestled inside Claire and kept her going. Whatever was going to happen, it was better than killing Amy. Even if the pack cast her out, made her a *seule*, she'd know that she'd made the right choice.

But the thought of facing the forest alone still made the familiar trees seem forbidding.

The fire was already lit in the clearing. Judith and Katherine sat near it, leaning toward the warmth.

Claire walked steadily into the clearing with her head held high. If she slinked in, hunched over like she was guilty, it would be worse. She'd look weak. Uncertain. And the pack would treat her that way.

Katherine and Judith stared at her as she approached the fire. Katherine had a look of simple relief scrolling across her face like a news ticker, but it was Judith that Claire was worried about. Her expression was complex—she looked conflicted. Happy, but also lonely. And there was a strong odor of regret coming from her side of the fire.

Before Claire could say anything, Beatrice came through the trees, a voluminous black shawl wrapped around her like a cocoon. She looked serious as death, but something unrecognizable glittered in her eyes.

The women greeted each other, and Marie took up her spot by the fire, raising her arms to bring everyone to attention.

"You are all aware of what has happened today. But I wish for Claire to tell us, in her own way, so that everyone understands. So that there is no risk of miscommunication. Then I will discuss the consequences for her actions."

Claire licked her lips, searching for the words to begin, but her mother cut her off.

"We will transform first," she said sharply. "Human words are a limited way to tell your story."

Claire snapped her teeth shut and nodded, vaguely irritated but in no position to argue.

"You may transform," Marie announced.

In a blink, the fire was ringed with wolves.

Wrapped in the comfortable warmth of her fur, Claire stared at the clearing, with its familiar trees and patch of sky. Her gaze traveled over the rough coats of the wolves who had become a sort of family to her. She didn't want to lose this—not yet. Not ever. But if killing Amy was the price she had to pay, it was just too high.

There was a brief rustling in the forest, and Victoria appeared. A stray leaf was caught in her hair, and she clutched Aura in her arms. Claire's heart began to race, thudding against the different but familiar shape of her wolf ribs. Victoria was supposed to be at home.

"I'm sorry," Victoria panted. "I couldn't stay away. I know—I know I'm excused because of the baby, but I had to be here. Wait—" She pulled a blanket out from under her arm and laid Aura on it. Once the baby was settled, Victoria transformed.

Please. I know I wasn't invited. She bowed low in front of Marie. *But Claire and I have gotten closer in the last several weeks, and she's done so much for me. I couldn't—I couldn't not be here.*

Claire shivered, feeling feverish. Victoria's presence made the possibility that she was about to become a *seule* all the more real, but having such an obvious ally sitting across the fire made Claire feel better.

Marie flicked her ears in Victoria's direction, motioning for her to get up. *You are a member of this pack. You are welcome to be a part of this, though I would encourage you not to exhaust yourself. You gave birth only a few days ago.*

Katherine gazed eagerly at the baby, her paws inching closer. *It's nice to see Aura, though. I hate to think that in just a few months, she'll be hidden away from us until I'm practically an old woman.*

I am fine. Victoria sat right up against the baby and met Marie and Beatrice's worried faces with a steady gaze.

If you're sure . . . Marie turned to Claire. *Begin, please.* Her mother sat gracefully by the fire, her ears flicking.

Claire closed her eyes for a brief moment, taking in a deep breath of the winter air.

Okay.

As simply as she could, she told the story of going to the bridge to kill Amy. The prickly awfulness of waiting and then the roller-coaster rush that came when she realized she couldn't go through with the pack's plan. She could feel her body twitching and moving, telling the story in its own way. The twitching noses of the rest of the pack told her that they were smelling the truth in her words.

She didn't flinch from it. She laid everything bare, knowing that the only way they'd be able to accept her decision was if they truly understood the way she'd felt and what she'd been thinking.

She told them about going to Matthew's and the conversation she'd had with him, looking for a way around the pack's law and Marie's order—before Amy had come over, before Amy and Matthew had talked and Claire had realized that there was never any reason to kill Amy in the first place.

She came to the end of the story, flinching a little when she realized that she hadn't called Amy yet. Tomorrow morning, she promised herself. She dragged her attention back to the wolves, who were staring at her.

So. That's what happened. I leave it to you to judge my actions. I stand by what I did, but I—I recognize that it was not in line with the will of the pack. I still think it was right.

She sat down heavily and turned to her mother, trying to look calm. Hoping that no one else could hear the panicked buzzing in her head.

Her entire future waited on the other side of the silence that hung in the clearing.

Marie stood up and faced the group.

Does anyone have anything to add?

Katherine and Beatrice shook their heads, but Victoria stood, being careful not to disturb Aura.

I do. I know that Claire's gone against the Alpha's command, and I'm not saying that it's not a big deal, but Claire has been an enormous asset to us as a pack and to me specifically. I want her to be a part of us—I want Aura to grow up to be part of a pack that includes Claire Benoit.

Claire dipped her head low, grateful for Victoria's defense. She wanted to butt her head against the hazel-colored wolf, but she knew it would look too impulsive.

Victoria lay down, pressing the warmth of her side against Aura.

Before anyone else could twitch, Judith stepped forward.

Before you make a decision, Marie, I would also like a moment.

Claire's mother closed her eyes briefly in assent. Judith paced close to Claire, and the scents of anger and frustration that were wafting off Judith made her cringe.

Claire has ignored our laws and an Alpha's orders more than once. And the pack is only as good as the laws we have—they exist to keep us alive, and we survive because we follow them. Claire has flouted that again and again. Something has to change.

The gray wolf sat down in front of Claire, their eyes level. Claire shivered, her skin rippling beneath her fur. Judith was going to condemn her. She stared at Claire as she continued. *Any law—any command—that would drive a human who doesn't know our identities to their grave at the hands of a wolf is unacceptably flawed.*

Beatrice interrupted. *Our laws are larger than this pack. We have no authority to change them.*

Judith turned to face Marie. *Then we must change the way we interpret them. You are very powerful, and you know our laws better than anyone. But hear this. If you use them without good sense, without regard to what it means for us —as a species, as a pack, and as individuals—then I* will *challenge your position. You may be strong, Marie, and you may love our pack, but I am no weakling. Claire has done the right thing. The thought of her living with the sort of agony that I carry, when her victim didn't deserve to die—it's appalling. There is a balance to be had here, and I urge you to find it—or I will do it for you.*

Judith paced away and resumed her spot by the fire, her

head held high and her eyes staring resolutely at the fire. Not challenging Marie, but ready to. Claire was too stunned to move—too stunned to breathe, almost. Both Judith and Victoria had stood up for her, and that had to be good, but Judith's threat to Marie shook Claire. She might have disagreed with her mother, but hearing Marie's position called into question made her feel shaky.

Without showing even a hint of nerves, Marie pushed herself to her feet.

I agree with Judith. And that is why, though the law authorizes severe punishment for what Claire has done, it falls to me, as the Alpha, to determine whether that punishment will be given. This is the second time Claire has gone against the pack. We have discussed—and I believe that she understands—that actions of this sort lead to very serious consequences. I cannot let this go unpunished. Even though it is a positive outcome, I cannot condone this sort of behavior from one who is supposed to be loyal to our group.

Claire's throat tightened. The edges of her vision blurred, but she kept her back straight, her ears up.

Her mother stared steadily at her. *At the next full moon, you will not be allowed to participate in the gathering. You will find your own protected place to transform. You will not come to the clearing. You will not hunt. You will be as a seule for that night. I hope, in the future, that it will be a reminder of how important this pack is to you. It will be a taste of the life you may face if you act without our consent again. Do you understand?*

Around the fire, the other wolves' tails curled close around their bodies, their ears laid flat against their heads. Katherine actually whined. It was a harsh punishment, but Claire was too relieved that they hadn't cast her out to be upset. After facing that possibility, one full moon seemed survivable. Painful, but survivable. Judith lowered her eyes, accepting Marie's decision.

I understand. Claire lowered her head. Accepting the punishment. Bearing its weight.

Good. Then let us return to our human forms. It is cold, and it has been a long week. I think we all need to return home and rest. Marie turned her gaze to the rest of the group. *When Claire has completed her full moon alone, we will not bear the memory of this against her. Though her transgressions are to be punished, her intentions are to be honored.*

Marie stood and transformed in a swirl of fur and skin.

The other wolves followed suit, and as soon as Victoria was on two feet and dressed, she handed Aura to Beatrice and came flying across the circle. She grabbed Claire and hugged her, squeezing until Claire's ribs ached with it.

"I'm so glad. Your mother is a good Alpha, Claire, and you are . . . you are wonderful. I'm so happy you're here."

"Me too," Claire whispered.

Victoria practically skipped over to Beatrice, and the two of them headed for home with Aura cuddled in the crook of Beatrice's arm.

Marie walked with Katherine to the edge of the forest

while Judith sat staring into the dying fire. Claire crept closer to her, until Judith was forced to look up. Though her body was rigid, her eyes were liquid.

"I—I'm sorry," Claire said quietly.

"Why?" Judith shrugged. "Because you escaped a fate that I didn't?"

Claire bit her lip. That was exactly what she was feeling sorry about. It seemed, somehow, that by not killing Amy she'd wounded Judith. "I know how you must feel—"

"No, you don't!" Judith snapped.

Claire froze, startled and hurt.

"I'm sorry," Judith said. "I—" She looked up at Claire and inhaled deeply. "It's a very lonely thing. I wouldn't wish this on anyone, but I'm strong enough to admit that I didn't hate the idea of not being the only one who'd been through it."

"You're right. I don't know how it feels." Claire wrapped her arms around her middle, wishing there were something better she could say.

Judith tilted her head to one side. "No, but you've come closer than anyone else. And that's something. You must be angry that I challenged your mother," she said, studying Claire's face.

"Not really," Claire said quietly. "My mother loves the laws, but that's not all there is. If I thought that way, I would have killed Amy."

Judith smiled with such brilliance that Claire was

surprised. She wasn't sure that she'd ever seen Judith smile before. Not like that, at least.

"Well. I'm glad there aren't any hard feelings. Now, go home and suffer your punishment like a good little wolf. When your night as a *seule* is over, we'll still be out here, waiting."

Claire nodded. She turned to go, aware of her mother's eyes on her back. She felt the forest close around her as she left the clearing, cutting her off from the pack. It ached, but in a not-totally-unpleasant way. Like a well-earned bruise. Sore but not permanent.

She went home quickly and quietly, bracing herself to face the human consequences of her actions.

Marie caught up to her just before Claire made it to the wall that marked the boundary between the woods and their lawn.

"Claire. Wait."

Claire turned.

Marie pushed back a stray strand of hair that had escaped her bun, then licked her lips. "I wanted to say that I'm sorry—I wish I hadn't had to punish you."

Claire shrugged. "I don't mind. I mean, I'm not *excited* about it, but at least I'm still part of the pack."

"You—you're not angry?" Marie's lips parted in surprise.

"I get why you had to do it." Claire reached out and grabbed a whip-thin branch hanging from a nearby tree. "I know I'm not the only one you have to look out for."

The look that passed across her mother's face was fierce and gentle in the same instant. "That's true," she whispered. "But you're the one I'm proudest of."

Marie reached out and gathered Claire into her arms. Stunned, Claire returned the hug, her face pressed against her mother's shoulder.

"It took great courage to do what you did—with Amy and in facing the pack. I want you to know that I don't take that lightly. I'm lucky to be your mother."

"Thanks," Claire whispered, tightening her arms around her mother's back.

Marie squeezed her briefly and then stepped away. The briskness Claire was accustomed to seeing returned to the set of her shoulders.

"Well. No use dwelling on it, I think. Let's go home and see what Lisbeth has left for us in the refrigerator."

Marie strode toward the brick wall and home. Claire followed, not even bothering to hide the smile that spread across her face.

Chapter Twenty-Three

THE NEXT MORNING, Claire dressed carefully, putting on her best, most normal human mask. She had two choices, and today she was going to have to pick one.

She could either become like Marie—like Judith—and cut herself off from the human world, or she could struggle to keep one foot in each life. She knew that in many ways, her mother's choice was simpler. There wasn't so much hiding. So much lying. But it was also an empty and lonely sort of existence.

Still, trying to have both things—a life in the pack and a normal human life—would mean stretching beyond the limits of being careful. It meant taking a risk, and after what had almost happened to Amy, Claire knew exactly what that risk entailed.

But her gut was telling her that it was worth it, that she wouldn't be happy any other way.

Matthew picked her up, eyeing her outfit appreciatively. "You ready for this?" he asked.

Claire nodded. Shrugged. "I think so. I hope so."

"You're going to be awesome." He reached over and grabbed her hand. She hung on for dear life.

Amy was at her locker when Claire walked into school. She could see the blond hair peeking between the shoulders of the passing crowd.

Matthew dropped a kiss on her cheek. "I'll talk to you after, okay?"

Claire nodded, her eyes fixed firmly on Amy. "Yes. Please."

She hitched her bag up on her shoulder and walked over to the bank of lockers.

"Amy." Her voice was barely loud enough to be heard over the shout and jostle of the hall, but Amy's head snapped up, her eyes widening.

"Claire!" She put a hand out, like she meant to touch Claire's arm and then thought better of it. "Listen, did Matthew tell you that he and I talked? Because I really need to say that I'm sorry. I totally jumped to conclusions, and I only said something to you because I was so worried, but I feel like I ruined any chance that we might have had to be friends." She was talking all in a rush, her thick eyelashes growing damp.

Claire leaned against the lockers. "It's okay. I'm not mad. I mean, I was sort of shocked, obviously. But I know you were just trying to do the right thing. It's not like you're the only one who's ever jumped to conclusions."

Amy mirrored Claire's posture. "I just want you to know that I'm not the kind of person who spreads stuff around." Her sure smile faltered. "I wouldn't do that. I thought you were in trouble, and I couldn't stand by and let you get hurt. I was just trying to be your friend, but I did a really crappy job of it. I'm sorry."

It was so exactly what Claire had been feeling over the last few months that it stunned her into silence.

"I hope that doesn't sound too needy or stupid or whatever," Amy stammered.

"Not at all," Claire said quickly. "I just—I've felt exactly that way before. And it sucks. I didn't mean to make it any worse for you. I haven't been . . . I'm not used to having to juggle things like boyfriends and stuff." She swallowed hard. "I'm the one who hasn't been a very good friend lately. Not to you and not to Emily. But that's going to change." As soon as she said the words, Claire knew she was right—that she'd made the right choice.

"Really?" Amy blinked in surprise.

"Yeah." Claire nodded. "Really. Maybe we can all go to Louie's or something soon?"

"That would be great." Amy raised a conspiratorial eyebrow. "If you can tear Emily away from Randy long enough."

Claire threw back her head and laughed. "Okay. I'll tear myself away from Matthew and we'll convince her to tear herself away from Randy."

"Deal," Amy said. "Maybe we can bribe her with cheese fries—"

"—and a Diet Coke," they finished at the same time.

Amy smiled at Claire, a genuine smile, and Claire found herself returning it.

"I've gotta get to class," Amy said apologetically, cradling her books.

"Sure," Claire said, waving her away. "No big deal. I'll pin Emily down for a girl's afternoon and then I'll text you, okay?"

"Perfect." Amy flashed her another smile and then disappeared down the hall.

Claire watched her go, feeling lighter.

There was a sudden presence at her shoulder, and Claire turned to see Emily, who was watching Amy's retreating back.

"What was that about?" she asked casually.

Claire looked at her best friend and grinned. "Us tearing ourselves away from our boyfriends long enough to have a fries-and-gossip session at Louie's this week. You in?"

Emily's eyes lit up. "Are you kidding? I've been dying to talk to you about Randy. I mean, Amy has great advice, but she doesn't exactly know my dating history the way you do."

"All twenty volumes of it?" Claire teased.

Emily swatted her on the shoulder. "Twenty-two," she

corrected. A shadow crossed her eyes. A hesitation. "Are you sure you have time?"

It made Claire ache. She'd found ways around the things she wasn't willing to do as a wolf. And in her human life, she wasn't willing to lose Emily, and she wouldn't keep hurting her.

No matter what it took, she was going to find a way around this, too.

She linked arms with her oldest friend, her best friend, and dragged her into the hallway fray. "I have time," she said confidently. "From now on, I'm going to have lots more time. I promise. No more crappy best-friend abandonment."

Emily hip-checked her. "Took you long enough to figure that out." She looked ridiculously happy.

"Amy helped," Claire admitted.

Emily nodded. "She's good at that. But she's no *you*."

Claire pursed her lips. "Yep. I'm one in a million all right. Don't you know that by now?"

Emily laughed. "And that's what I love about you. Now, come on, before we're late."

Arm in arm, they hurried down the hall. The day was waiting. Everything was waiting. One little thing at a time, she would make a life for herself. She knew it was going to be difficult—that she'd picked the thorniest, most rock-strewn path there was—but she didn't care.

It would be worth it, in the end.

Acknowledgments

First of all I want to thank Anica Rissi, Emilia Rhodes, and everyone on the Simon Pulse team, who have been so fabulous to work with. They have been cheerleaders, hand-holders, and made endless fabulous suggestions. I may start having them dress me. That's how good they are at, well, everything.

Of course, my wonderful agent, Caryn Wiseman, handles all my weirdness with grace and humor. In the high-wire act of literary life, she's my net. I'm eternally grateful for that.

Then there's my family. My husband and parents did so much to give me time and space to write this novel. Having a toddler, a baby, and a deadline was an intimidating combination. Without my family's love and support, I'd still be whimpering in a corner with about three finished paragraphs.

And that brings me to my writing family. Lisa Amowitz, Heidi Ayarbe, Trish Sanders, Jean Shriver, and Mandy Silberstein, who talked me down when I needed it. Pippa Bayless, Linda Budzinski, Dhonielle Clayton, Lindsay Eland, Cathy Giordano, and Kate Milford, who welcomed me with open arms. A special thank-you goes to Cyndy Henzel, who saw the draft of Nocturne when it was a gelatinous lump of a novel. Without her, it might still be jiggling.

Then there are the authors who were so warm and wonderful after my debut. In an industry that's rumored to be harsh, so many other writers—Saundra Mitchell being chief among them—made me feel like I'd found not just colleagues, but friends.

I can't leave out Jami Slack, the fantastic book blogger who suggested Nocturne's title in the first place.

Which brings me to the readers! All of you! Who read Claire de Lune and now Nocturne. Every e-mail and tweet and blog comment I've gotten from you has made me giddy with happiness. Really! My mom always says she likes my books because she has to. It doesn't count. Hearing from total strangers that they think Claire is awesome is better than cupcakes. And I really love cupcakes.

And finally, thank you to Erin Fehskens for so many years

of friendship, and for letting me steal that one crucial detail.

If I really thanked everyone who deserved it, these acknowledgments would be about three pages longer than the novel itself. So to everyone I've left out, please know that I truly do appreciate you!